Anna

by Melissa B. Severance

"Melissa Severance's novel *Anna* is a coming-of-age story that delves into the legacy of child abuse and its effect upon relationships. The author writes with compassion and nuanced psychological understanding, creating an intimacy between Anna and the reader that opens humanity to its core."

~ Hollie Hannan, Ph.D., Marriage & Family Therapist

"Melissa Severance delivers a courageous and compelling journey down a long, dark gravel road. This poetic tale of struggle and redemption wouldn't leave me alone, I read it cover to cover in two sittings."

~ John Seffl, Artist

"*Anna* is a harrowing, gripping novel of love and violent obsession that won't let you stop reading till the end. And through it all one is left in awe of the faith and resilience of a deceptively powerful woman."

~ Steve Chandler, author of *Time Warrior*

Anna

Anna

Melissa B. Severance

Blink Books

Anna

Contact the author: melissa@besomebodyinc.com

Editing by Chris Nelson, www.prose-alchemy.com
Cover art by Melissa B. Severance

Lake Elmo, MN

ISBN: 979-8-9870431-0-3

Library of Congress Control Number: 2023919787

First Edition

For Carol Bly

Chapter 1

The strange thing is that no matter where someone sticks me or where I find myself, I always find someone to love. The second time I noticed this was when the judge sentenced me to St. Joseph's Hospital psych floor, suicide ward, in St. Paul. He said it was for evaluation. I wasn't suicidal, but the suicide wards have locks. The judge wanted to be sure I would stay.

The intake nurse had me spread the contents of my suitcase and purse onto what was to be my bed. She took my comb, tweezers, fingernail file, toothbrush, and toothpaste. She secured my belongings with a padlock whose key I didn't have in one of the lockers along the wall in the day room and told me I'd have to locate a nurse or an orderly to use any of these items. Nurses and orderlies all jangled with keys for opening things on request. I was required to ask a nurse or orderly to watch me brush my teeth after asking for my toothpaste and toothbrush from the locker.

"Why do you have to watch me brush my teeth?" I said.

"You could stick the handle of the toothbrush in your ear and kill yourself. We can't let that happen," the nurse said.

"I never would have thought of it," I said.

I learned a new way to kill myself almost every day.

Toothbrushing was potential death. Besides putting the brush in my ear, I could tear the tube and slit my wrists. This was especially possible with Vademecum tubes (the toothpaste I used) because they were made from a sturdier metal than other brands of toothpaste. I used Vademecum because the paste was pink, not because the tube was sharp. At age fifteen, what I needed and continued to seek was to learn not how to die, but how to live.

Most of the patients were nearing the end of their lives and awaited nursing home placement. I was younger than everyone by at least thirty years. I made friends with Sarah McIntyre, who was eighty-two, so I figured that she'd been born in 1890 or 1891. Sarah McIntyre was as old as the two antique Mason jars my mom and I got as a gift from my neighbor, Tommy Erikson. Sarah had charcoal-gray, deep-set eyes and thick, coarse, gray hair to match. Her evenly-parted hair moved easily, like a horse's mane; her pleasant character matched this easy movement. I loved her right away.

If we weren't in our bedrooms, we were in the day room. One morning Sarah wasn't in the day room. I found out she had fallen the night before. The staff restrained her in bed, for her protection they said.

"Help me! Help me!" she yelled from her room. "Would somebody please help me? Let me out of here; I can't get out. Please! Help me!" The hallway leading to the bedrooms wasn't long. It was easy for everyone to hear her screaming. She yelled for so long that eventually the staff let her come out. They strapped her in her wheelchair and chained the chair to the support beam in the center of the day room. The chain went around the beam and through the right wheel of the wheelchair, and it was locked tight with a padlock.

"Let me loose," she said, shaking the padlock, which forced her into an odd, bent-over posture. Her gray eyes were no longer wise but pained, weakened, pleading up at me.

"I can't release you. I don't have a key. I'm a patient, too," I tried to explain.

It was astounding how quickly she had changed. She'd forgotten that we were friends. Now she didn't understand the difference between staff and patient. We were all the same to her—tyrants, jailers, thieves. I wondered what drug they were giving her.

The day room had two aqua vinyl-stuffed chairs, three church-brown Formica-topped tables with folding chairs, and a large window along one wall. Patients entered the ward through the day room, so I generally saw the new people right away.

A nurse joined the unit as a patient. At least that's what I heard her say.

"I'm a nurse," she said to the woman behind the desk. I know I was eavesdropping, but there wasn't that much else to do.

Later the nurse as patient sat in one of the aqua chairs. She stared out the window all day. The nurse smoked constantly; she inhaled the last of the tobacco from a white filtered Salem 100 and then lit another one with the remaining coal. She inhaled deeply and exhaled in a slow, deliberate way, making me think of Old Man Winter initiating the wind. She didn't lift her gaze from the window. I wondered what she was staring at. Was it the sky? Was it the dome of St. Paul's capitol, about two miles off on a hill, and about even with our sixth-floor perch? Or perhaps the statue of the four gilded horses at the base of the dome caught her interest.

"Hi," I said. "I'm Anna Books. What's your name?"

"Avis. Avis Otto. I'm a nurse," she said.

I didn't tell her I already knew that she was a nurse. "What are you doing?" I said.

"I am purifying my lungs as I watch God. Can't you see him there at the capitol?"

I looked out at the white capitol building. I could see the four tarnished horses standing in for the power of nature: earth, wind, fire and water.

"I've never seen God," I said.

"Oh," she said, but without moving her eyes.

It bothered me to see so much smoke around her face. I thought she'd do better if she had something to do with her hands.

Occupational Therapy was outside the suicide ward, but still on the sixth floor, the first door on the left. We were locked in that room, too. Some of us attended O.T.— that's what we called it—in shifts during the morning. In O.T. one could make a number of projects: leather tooled belts or wallets, copper pictures, ceramics.

At O.T. the next morning, I brought back some yarn and two crochet hooks. After lunch, I sat in the other aqua chair, and I taught Avis how to crochet. I don't know why crochet hooks and yarn were allowed without supervision. I was already catching on to think that I could hang myself with the yarn, or stick the hook in my eye, but for some reason the staff didn't say anything. I didn't point out the inconsistency. I showed Avis how row one was the hardest because of inserting the hook into the initial chain. She had trouble remembering to chain two at the end before she turned the work around in order to begin the next row.

"Crocheting is easy," I said. "If you don't like it, you can just rip it out and start over. Just take your time," I said. We did take our time. We didn't have to hurry; all we were waiting for was supper. It took us all afternoon, but she learned. Avis made progress on a green acrylic yarn potholder. She still lit one after another, but many of her cigarettes burned up in the ashtray. "Thank you. This is fun," she said with a soft voice.

Avis didn't mention the need to purify her lungs. Maybe if she felt useful she didn't worry so much about being pure.

I was compelled to make things, as if the act of moving my hands kept me safe. O.T. was fun. It was a place to make a mess. The tables and floors were dull, coated with glue and paint splats.

The cupboard doors had nicks and dents. I picked out a wide piece of chestnut-colored leather and decided to make a belt. The O.T. teacher showed me how to get the leather wet and put designs into it with metal stamps. I chose a simple leaf pattern and carefully pounded the design all around the edge of the belt. I thought it turned out well.

Back in the day room, a nurse asked, "What did you make in O.T. today?"

"I made this belt," I said. "I'm proud of it."

"We'll have to take that from you," she said.

"But why?"

"So you don't hang yourself," she said.

One afternoon a younger woman entered through the locked double doors, escorted by an orderly. She was younger than everyone else except me. I guessed she was in her thirties. She sat at my table. "My room isn't ready yet," she said. "Can I borrow a tweezers from you?" she asked.

It seemed an odd thing to do on your first afternoon in a suicide ward, but I asked a nurse to get my tweezers from the locker. The new patient had to pluck her eyebrows in the day room, under supervision. The young woman was unsteady—she was as likely to pinch her skin as an eyebrow hair with the tweezers, so before long she was bleeding above both eyelids. I wondered if I should offer to help her.

"These pills make me shake," she said.

I refused to take any medication, though the staff suggested that I "take something" for my depression. I had been taking drugs and alcohol for three years. What made *their* drugs acceptable? It seemed like a trap.

I'm not sure what they would have given me, but plenty of dull-faced people were dragging their feet down the hallway in what patients called the "Thorazine Shuffle." I didn't want any part of it.

"Your eyebrows look fine," I told her.

I asked her about her wooden leg, attached by a brace just above her left knee. She told me she had fallen off her porch swing and injured her knee while she was on an acid trip. The wound never healed, she said, so her leg had to be amputated.

She screamed the next morning. "I want my leg—give me my leg!" The nurses and orderlies were telling her, "You lost your leg, dear; it's gone," thinking of course that she was confused and meant her real leg. They scurried out of her room and back to the nurses' station to see what drug they could give her for her agitation. She persisted, insisting that she did in fact have a leg. But she couldn't get out of bed without it, or perhaps they had her strapped down, too. She was screaming like Sarah McIntyre, with the same frantic tone.

It was ironic, now that I think of it, how many people started screaming so soon after going into the hospital for help.

I was still in my pajamas but seated at the table in the day room, smoking.

"She walked in here, yesterday. Yesterday, she had a leg," I said to the nurse in the hall as she hurried toward the office.

The nurse walked over to my table. "She did? Did you see what they did with it?"

"No. It was made of wood. It attached to her leg just above the knee; she showed me."

A group of staff nurses and orderlies returned to her room. They found the wooden calf and foot in the closet. The night staff had forgotten to note in the chart where they put it. The woman had been so heavily drugged that she was asleep when the leg had been removed along with her street clothes. Now that she had her leg, she stopped screaming. I didn't hear them call her "Dear" again.

Avis Otto, the nurse patient, and I became friends. She was fifty-four and from White Bear Lake. Though she emphasized that she had a loving family, she had been in the hospital several times before.

"They tell me I'm nervous," she said. "I have bad nerves."

We walked arm in arm up and down the short hallway. When we walked up the hall, we looked out the window down the six floors to the street. We saw a couple of drunks leaning against the wall below, smoking cigarettes.

"On the outside they look lost, but from in here, up here, they look free," Avis said. Though she never made it clear to me, I guessed that Avis was, like me, in the psych ward at least partly against her will.

Avis and I measured one of the industrial vinyl floor tiles with a ruler. We counted the number of tiles in the hall's length, from the nurse's station to the window at the end of the hall, and then multiplied the number of tiles times the inches of a single tile. While sitting at the table in the day room, we calculated that if we walked the hall from the nurse's station to the window up and back thirty times, we had walked a mile. We walked a mile then, briskly, arm in arm, as an after-meal ritual. It was fun. The staff hushed us when we got too boisterous with our laughter. We immediately stopped talking loudly and went to whispering.

"Happiness," Avis whispered, "is easier to stop than misery." The staff didn't get such obedience from the screamers.

Chapter 2

It wasn't exactly clear why the judge wanted me to get "evaluated" in the psych ward. I wasn't getting along in school. Mr. Stark, my history teacher, said I was incorrigible. I needed to look up the word. Dad wanted me to quit smoking pot. I said, "Dad. I'll quit pot, if you quit drinking." That's where we left it.

One night just a few weeks after I learned I was incorrigible, I fell asleep in front of the TV. Mom woke me and told me to go to our neighbors, the Stones, where my friend Susan lived.

"Don't change your clothes, just get Janice up. Get your coats on and go now," she said.

Even though I'd been asleep, I knew it was because they were fighting. I could feel it. Janice, my sister, two years older than I, was not asleep. She'd been listening to the whole thing, and she was crying. Janice put her coat on over her pajamas. We walked to Susan's house.

I could see our house through the woods from Susan's kitchen.

For a time I could see my mom struggling outside in the snow with my dad. The outside light on the garage lit their silhouettes—more than once I saw the larger figure knock the smaller figure down.

When that happened, Mrs. Stone told us to go into Susan's room. The two of us sat, legs straight out in front of us, backs against the wall, on her bed. We knew to be quiet without saying anything to each other. We even stilled our breathing so it made it easy to hear anything happening outside of the room. I stayed with Susan until I heard my mom's voice. I moved into the hallway, still out of sight, straining to hear. I was afraid that if they saw me, Mrs. Stone would make me go back into Susan's room.

I dared to peek around the corner and saw that my mom was sitting on the couch in the living room, holding a cigarette. She had quit smoking, so the cigarette was unlit. Would she light it? I crept closer to the room. I saw my dad then. I just happened to move forward and look left, and he was there at the porch door. The door was open about one foot. He would have had to move it in order to come inside, but it was already open. He was motionless; he was just standing there. I could see how sad he was, even though I'd only seen him sad once before, at dinner when he talked about his dead grandmother. I noticed something else about him. He was as lifeless as a plastic doll, with the same blank face. It scared me and hurt me to see him that way: it seemed like an emergency to me. Mr. Stone, who had been in the living room with my mom, finally saw my dad, too, and went out on the porch. The conversation was serious but matter of fact. No one acted as if they saw the emergency I had seen in my dad's face. My dad needed help. He needed someone who could understand him; that was clear to me. No one ought have that look on their face.

The next day when we were home again, I dried the dishes while she washed them, which she rarely wanted me to do. "Dad needs help, Mom. Are you going to get some help for Dad?" I asked.

She was watching the dishes in the sink, and I was watching whatever dish I was drying or putting away. We didn't look at each other. I could feel that she heard me, but she didn't say anything.

৵

I don't understand now, looking back on it, any better than I did then. I don't understand how it was that in the quiet weeks after I told my mom that my dad needed help, he never got any help. I don't understand how it was right after that my mom made an appointment for me and took me to see a psychiatrist. Some illogical twist as quiet as the swinging chain of a hypnotist's watch changed reality—so that except for a nagging feeling, I could barely remember a time when anyone had thought my dad's behavior was strange, or a time that the family situation was not all my fault.

The psychiatrist asked me questions in his tan room, with tan chairs. He sat on a padded desk chair with a huge cherry desk behind him. I didn't like it because the window was behind me. I faced him and he faced me but he might have been looking out the window instead of at me; I couldn't tell. He had a flat mouth and a faraway look. I wasn't sure he could even see me.

I told him that my teacher, Mr. Stark, started all of my problems; he didn't like me. I didn't know what made Mr. Stark so mad. It seemed to me that he picked on me. He put remarks on my report card that said I was incorrigible and he gave me a C grade. That was more than my dad could take. We had fights about it, I said.

"Do you mean Ken Stark? Is your teacher Ken Stark?" he said.

"Yeah. Mr. Stark. I think his first name is Ken. Why?"

"I know Ken Stark. We were in the Marines together."

There you go. The psychiatrist was a friend of my enemy. I was quiet then. I stopped wondering if he was looking out the window, and refused to go back.

We saw another counselor. I talked to her by myself for half the hour. She had delicate hands with mauve, enameled nails. Each nail was perfectly shaped and precisely the same length as all of the others, and these nails made her hands seem extraordinary. She had wide hips that made her seem comfortable while she asked me one question after another and listened carefully to every answer. As far as I knew she didn't think I was incorrigible. She never said so.

Then my parents talked to her for half the hour while I sat in the waiting room. It was tense in the car on the way home. My parents were stiff in the front seat and didn't talk to me. I would have gone back to that counselor, but I didn't have to.

The day after I saw her, I didn't go to school. I was too tired to get out of bed. I was fifteen, in tenth grade. Mom woke me at 10:30 a.m.

"Mr. Wies called. He wants you to come to school," Mom said.

Mr. Wies was the Assistant Principal at the high school. This generation had overcrowded the junior high and high school. A new high school was built, but not a new junior high, so the new high school filled with eighth through eleventh grades. I started senior high in eighth grade.

"What does Mr. Wies want?" I said, feeling annoyed and afraid.

"He didn't say," Mom said.

We drove to the principal's office in Mom's green Volkswagen hatchback.

"You were caught smoking pot," Mr. Wies said.

"When?" I said.

"Yesterday," he said.

"When was I smoking it?" I said.

"Yesterday."

"I don't recall being caught. What did you do—take footprints?"

I did smoke pot at school, but I hadn't been caught doing it.

"I don't have to tell you how we know," he said. Then he turned to my mom.

"The standard procedure for students caught using a controlled substance is for them to be placed in our afternoon school program for a period of three weeks. Regular daytime class attendance is prohibited," he said.

"What time is she supposed to be here?" Mom said. She was polite and calm.

"Anna will arrive at 3:00 p.m. for school. Her class will end at 5:00 p.m."

I hated everything that Mr. Wies did. I wanted to scream at him. I didn't, though. I just glared at him and wondered how he talked to his own children.

"Is there a bus?" Mom asked.

"She will need a ride to and from class. She may not loiter here or associate with other students on the grounds."

"How does she get back into school?" she said. I sat next to my mom, watching her talking to Mr. Wies as if I was a houseplant and she was seeking instructions for my care.

"She will be evaluated during the three-week suspension. During that time we will decide whether she will be able to return to daytime classes. We will notify you in writing."

We rode home in silence. Neither of us said anything, but Mom's disappointment in me was loud.

❧

I wasn't surprised to see Harry Homer, David West, and Tessa Moe, David's girlfriend, at detention school the first afternoon. I walked in the classroom, and there they were.

The day they had been caught, we had smoked my pot with their pipe. They had approached me that day and asked if I had any pot. We went to Harry's car over lunch and lit up. I left them in the car and went to class. They got caught. One or maybe all of them told on me, and that's how I got in trouble. They probably got something for turning me in.

Mrs. Koski taught afternoon school. Nobody liked her daughter, who was my age. The rumor was that someone looked over the stall in the bathroom and saw her daughter masturbating. I didn't believe it. And anyhow, it seemed more terrible to spy on someone than to masturbate, so it didn't make me dislike the girl. But I still didn't believe it. Granted, she was plain and had an unpopular mother, but she looked as if she could wait to get home to masturbate. I even tried to talk to her. She was so used to ridicule I don't think she realized I wasn't teasing her. No one wanted to go to "night school," as we called it. We met in a tiny room in the back of the library. It was more like being baby-sat than going to school. No homework. No lectures. Mrs. Koski, four students, no one else.

I thought David West was cute, but he was there with his girlfriend, Tessa. Tessa had bad skin and giggled too much, a shallow, horizontal giggle like a rock skipping across the water. Harry parted his shoulder-length hair in the middle and played in a rock band. I wasn't interested in talking with them, since I was sure one—and probably all of them—had given Wies my name.

While attending night school, I didn't get out of bed until noon or later each day. I drew pictures of plants and embroidered. I finished cross-stitched dishtowels, one for a household chore for each day of the week. Monday: Washday, Tuesday: Ironing, etc. Then I sewed a plain muslin shirt and embroidered a dragon on the front of it. I walked alone for hours. I brought my sketchbook to class. My mom was there with me during the day. She was busy with her housework and cooking. The only thing I remember about her is the heavy, silent disappointment. Without admitting it to myself, I felt condemned.

I knew I couldn't get back into day school until three weeks had passed. At the end of the three weeks, on the last day, I watched from the kitchen window down the hill to the road for the white and blue mail truck to stop at our mailbox. I walked down to the end of the driveway and got the mail as soon as I saw it come. The envelope was addressed to "The Parents of Anna Books." I opened it as I walked up the driveway.

The letter said that I had been evaluated top to bottom by everyone from the superintendent to the school nurse. That was a shock. I hadn't talked to *anyone*. Mrs. Koski was the only adult I had seen at school in the three weeks. The second shock was that the letter said it had been determined that I was not suitable for the day school program and would have to remain in detention.

When I got to school that afternoon, I learned that Harry, David and Tessa had been readmitted. They were delighted to be going back to day school.

Here is where the injustice of it began to sink in. After class, I marched, my anger making me stiff, right into Mr. Wies' office. His office was a closet, with a wide desk keeping us apart. His bald head shone from the fluorescent light above it.

"Why aren't you letting me back in school?" I said.

"Because I don't like you. I don't like your kind. If it was up to me you wouldn't be in my afternoon school either, but you aren't old enough to expel. I don't have a choice."

I walked out to the car where my mom waited patiently. I told her what I said to Mr. Wies, and what he had said to me.

"What am I going to do? I can't stay in afternoon school. If I ever get back in, he'll make up some reason to kick me out again. I quit."

"You're probably right," she said, her expression as hopeless as I felt. "I don't know what to tell you."

Before I had noticed that my dad needed help, he had yelled at me for getting a "C" on my report card. Now, after that, I had quit school entirely, and the whole house was peaceful. I don't remember any yelling at all.

The next letter to arrive from Mr. Wies said that he noticed I wasn't in attendance in the afternoon school. The law is that you have to go to school until you're sixteen. Mr. Wies was taking me to court for truancy. The court date was set.

When I got to court, the judge sentenced me to the hospital for evaluation. "We have to find out what's going on with you," he said.

Even though it doesn't quite make sense, that's how I got to St. Joseph's hospital.

⚭

As the judge said, I was hospitalized for evaluation, so I got evaluated and examined. Sometimes I took tests in the day room. I took the long M.M.P.I. for the first time, more than five hundred true or false questions. True or false: I like mechanics magazines. False for liking mechanics magazines was easy. I'd never seen a mechanics magazine, but it was clear to me I wouldn't like one. True or false: I loved my mother. I spent time worrying about that. I did love my mother, but she was still alive. The statement was I *loved* my mother. I didn't love her in the past tense, did I? If I loved her in the past, would they think I didn't love her in the present?

We had our three meals in the day room. We ate, sat and waited in the day room. In the day room one could talk, crochet or play cards. Staying alone in our hospital rooms was discouraged. If I stayed alone in my room too much, either reading or staring out the window at the sky, I was told to get up and go out.

The first meeting with my psychiatrist took place in my hospital bedroom, with the door closed. He told me to take off my clothes. "Everything except your underwear," he said. He told me to touch my nose with my finger. Next he said, "Follow my finger with your eyes."

I touched my nose, followed his finger with my eyes up and down, and hopped on one leg and then the next in my underwear. I was embarrassed. It didn't seem right that I had my clothes off. He didn't listen to my lungs or anything. I was cold. Most of the people in that ward were on their way to a nursing home. I wondered if Avis had to stand in her underwear during her test. He asked me questions for over half an hour while I sat on the hospital bed in my underwear. I didn't like that.

I didn't understand this evaluation. I thought they were trying to find out if they could help me, but I never learned anything helpful.

The only information I got from anyone on the results of the court-ordered evaluation that lasted five weeks came from my dad.

"What did they find out about me?" I asked.

"You are oversexed," Dad said.

It wasn't easy to talk to my dad anyway—but when he told me that I simply couldn't think of a thing to say to him. What was oversexed? Who told him that? Did anyone tell him that? How did they know? How did I have so many questions that couldn't find a way onto my tongue? The words crowded my mind like musty, ill-fitting coats stuffed in a back-room closet. I was oversexed. At fifteen, a part of me believed anything adults said. It would be five more years before I even considered that someone might be lying, and many more years before I understood projection. If I had been a china cup most of me had already shattered in a busy parking lot, leaving some of me shards, and some other parts of me ground to dust by passers-by, but I didn't know that yet either. Being described as oversexed didn't feel good.

Most teenage girls must seem oversexed to the men who lust for them. Perhaps it's just a thought that comforts their desire.

$$\mathcal{A}$$

Between shifts, the nurses and orderlies met in a closed room by the nurse's station and discussed how we were all doing.

Following the meetings, they wrote in our charts. This procedure was called "charting." I got this information from one of the orderlies.

I'm not sure how all this was arranged; I assumed it was part of the charting meetings, but my parents told me they would like me to go to an intake interview at the Holy Mary Home for Girls. The home was on the edge of North Oaks, fifteen miles northeast of my parents' home, in a suburb of St. Paul. The Holy Mary Home for Girls had traditionally taken in pregnant teenagers, but in the 1970s they expanded their services to the incorrigible and to girls on drugs. I didn't understand what the Holy Mary Home for Girls meant, but Mom said if I agreed to go to the Home, I could get out of the hospital for Thanksgiving.

Mom and Dad picked me up at the psych ward and took me to the Holy Mary Home for my intake interview. I trembled in the car because along the freeway there were no walls. I was shocked by the space.

I had forgotten that space was friendly, the way Mrs. McIntyre had forgotten that I was. Mom told me that Tommy Erikson had been caught smoking pot. "Is he in night school, too?"

"I don't know," she said. "I imagine."

I don't remember how it got decided. I was seduced by the idea of going home for Thanksgiving. But right after that I was going to live at Holy Mary's home.

When I was released from the hospital, the staff couldn't find the tooled leather belt I had made. It had been lost. Also lost were my birth control pills. The pills had been confiscated at intake. "To prevent an overdose," they said which made me laugh. I could see the headlines:

INCORRIGIBLE GIRL DIES:
BIRTH-CONTROL PILL OVERDOSE

Chapter 3

The first time I noticed how easy it was to find someone to love was when I met Larry across the lake.

Larry was sixteen, a junior in high school. I would start eighth grade in the fall. We both lived with our families on Lake Elizabeth, north of St. Paul, Minnesota. Lake Elizabeth has three bays. I lived with my parents and sister on the shore of what was known as the first bay. Larry lived along the shore of the second bay.

I loved Larry. I met him the same year I started drinking, a couple of years before I landed in the psych ward and the Holy Mary Home for Girls. On Friday nights, my parents were either having a party or going out to dinner. One night when they were out to dinner, I drank gin at home alone, the way I had seen my dad drink gin: just straight in the glass, no ice, though I didn't add an olive or stir it with a plastic stick with a Playboy bunny on top, the way my dad did. I regularly downed several glasses like this and threw up in the toilet in the upstairs bathroom.

Larry was screwed up, and I loved being near him. He suffered. I loved suffering for some reason. Larry drew cartoons of G.I. Joe and Alfred E. Newman outlined with paisley scrolls in India ink on clean, white paper. I loved the sleek gloss of the ink. He cried as he talked about how much he missed his mom and his half brothers. He knew his life wasn't fair. It wasn't fair that his stepmother didn't like him.

It wasn't fair that he had to be separated from his mother and half brothers just because his parents didn't get along.

Larry and I were girlfriend and boyfriend all summer. I saw him almost every day; I either drove the speedboat seven minutes to the second bay of Lake Elizabeth or I walked the three miles by road to his house. In order to be out of the sight of Larry's disapproving stepmother, Larry and I sat around smoking Marlboro cigarettes, with KDWB on the transistor radio, and talked about life as it was in the summer of 1970, on the road by Rick Davis's house.

Rick lived three houses away from Larry on the same side of the street. The road on which they lived circled "The Island," which was actually a peninsula of land between the second and third bays of the lake. Most of the homes were originally lake cabins. The Island was the rural equivalent of crossing over to the wrong side of the railroad tracks.

I was lonely as a baby loon for two overlong weeks when Larry visited his mother. He sent me letters from Blackduck, Minnesota, where she lived with Larry's half brothers. It was the first time he had got to visit her in years. It was the first time I had ever heard of anything that said, "Where the Hell is so and so?" He sent me a bumper sticker: "Where the Hell is Blackduck?"

❧

Many times in the years before I met Larry, I went with Susan, my neighbor and best friend, out on Lake Elizabeth. We rowed near the end of the first bay to The Channel, which connected Johnson Lake to Lake Elizabeth. We found sleepy mud turtles sitting on dead trees that lay near the shore. The turtles plunked off the sun-warmed wood. We captured them by reaching into the water and lifting them into the boat while they continued to swim in midair. We lovingly gathered as many as we could catch. The edges of their painted bellies clapped against the rounded sides of the boat, and their clawed feet whined along the sandy aluminum.

Every few nights we looked to the summer sky as if we were part of a chorus, and said, "Is that a UFO?" We saw many falling stars and no UFOs before we drifted to sleep in bags on lawn chairs outside on the deck above the garage at my house. I brought the pillow from my bed and loved how cool the cotton case felt against my cheek when I slept outside.

I walked alone, with my sister, Janice, or with Susan along lakeshores, wooded paths, and unpaved roads in the day or in the night. People were still talking about Ed Gein and Eugene Thompson. Though Ed was from Wisconsin—close by—Susan and I talked about how close he was; I didn't think it counted as scary because he didn't kill people. He just used the already dead. Susan thought he killed people, and she was scared. I was curious about the things Ed Gein made from human flesh. I imagined the lampshades: skin pink, with a ruffle at the edge.

People didn't get murdered much in the Minnesota in 1969. When Dave Moore from television news reported a murder, a current one, in general he was talking about a story from New York or Chicago.

Salamanders gathered in the window wells of our house; I saw frogs and snapping turtles in the yard. We found praying mantises and walking sticks, not in the deep woods but on the oaks six feet outside our house. Almost any summer evening if I wanted to I could capture fireflies in an empty peanut butter jar and watch them glow yellow through the glass in the unlit hallway outside my bedroom.

Still, I spent a lot of time afraid, not of Ed Gein, or murderers, but of the invisible. A few times I opened my eyes in the middle of the night. It was quiet. The busiest road near our house had not yet been upgraded, so there were no traffic noises, even at night, even for the short time in the early spring when the oaks were without leaves.

My bunk bed had a wooden headboard, and my bedroom was paneled with wood. The room had a wooden floor and ceiling as well, so I slept in a wooden box. Janice slept in the bunk above me. We shared a room until I was ten years old. I knew she was directly above me, but I didn't hear her. I didn't even hear myself breathing. I didn't want to, but I made myself look up to the wall just above me, to the window. I saw the calm moon behind the silhouette of an oak tree.

Then a voice said, "Come out."

I heard this voice several different nights—it sounded as if it was right outside my window, speaking from the woods.

I tried to get back to sleep by rubbing the soft inner part on the arches of my feet together, and by rubbing my cheek on my pillow, the way I did when I was sick, or afraid.

Some things happen and you don't know what they mean or why they happened, and you're never going to find out. This was one of them. That voice came to my window through the vaporous light a half dozen times. I never mentioned it to anybody. I never asked Janice if she heard it. I never decided whether I had dreamed it or whether it had happened. I lived in a state of unease, as if any minute reality could cease to make any sense at all. I didn't know that a voice like that could be a calling.

I can remember summer days on the beach as clearly as the Bible verses I memorized in order to get a copper cross for my Bible—packed as if all the days were a verse.

Our mothers read novels and sat in greasy lawn chairs, summer after summer. One summer day, as on most, Janice, Susan, and I had been swimming. In the late afternoon, the sun fell behind the trees and barely reached us on the eastern shore. The three of us were in an inner tube, hanging over it as if our heads and upper bodies were the petals of a water lily. When we were still, the sunfish would nibble on our feet or bare stomachs. We swam up through the center of the tube from underwater—careful to miss the valve stem.

I dove through the top at the same time Susan and Janice swam through the middle. We got stuck. I got caught face down in a foot of water—I could not get back out, nor continue through the tube. I struggled, opening my eyes, kicking my feet, and choking.

Susan finally noticed me struggling. She wriggled her way out of the tube and set me free. I sat in the mud along the shore near my mom, where I caught my breath and told her what had happened.

I collected wounded rabbits, birds, and squirrels. I'd save them for a while to make sure they were all right and then let them go. One squirrel I had in my room got out of his box. I captured him with a flour sifter and pulled him carefully down the hall to the front door where I set him free. One day, while on a walk, I spotted a nest at the top of a tree. I climbed the tree and looked at the babies. A few days later I climbed the tree again and the birds were dead. I never knew if I had disrupted the nest so that the mother didn't return, or if she was already gone the first day I looked. I wondered if I could have saved those birds.

Being in love or being in danger make life specific. For example, I'll never forget when Larry got home from Blackduck. Many times, I drove our new speedboat with Susan over to Rick Davis's shore. She liked Larry's younger brother, Cliff. We stayed all day, and in my memory all of the days seem similar. But when Larry got home from Blackduck, I went over to get him in the boat by myself. I stopped the boat on Lake Elizabeth. We lay under the bow and floated while we kissed.

I remember two other events perfectly. The summer I met Larry, I found a baby robin. I could not find her nest, so I kept her. I spent the day with Larry in the boat. When I got home the robin was dead. I cried.

My mom let me bury the robin in the corner of her garden. The worst part was that I hadn't even thought of the bird all afternoon.

The second was, one day, Mom told me she was going to have a nervous breakdown. Why was I gone so much? she asked. I wanted to help her. I didn't know how to help my mom not have a nervous breakdown, and I didn't stay home more. Though I don't know how I could have helped my mom, I don't know why I didn't even try.

Chapter 4

Occasionally we played ball with the island neighborhood kids at the field at the intersection of Johnson Lake and Elizabeth roads, just past Tommy Erikson's house. Tommy's house was before The Island, so he was known as a boy from our neighborhood.

I often felt tense and clunky around Larry; he was older, and I wanted to impress him. I listened to the same music, smoked the same cigarettes. He acted as if he liked me. He brought me a Black Sabbath album and a yellow (I never liked the color) brandy snifter that he got at the Minnesota State Fair. I didn't even know what to do with a brandy snifter. I put it up on the highest shelf in my room, where it collected dust in the deep bowl of the glass.

Larry's life was a version of Cinderella, as Larry and his brother had lots of chores to do, and they had a stepmother. She was a square woman with long hair pulled into a tight ponytail, as if she was being held back by her hair. They could never have anyone over without sneaking, especially girls. Larry's dad and stepmom didn't go out to dinner as much as my parents did, but they did go out occasionally. Larry's bedroom took up about half of the second floor of a barn-shaped house on a hill overlooking the lake, across the bay from the Society of Jesus retreat house. Catholic businessmen visited the Society for rest and solitude; the place hired kids to help serve meals. Susan worked at the retreat's kitchen on weekends.

Once when his parents were out, I got up to Larry's bedroom. He shared it with his brother, Cliff. Larry's drawings hung on one wide wall where he had inked quotes from Malcolm X. Some places he had America spelled with a "k." In one of his letters from Blackduck he inked my name: TO ANNA BOOKS. Then he copied the words to Bread's "Make It with You." It was so beautifully done it could have been framed. No one else since has ever copied the words to a song and sent them to me.

He worked in North St. Paul as a dishwasher at the King High drive-in. One time he came to my house after work. I crawled out the high window in my bedroom and he helped me down to the ground.

We parked in his '61 Corvair with the rear-mounted engine and red interior on an unpaved road off Doe Lake Trail, about a mile from my house. We kissed, talked, and kissed some more; the car floated in the timelessness of kissing. We might have stayed all night but saw a car coming. I knew it was going to be my dad, and I was right. I don't know how he found us, why he thought to drive down this road.

Larry started the car and put it in reverse as though he was going to try to escape. I watched his eyes, while he watched the rear-view mirror. He backed up about fifty feet, and then put the car in park.

Dad knocked on the window on the passenger's side of the car. I opened the door.

"Better come home, Charlie Brown," he said. My dad sometimes called me Charlie Brown.

I rode home in silence in Dad's Ford LTD. Dad wanted to know whether he should take me to the hospital, but I didn't know why. He was talking this over with my mom. "Should we have her checked?" is what they said. Some unexplained quick change in tone occurred, and I didn't have to get checked. Nothing worse than my parents' silent disappointment happened to me for getting caught sneaking out with Larry.

꙳

One late afternoon Larry and I met near the beach at my parents' house and talked. We sat in the shaded woods instead of at the shore. I thought he was handsome. He had blond, curly hair, and a long, thin nose, which moved at the nostrils just a bit when he breathed; something about his nose made me feel sorry for him.

Larry carried a condom with him. Here's how I found that out.

He took his slippery black wallet with a driver's license, a five-dollar bill, and pictures of friends from his pocket. He slid out the packet.

"What's that?" I said.

"It's a rubber, Anna," he said.

"Oh," I said. I tried to act as if I expected it, though I was completely surprised. I barely knew what a rubber was.

"I'm ashamed of myself," he said.

"What's the matter?" I asked.

"I'm in a bad mood."

"Why?" I was interested in the condom and afraid of it, too, the same way I felt about anything "down there" or "about that," the way we'd all been taught.

"I haven't been telling you the truth."

"About what?" I was confused.

"I haven't told you everything. I've been to the doctor," he said.

"What for?" I said, sincerely. I did care. If you had asked me, I would have said Larry was somebody who needed help.

"You don't understand. I haven't let you understand. The doctor said if I don't have children in the next few years, I won't be able to. I'm nearly impotent."

I wasn't even sure what that was, but it sounded serious. You had to have confidence to use the long words that Larry used. Sometimes he talked about people who were "melodramatic."

"Oh," I said, trying to match his depth.

"I have a low sperm count. I may never be able to have children. I have a greater chance if I start now. The doctor says the situation will worsen with age."

He ran to the shore of Lake Elizabeth and threw that condom into the lake the way you pitch a baseball (not the gentle way I used to skip flat rocks I found on the shore). I didn't know what he wanted me to do.

"Oh, how unfair that you can't have children," I said.

"That's not true. I might be able to have children if I get started soon enough."

I was so confused. I had just turned thirteen years old. Did he want me to volunteer to have his baby? Did he throw the rubber in the lake because he didn't need it?

Just after that conversation, I started having cramps. I had a fever. I stayed all week on the foldout couch in front of the TV.

Mom took me to her doctor at the Central Medical Building in St. Paul. I had my first pelvic exam. The doctor said I was acting as if I had a cyst on my ovary. But he said I was too young for that. I must have been too young to be sick, because he didn't check for anything. Was he saying that I wasn't sick? That I didn't have a fever and pelvic pain, and I didn't spend a week on the couch?

These paradoxes were so many I just left them in my mind as if it were normal to have blatant clashes of logic in a standoff.

❧

Larry said he couldn't stand it with his stepmother anymore. He moved to Stillwater to stay with a friend, Sid. Sid was a cool cat, Larry said. Sid was screwing Lorna; that's how Larry put it.

School started. I missed Larry. Shortly after he moved to Stillwater, he invited me on my first date, in a car, in the evening. Official. It was a double date so my parents said I could go. Larry was mad that my curfew was midnight. He didn't have a curfew at Sid's house.

Susan braided my long blonde hair in tiny braids all the way down to the ends. We used her orthodontist bands to hold the braids, while my hair was still wet. I slept on the braids, and took them out in the morning. My hair was a thick wavy mass. Susan lent me her black cape, with a red silk lining. I wore eye shadow, liner, and mascara.

Larry introduced me to Lorna and Sid. They were all sixteen. Though Sid was supposed to be suave, he had an annoying twang in his voice that I couldn't get past. Lorna's arms and legs were graceful but long. She reminded me of a daddy-long-legs spider. Sid, Lorna, Larry and I saw Donovan in concert. I was nervous, and shy. I tried to pretend I was older. I felt awkward. We smoked pot. Larry fell asleep.

We went to Sid's afterward. All in all, it was a boring evening, what with Larry sleeping and me feeling young and out of place, even with pretty blond hair and a silk-lined cape.

❧

One Saturday, I called Larry from my bedroom with my yellow princess phone with the lighted dial in the receiver.

"Hi, Larry," I said.

"Hi, Anna," he said.

"How's it going?"

"Okay."

"I miss you. I'm lonely today. I haven't heard from you since we saw Donovan."

"I know. I haven't felt like calling."

"Do you know why?" I said.

"I've been spending time with Lorna."

I could be understanding, but I couldn't be older. I couldn't be free to go on dates and stay out indefinitely, the way Lorna could. I felt the panic of being replaced.

"Oh. Why is that? I thought Lorna was dating Sid? What happened to Sid?"

"I don't know what you mean," Larry said.

"I thought we were friends. What happened?"

"I might have more to do with you if you were more like Lorna," he said.

"Do you mean you would still be interested in me if we were having sex?"

"Yes. I think I would."

I didn't hear from Larry for months, and for months our last conversation left a bee's lingering sting in my brain.

❧

Late in the spring of 1971, before I turned fourteen, Larry called me. He was going home to visit his parents. I walked over and met him on the road by his house. We sat down by the pine trees near the baseball field and he kissed me. I got completely naked, though he didn't, and we screwed in the weeds at the edge of the ball field outside the boundaries of the island at the intersection of Lake Elizabeth and Johnson Lake road.

It was the first cold action of my life, the first of many. I didn't even realize it was a decision; maybe it wasn't. But it *was* cold. Sex was impersonal. It didn't hurt. I was numb. I was embarrassed out there in the weeds in the light. A new house had been built near the ball field.

As we lay there for a while, a man came up from that yard and yelled at us. For all I know, he had watched us have sex.

I walked home deep in thought, as if I were trying to understand what had happened to me by listening carefully on the inside, by remembering. My legs were heavy, as if sloshing through mud. My mom said I walked funny, as if she knew what had happened. Larry never called me again.

Chapter 5

After six weeks in St. Joseph's hospital, right after Thanksgiving and more than a year since I had last seen Larry, I moved to the Holy Mary Home for Girls. The afternoon my parents left me in the barren upstairs room with a carton of Newport cigarettes and my suitcase full of clothes was a desolate afternoon. When I realized they were leaving and I was staying, I felt a terror I couldn't name nor contain, like being eaten alive without the hope of death.

The home wasn't for pregnant girls; in the seven months I was there, only one girl was pregnant, and she didn't arrive pregnant. She got pregnant on a visit home.

It wasn't a home either. It was five homes—"cottages" they were called—a school building, a church, and a convent. Each of the five cottages on the grounds housed fourteen "wayward" girls—that's what we were called. The cottages were located in a flat, grassy area at the outer edge of North Oaks, an enclosed private community for the well-to-do. It was a perfect geographical oxymoron putting the Home and the wayward girls it housed right next to the vast woods and mansions of North Oaks. Sometimes the police would have to scour those woods to find runaways. Most girls who ran away were caught in just a few hours.

When I thought of a cottage or a cabin, as these structures were interchangeably called, I thought of wood and logs and lakeshore, not the locked place in which I found myself. The cabins were made of brick and concrete. A long cement tunnel connected all of them to each other. The tunnel also led to the building where the schoolrooms, the nurse's office, and the cafeteria were contained. The tunnel did not go to the building where the nuns lived, or to the chapel.

The cottages were named: P.H., which stood for Pelletier Hall, named for the Home's founder, Sr. Mary Euphrasia Pelletier; Kari, a Japanese word meaning bridge; Keller, named for Helen Keller; Mary, which stood for Mary, Mother of Jesus, and Waybun. I was assigned to Waybun cottage. Waybun was an Indian name for peace. Each cabin contained its own family, and we lived separately from each other. I didn't get to know any of the girls from the other cabins.

We made our own breakfasts and lunches in the cottage, and every night we picked up our prepared dinner from the cafeteria. Girls were assigned jobs. Those assigned the job of picking up the supper would go to the cafeteria where it was made and carry all the food back to the cabin on large trays. The times for these pick-ups were scattered to prevent girls from meeting with and talking to girls from other cabins while in the tunnel. Girls also picked up supplies for breakfasts and lunches the same way, on trays. The trays with the milk cartons were hard to carry. Waybun was farthest from the cafeteria, so our dinners were always cold, and the milk wasn't.

The main floor of Waybun had a living area, kitchen, and dining room, the entry, and a staff office. Upstairs were individual bedrooms made of concrete. Each one had a window, a single bed, a desk, and a closet. We were locked in the house during the day, and doubly locked upstairs at night.

I brought my pillow and case from home, which helped. I macraméd a white plant hanger, and my mom got me an ivy to put in it. I had packed a few of my favorite bottles from my antique collection, along with the teal-colored enamel vase I had dug up from the dump at the old farm on the point of Lake Elizabeth. It was dented in a few spots, but dear. I placed it on the window ledge, along with the clear bottle with the tarnished silver cap. Mom got me some sheer curtains to soften the light, and a gold bedspread to warm up the white room. At home, right away, she began tearing, sewing, and balling rags for me.

Then I started crocheting a rag rug from her balled rags for the floor of my cell.

I had a yeast infection again. I decided not to tell anyone. Even though I was up night after night with such an itch, I didn't get it treated. I thought I might get sick and die, and I liked that idea.

I got to sleep at night by imagining myself outside on the concrete apron near the entrance to Waybun, spinning as fast as I could with my arms out like helicopter blades until I imagined one arm hit the brick edge and cracked the bone in my forearm. This fantasy gave me comfort night after night.

We had a weekly mandatory meeting called "group" on Mondays, from three to five in the afternoon, with the counselors and the other residents. The counselors used terms such as "direct communication" and "confront." All of the problems and decisions of Waybun were handled "in group," unless they couldn't be talked about in a normal tone of voice. We talked in serious tones about our problems. Diane had the most problem with yelling. Yelling had to be done privately she was told. Sue Terwilliger—I loved her name, and usually called her Sue Terwilliger, while other girls didn't—got corrected for wearing her pajamas downstairs. Staff would say without singling her out that we must make sure we were fully dressed on the main floor. A plump red-head named Sue, and Stacy, the youngest in the group, couldn't understand why staff didn't want them walking around on top of the dining room tables even if they were in a good mood.

When I asked, though asking was mostly a formality, I usually received permission to go home. Home visits started first with my parents visiting me for an afternoon, then with me visiting them for an afternoon, next expanded to one overnight, and then the whole weekend, first every other weekend, and then every weekend.

❧

My first afternoon home visit, I saw my neighbor, Tommy. He

picked me up in his dad's car and we drove to Spring Lake State Park and walked around.

"I heard you got busted, too," I said to him. What happened?"

"Marty Farr, Pat Rusco and I were going to smoke the seeds that I had and the half joint that Pat had. Pat knew how to pry open the door to the gym. We got up to a loft area above the stage and started smoking. In a while we heard a noise. Mr. Wies came up the ladder. He took us to the office and expelled us."

"Did you have to go to night school?"

"Yes."

"With Mrs. Koski?"

"No. I had Mr. Griggs."

"Oh. Mr. Griggs. Did you have interesting classes? Did you get homework?"

"We just sat there for two hours, waiting, like a long homeroom."

"Were you alone with Mr. Griggs? Were there other students there?" I asked.

"I wasn't alone at first," Tommy said.

"This is sounding so much like what happened to me, Tommy," I said. "Tell me more."

"We had a hearing about a week after we got busted. Each of us had a separate hearing. Marty Farr got back in school after about a week, just after the hearing. I'm not sure how long Pat was suspended; he was with me for a while, several weeks. I was suspended for almost an entire quarter. Mr. Griggs finally called the Minnesota Chapter of the ACLU, and a lawyer took my case. I was allowed to return to the main school the day after he called."

"How did you find out, about the lawyer I mean?" I said.

"Wies showed up at night school and asked me if I'd like to come back. I said I would. He said, 'You can start regular classes tomorrow.'"

"Did he say anything else? For example, why you were being let back in?"

"No," Tommy said.

I told Tommy that Mr. Wies told me that he'd never let me back in day school. That's how I got sent to where I am now. I wondered what an ACLU lawyer would have done with that.

"I think that's the way it is. If Wies doesn't like you, you're out, unless you narc on someone he likes less than you," Tommy said. "Cops, administrators, and my parents were at the hearing where they decided what to do with us after we got busted. They said, 'Tell us who else you know who takes drugs, so we can help them.' 'You mean the way you're helping me?' I asked. They didn't like that much. I'm sure that's why they didn't want me back. But I noticed that Marty Farr must have had quite a lot to say to help them to help others, since he returned to school with only one week of detention, the week we waited for our hearing. We were all caught at the same time doing the same thing, but we all got varying punishments."

"That's just what happened to me, Tommy," I said. "I didn't even get caught!" I felt close to Tommy, as if he understood what it was like for me.

Tommy dropped me off at home about 4:00 in the afternoon. I was due back at Holy Mary by 7:00 p.m.

⚘

I talked to my mom while she made supper. I sat on the counter in the kitchen while she cleaned the vegetables for the salad.

I had just learned that Janice had been caught selling LSD. My parents had her bankbook.

"Are you in trouble with Mom and Dad?" I had asked Janice.

"No. I don't think so. They haven't done anything to me yet," Janice said.

"What did you tell them?"

"I told them it was Susan's deal. I just lent her the money."

"And they believed you?"

"I don't know."

It seemed to me that getting help was my job. The rest of the family didn't want any part of it.

"Mom," I said to her in the kitchen, "I'm getting straightened out. I'm learning to use more direct communication. It's better to be honest, to tell people how you truly feel. Stuffing your feelings isn't healthy. I think we might get along better if we used direct communication. Do you think that would work for our family?"

Mom moved the pile of carrot tops, then celery tops, then lettuce leaves closer to me.

Janice came into the kitchen. She looked at my legs.

"Oooh! Look at all that hair on your legs. You're obviously not looking for a man," she said, as she took a carrot from the drainer, and then left the room.

I don't know why Janice was cold to me that way.

"Is Janice going to get help, Mom?" I asked.

"I don't think so," she said looking out the window over the sink.

"Let me see—someone says I was smoking pot, but I wasn't caught. I do smoke pot, but I didn't get caught doing it. Janice sells drugs, Mom. She sells them and takes them. You found the drugs and her bankbook. Why doesn't she need help, too?"

"She doesn't give us so much trouble," she said.

"By that do you mean that she'll lie to you about what she's doing?" She didn't say anything, but I kept up, frantic from this latest contradiction heavy on my chest.

"I'd rather tell the truth. They teach us that at Holy Mary, Mom. They say it's better to tell the truth. It's better for your mental health," I said.

"I suppose it is," Mom said. Her tone was neither resignation nor interest. I hadn't given up on the idea of a fair application of the concept of being helped. I didn't yet see that their idea of my getting help was helping them to get me to shut up.

Chapter 6

I had so many things to wonder about. My dad still hadn't got any help, so far as I knew. Tommy had missed a whole quarter of school for doing the same thing that Marty Farr had done, yet Marty only missed a week for it. Janice was selling drugs—LSD and speed—and she wasn't going to have to get a single evaluation. I wondered if someone would think she was oversexed. Why I was getting help and what was helpful about it never made sense. People seemed happier with me when I agreed with them and asked few questions. Monday, after my first home visit, after school, I got summoned to the staff office in Waybun. Mary Malone, the counselor, said that Sr. Laura, the administrator of Holy Mary, had heard from Tommy Erikson's psychiatrist. Mary had a permanent look of concern on her face, but she put a special crease between her freckled brow and said: "Tommy is dangerous. You aren't allowed to see him anymore."

"Dangerous? He doesn't seem dangerous to me," I said.

"His psychiatrist says he's dangerous. He doesn't have a conscience—there's no telling what he might do. He's not good for you—and we want you to make it, so you can't see him any more on home visits." When they were concerned about whether a girl was going to "make it" they meant they were concerned if she would ever be able to go home. They were telling me that if I didn't stop seeing Tommy, I wouldn't be going home.

I was going to be lonely without Tommy.

If we were in good standing with the staff, we could ask permission to use the telephone in the evening after dinner. The phone in the staff office had an extra-long cord on the receiver, so once you dialed the number you could move out of the staff office, and onto a bench in the front lobby. I sat on the floor close to the coat closet.

I called Tommy. "I can't see you anymore. They tell me that your psychiatrist says you are dangerous."

"What? Are you kidding? I don't have a psychiatrist," Tommy said.

I didn't know whom to believe. It seemed unlikely that Tommy would lie to me about not having a psychiatrist.

"Who could it be then? Who is calling the Holy Mary Home for Girls telling them to keep you away from me?"

"I don't know," Tommy said.

Tommy and Mr. Griggs had done a lot of talking when they were alone together in the night school, after the others left. He had talked about me. Later that year, Steve Griggs, the one who had helped him get an attorney and get re-admitted to school, propositioned Tommy for sex. Tommy said he turned him down. We guessed that Mr. Griggs had helped Tommy get back into school, posed as his psychiatrist and kept him away from me so he could have him for himself.

Chapter 7

I got out for two hours a day for math and history class at Moundsview, the local high school. This freedom was a rare privilege. In the time I was there, I was the only one who had it. I had a break between the two classes and spent the time in the bathroom, smoking.

I happened to meet a girl named Karen in that bathroom at Moundsview. I'd heard about Karen. She had been released at the end of the summer from the Home, but before that she had, like me, been allowed to go off-site to Moundsview for classes. The counselors said she was beautiful, and she had done so much work turning her life around. When Karen found out I lived at Waybun, she gave me a hit of blotter acid—LSD dropped on blotter paper. I took the acid the next morning, by placing it on my tongue and then grinding the tiny piece of paper between my front teeth.

It was my job to make breakfast. A counselor slept upstairs with us every night. Joan Jessop was "on," as we called it. She unlocked the cage for me early, at 6:30 a.m., and let me downstairs thirty minutes before everyone else. I heard the cage lock again as I went downstairs. I found the electric fry pan in the cupboard and set it on the counter. The girls never put the dishes away in the same spot, the way they were supposed to. I took the eggs from the refrigerator and got one out of the package. I held the egg in my hand—and had the sense that it contained the answers to all my questions. It's hard to know how long I stood there holding the egg.

Morning was always chaotic. The counselors had a meeting between shifts; "staffing" they called it. The girls were left without any supervision during staffing.

I knocked on the door, still holding the egg in my hand.

"Yes, Anna," Mary said, irritated with me because of the interruption. Joan sat next to her with some papers in her lap.

I said, "I think you should talk to me."

"Why?"

"Privately," I said.

They let me in the office and closed the door.

I said, "I've taken some blotter acid and I don't think I should go to school. I'm afraid I might wander off or not want to come back here. I don't want to do anything that I might regret. I don't think I should go to school."

The counselors were shocked and nervous. I thought they were worried I might have a bad trip. I was worried, too, about how it would be to spend the day locked up high on LSD.

Luckily for me, two girls ran away that day. Taking acid was one of the things you got in trouble for, but with all the commotion at group when Toni and Rita got back, the staff must have forgotten.

Several weeks later Joan Jessop, the counselor, remembered it.

"Didn't we ever confront you about that?" she said.

❧

Life went on for me; no more near misses, no more trouble. Even though I thought it was unfair, I didn't see Tommy when I went for visits home.

On one home visit, Rick Davis took me to see Larry at Larry's new apartment. I combed my hair and parted it on the side. I wore a pretty embroidered top with my blue jeans. I wanted Larry to notice me. I wanted to feel special to him the way I had felt before. Larry gave us a tour of his place: a two-bedroom with gypsum walls, a galley kitchen and a dining room. We sat on the floor around a short coffee table, drank beer and smoked pot and cigarettes.

"I'm in love with a beautiful woman," Larry said. "She has money, too."

He showed us a picture of her. She wore long, dangling earrings, and seemed tall. I wanted to wear large earrings, but I thought my neck was too short. I felt sad, but I didn't move or say anything. I think I turned to dust.

❧

I went home for good, not just for a visit, on Friday, June 7, 1974. At my entrance interview, they had asked me when I wanted to get out, and I told them June first. You will stay at least six months they said. June first was exactly seven months. I was the only person I had known to get out on the date they picked at entry. All the other people did bad things that got them longer sentences. I did not want to be bad. I wanted to be good.

I wanted my parents to like me. I don't know if they knew that it was an achievement to get out the day I had planned, with no revisions. I didn't tell them.

The home had a consecration in Waybun, what they called a party, on the day I left. Sr. Laura, all the counselors, my parents and sister, Susan Stone, and all the wayward girls of Waybun were there. We sat in the living room in a big circle, and people told me how much I had grown. Then we sang songs and ate cake. My parents had a party for me, too. Rick Davis, Larry's closest neighbor, came to the party, though Larry didn't. Tommy Erikson wasn't invited. Susan was there. Janice and her new boyfriend, Eddie, stayed only about thirty minutes, looking bored the whole time.

It seemed that my parents approved that I had gotten help. My dad bought a bottle of champagne, and I filled glasses.

It made my parents uneasy that I had friends. They said that I picked bad friends. I tried not to have any friends all summer. I walked alone, mostly, though I sneaked a few times to see Tommy.

Tommy told me he'd seen Larry at a party, and that Larry had bragged to him about screwing me. "He knew he could do it," he said.

All these years later, I still feel badly about that. I loved Larry. What I loved were people's wounds. I'll never know if he meant to hurt me, or if the summer I met him was just the last summer he had an opening in his own heart, and maybe somewhere deep within he's still hoping to be reached in that sad part of his heart. Maybe the opening closed right after I met him—and saw that part—and he went for the hard safety of cool cats like Lorna and Sid, and to bragging about getting somebody like me. If so, the joke is on him. Bragging about getting somebody like me is like bragging about killing ants.

Chapter 8

I worked for my dad on Mondays the whole summer. He was a salesman. I was stiff as frozen pizza, and felt flawed because of it, as I rode to work with Dad. It would be decades before I realized that these body sensations were trying to help me. On a normal day at home it often felt as if I was falling short of expectations, though I couldn't have said that. This was work, a whole new place to fail. I noticed the liquid shimmer on the highway, but by the time we got close to it, it disappeared.

"What is that?"

"It's a mirage," he said.

"I thought that's what you saw before dying of thirst in a desert."

"I think it's the refracted image of the sky," he said.

It impressed me that Dad knew things like that, but I didn't ask more about it. It seemed that anything he knew that I didn't was just another opening to fail.

Dad's office was in a building with other businesses. As I waited for him to unlock his door, I noticed a door to an advertising agency across the hall.

My dad said, "Why don't you go over there and ask them for a tour? They give tours."

"They do?" I said, but I couldn't imagine going there. The idea of it made me tense.

He mentioned it several more times over the summer.

"I want you to have some interest in the world," he said. He didn't say interests, he said interest—a general thing. Most of what my dad said was general. "When I was your age, I was interested in the world."

I knew I was disappointing him, but I couldn't explain myself. I didn't know what to say. I was too shy to tell him I was too shy. One day I would understand I didn't feel safe around my dad because of something that came off of *him*, but here I still put it all on myself. I never took the tour.

My dad's secretary, Christina, helped me learn the routine. She was a Hindu from Germany who drove a 1961 yellow convertible Karmann Ghia.

I rode in her car with her to a mall for lunch. She ordered a blended vegetable drink.

"Order a sandwich, please," she said.

"Okay. I'll have a turkey sandwich," I said, practically levitating I was so uptight.

She watched me eat it then, as if she could hear the turkey scream with every bite. I lost my appetite and couldn't finish the sandwich, and that seemed to bother her even more.

"Aren't you going to finish?" she said.

I wrapped it up as if I were swaddling a baby and told her I would eat it later.

My mom said Christina didn't have any furniture in her house, just a refrigerator and a yogurt maker.

Christina told me she could see my aura. "There's something special about you," she said. I never forgot that.

One day, a man came to see my dad. He greeted Christina and me and went in my dad's office and closed the door.

Later that night, when my dad was mixing himself a drink he said, "You know that man came in and asked me, 'Who is that braless babe out in the front?' And I told him that she was my daughter."

My dad had a way of speaking as if each word were a punch. I remembered then that I was oversexed; that's the feeling I got from my dad. I felt like a piece of onionskin typing paper that I rolled in the

Smith Corona typewriter at work. I put band-aids over my nipples on all the Mondays after that, a trick I had learned from Susan.

Chapter 9

The second full week of August, 1973, Janice and I camped for the weekend on a sand beach at the bottom of a steep hill along the St. Croix River, south of Stillwater. The first evening, a red-haired kid came by on a dirt bike. He rode through our camp within inches of our tent. I motioned him to leave, and he kept circling back. Finally on his way through, I jabbed him under the arm with a long-handled roach clip, which contained a joint of marijuana. He looked at me as if I were crazy, but he rode away.

Later we heard motors in the distance. This time the kid was with an older man on a Harley, a serious motorcycle. I was afraid. They circled around but not closely, and they left without bothering us. Maybe it was enough for them that we looked afraid.

The next day, after breakfast, I gathered pop cans, foil wrappers, and broken beer bottles along the shore, and in the woods nearby. The farther I got from the shore, the more noticeable was the smell of rotting fish, and I felt sick from it. Yet, I was pleased to find three individual fish vertebrae. The white backbones were interesting shapes, with a natural hole for stringing as beads.

The second night, I didn't sleep well and got out of the tent. I was thinking about what to do with my life. The moon was full on Tuesday, August 14, 1973, and it was as high in the sky as I'd ever seen it, with its lovely light splattered all over the moving river. Watching the moonlight, I got the idea that the world needed help. Like being called to be a fireman or a mechanic, it was clear as the sky that I should take on the job of helping the world.

In the morning, I told Janice what I figured out.

"Jan, the world needs help. We can't keep dumping garbage everywhere. I think I'll do something about that. That's what I am going to do with my life. I want to help the world."

"You're weird," Janice said. That's what Janice usually said to me. Worse was when she said nothing, as if I hadn't spoken, or wasn't worth a response. Worrying about getting Janice's approval was an irritation. The world was screaming though. I could hear it in the sky and feel it in the trees.

Chapter 10

We had two family meetings. One time we met to discuss whether we needed to get a color TV. Janice and I said we didn't care. We didn't need to get one just because Susan's family got one. The next week, we got a color TV in a console and put it in the basement. We watched the Wizard of Oz in color and saw the ruby slippers clicking three times in their red splendor. We all admitted that we hadn't needed a color TV, but it was a fine thing to have.

We had another family meeting when Dad decided to go into business for himself. My parents weren't looking for an opinion here. They just wanted us to know that they were not playing around with any of the money they had saved for our college.

The fall after my release from Holy Mary, I returned to high school. I assumed Mr. Wies tried and couldn't find a law to stop me from being there. People had complained about Mr. Wies' style, so problem kids were now assigned to Mr. Rhodes, the high school counselor. Lane said that Mr. Wies was more suited to work sticking sticks in apple cores at a caramel apple factory than he was to working with kids.

Mr. Rhodes had a file cabinet filled with college catalogs. I browsed through them during one of my free hours the fall of my senior year. I picked the brown and white brochure describing Alma Community College in Alma, Minnesota, north of the Laurentian Divide. Alma Community College had a two-year program training Conservation Technicians. I liked that word "conservation"—it appealed to my idea of saving something. Here was a brown and white brochure, nothing flashy. Though I couldn't have said why, and no one had asked anyway, it appealed to me.

"I'll take this one," I said.

But when I told my parents where I wanted to go to school, Dad drove me to the University of Minnesota campus in Minneapolis. Mom had helped Dad through college at the University of Minnesota. They got married between his first and second year of college. College was important to my parents.

We walked down the long brick walks lined with enormous trees. He showed me some of the classrooms where he studied, and a wooden plaque on the wall, which honored him for scholastic achievement in 1950.

I was so self-conscious I could barely look at him. It's hard to describe how miserably weak I was walking on the sidewalks of the campus with my dad. It was as if I were a shadow and everything around me were darkness. I had some sense as to how moss may feel on the north side of a redwood. Without being able to think it or speak it, I knew I could never make it at the university. I've heard a person cannot fail if they keep trying, but I was a failure before trying; I was a failure *at* trying.

❧

Janice and Eddie got married just before Christmas in 1974. I got drunk at the party after the wedding and didn't drive home. I knew that upset my mom. Her disappointment in me was so loud I withdrew deeply inside of myself where it was quiet.

To everyone's surprise, including Mr. Wies', I graduated high school in the spring of 1975. I waited a year, and in the fall of 1976, I moved to Alma to start college. My parents were going to pay for my living expenses plus tuition.

Janice's husband Eddie had a friend who was in technical school learning to apply vinyl roofs to cars. He needed to practice. He put a vinyl leopard-pattern roof on our green car. People commented about how unique it was. Sometimes unique is ridiculous. The car was ridiculous. Though she didn't say so, I thought my mom was relieved to give it away, rather than to be seen in it. My parents gave me the Volkswagen hatchback with the black-and-white vinyl leopard-skin roof.

I packed my delicate bottle collection carefully, wrapping it with Kleenex first and then newspaper wrapped around each bottle. I had no idea how long it would be before I could unpack them and I didn't want anything to break. I piled the hatchback, the back seat, and the passenger's seat, with everything I owned, so I couldn't see to my right in the car, but I didn't think that mattered too much since the trip to Alma was mostly highway, and only required that I look to my left or straight ahead, as long as I stayed in the right lane. I drove the two-hundred fifty miles north from Spring Lake to Alma, Minnesota.

Alma Community College had fewer than three hundred students in the school, fewer students than were in a single grade in my high school. Students rented the tourist cabins at resorts in the winter because Alma did not have student housing. The school helped match you with other students moving into the area and looking for roommates. Ellie Lott, my roommate, was coming from Colorado but she wouldn't arrive until Monday. I wanted to be settled before she got there. We were going to rent one of the cabins at Grahek's Wilderness Lodge, but we couldn't get in until after tourist season. So we had a trailer for a month. Nothing was rented to students in the summer; they either left town or found other places to live.

When I got to Alma, I checked into Grahek's Wilderness Lodge, got the key to the trailer where I would be staying, and unloaded the car. I hardly thought about what I was doing, why, or what I felt about it.

My first night, I walked up the road. I wasn't prepared for how dark it got in Alma when night fell amongst the trees. With no major cities around, and no moon, and an overcast sky, I couldn't see my hand before my face. I wasn't prepared for that either. I found the road by hearing the sound my feet made on the gravel.

I was almost back to my trailer when a creature screamed at me from the side of the road. I stood frozen in space, unable to see. The creature seemed powerful, like a lion, but it sounded like a bird. Here's how I imagined it: a bird-like creature as tall as me with long bird legs, but cat's teeth and frightening black eyes, as cold as a reptile's.

Whatever it was, I didn't like it, and it didn't like me. It was screaming *Don't be here!* Except for my chattering teeth, I couldn't move. It screamed again and moved closer. I couldn't see a thing. Though I was afraid to move, I realized moving was my only hope. I took a step. The creature screamed again, and I imagined it lunging at me. I had the same feeling I had had at home: it was as if I wore a target on my back that glowed to predators at night. I made it to my trailer, where I was alone with the quiet and fear, and I cried myself to sleep. I hadn't noticed it until I got into the quiet loneliness of the woods, but I had emptiness in my heart and stomach as deep as eternity. I cried instinctively, against my superficial will, so much that my eyelids remained swollen the whole next day.

I was surprised. I hadn't expected to feel so sad.

❧

Ellie arrived from Colorado. She was nice. She had long brown hair and white teeth. I noticed people who were able to show their teeth, because I thought mine were ugly. I tried not to smile, not even for pictures.

I accommodated her easily because I felt inferior to her. I felt inferior to everyone. It was hard to know why I felt this way. I always had. Without realizing it I felt like a low form of life. Anything I had going for me was merely a way I wasn't living up to my potential. Maybe mushrooms settle in their cool hidden place and never long for the light. Part inferiority and part politeness had made me leave the large bedroom in the trailer for her. I was on the couch that folded out to a bed in the living room. She was happy I gave her the bedroom, and so was her boyfriend, Michael.

We got on well that first month, with few upsets. One came when I opened the silverware drawer and saw a mouse in the spoon slot. My solution to that was to close the drawer and ignore the shame and fear I felt. Another was when I had a three-fourths-finished, macraméd lampshade, which had three Hawaiian Kakui Nut beads, tied in the finished sections. I discovered one of the three nuts was missing from the work. The missing nut remained an upsetting mystery. Because the string was cut flat, not frayed, Ellie and I suspected foul play, instead of a mouse. Yet it was such an odd act of vandalism, we weren't sure. Ellie and I talked about it. We were united in our speculation and suspiciousness. We started to lock the trailer when we left home. It wouldn't stop a mouse, but we thought it could stop a rat, so-to-speak.

Fifteen people made up the new entrants into the Conservation Technician program at Alma College. Ellie, Sally Lies, and I were the only females in the program.

I had plenty of homework in three classes: Introduction to Conservation of Natural Resources Field Lab, Writing from Personal Resources, and Environmental Science. I loved having the books and notebooks and office supplies. Books contained authority I could admire without feeling judged. I felt safe with books.

I got a job as a waitress at the New Moon Cafe in Alma. I would get off work in the middle of the night. I took in the inexhaustibility of the sky. The sky was a part of the world I could understand, and seeing it made me feel understood. Though in some ways I have never been more lost than I was back then, I also have never seen such incredible starry nights. I miss them.

Sally Lies was a natural food buff and teased me publicly in the school cafeteria for my food choices. She ate a lot of soybeans and yams and talked about how regular her poops were. All of the "Con-Teckers"—people enrolled in the Conservation Technician program—got invited to her house one day. Nearly all of her food was in jars. You could see the food in the jars, and the jars in the open cupboards.

I found out that food stored in jars came from food co-ops. The co-op was a grocery store with an attitude. All customers were not equal. Sally fit in. People who smoked cigarettes weren't welcomed at co-ops. Pot smokers were okay.

One day Sally Lies asked me if she could bum a cigarette. I have never forgotten that. She said she felt comfortable asking me because she knew I wouldn't judge her for it. Even that remark came off as an insult, as though she knew I wouldn't judge her for it because it took self-respect to be judgmental.

Being in Alma was like being at Holy Mary Home for Girls, in that it took me years to shake the feeling that I was always in trouble, that my life was in some way an ever-unfolding punishment. My mom wrote me almost every day. Sundays were lonely. I looked forward to her letters. I wrote to her about how hard my life felt. She said I'd have to find out so many things for myself. She wished she could get me to believe that life didn't have to be this hard.

She said she was trying to keep the plants blooming outside as long as possible, but the impatiens, coleus, dahlias, and zinnias had all shriveled in the garden in the last frost. She carried the pots of geraniums up close to the house, and they were still alive. I've spent my whole life trying to live in my mom's orderly and rhythmic manner. I still haven't done it.

I told her that I cried when I read her letters. She said she cried when she read mine, too.

In late September, our Field Lab class took a bus up the Arrow Trail to Hegman Lake to see an especially old stand of red pines and some Indian cave paintings along a stone cliff. It was a stupendous fall day with cool, dry air. The blue sky coaxed the colors from the yellowed aspen and birch—burgundy, red, and gold maple—and the varied and everlasting greens of the white, red, and jack pines. The trees, mostly *populus tremuloides* and *betula papyrifera*, were protected by the overgrowth. One could feel the patient waiting in the smaller trees. One tree we saw was so large that three of us couldn't get our arms all the way around it, even though we tried. Beneath that tree was a boulder-sized fungus, as smooth as a bald head.

Jerry Beck, the teacher, said, "They call this God's country."

❧

I drank with Ellie. We sat in the bar. I noticed people looking at us. I thought it was Ellie's pretty smile, or long hair. I did feel people wanting something from me, but I didn't know what. A stranger sat next to me for a while. He was tender. I could spot kindness swiftly, the way a cactus finds water. "You're young," he said, "You don't have to act as if you know everything already."

In the bar that night, I realized that the tourists were almost gone. Just a few bow hunters straggled in for bear season. I walked past a dead bear on my way to the Lodge. "The Lodge" was what the Grahek's called the walkout basement part of their house. The bear's chest had been split, and his rib cage exposed. He was somehow attached to a pole, so he was standing.

The bear stood about five and a half feet tall.

The tourist said, "Looks like a person, doesn't it?"

"What do you mean?" I said.

"A dead bear looks a lot like a person. They have a similar rib cage."

"I thought bears were related to dogs," I said.

The dead bear put me in a bad mood. I knew of a dump nearby. It's easy to shoot a bear in the dump at the edge of town. I wondered if the bow hunters had just gone to the dump and shot their limit.

I got to meet nature writer and conservationist Sigurd Olson at the college. Though he hadn't taught full-time since 1936, he gave some lectures for us in the conservation course. He smoked his pipe in the cafeteria after class, with a circle of smoke and students around him.

He read to us, "Unless we can preserve places where the endless spiritual needs of man can be fulfilled and nourished, we will destroy our culture and ourselves." His weathered skin and the dreamy confidence of his words mesmerized me. He signed a copy of his book *Reflections from the North Country*. I wrote my dad about our meeting. He wrote back saying he was glad I got a chance to meet him. My dad was curious about Sigurd Olson's life, as he said that all great persons have suffered before they prospered.

Chapter 11

Ellie and I moved from the trailer to a cabin in mid-October. We each had our own bedroom in the cabin (I took the smaller of the two). The new cabin had a spare bedroom as well that we (mostly Ellie) used for storage. Our cabin wasn't as romantic as we'd hoped. The landlord hadn't told us in advance that we had to pay additional money for heat and electricity. Temperatures were way below normal already. The resort cabins weren't winterized, and the Graheks didn't seem to care about the holes along the base of the cabin, increasing our heat bill with each waft of Arctic air. The heat bill was already equal to the rent.

The last weekend in October, Ellie and I participated in a deer drive, organized by Jerry Beck, the biology teacher. The purpose of this was to get an accurate count of the number of deer per acre. I invited my parents, but they couldn't make it. A large group of people got in a line a mile wide, arm's length apart. We walked on the command of the leader straight ahead into the undisciplined alder brush. Another group stood on the road at the other side, quietly, and counted the deer and rabbits that ran out, chased by the line.

It sounds simple enough to walk in a straight line right through the woods, until you try it. Walking through alder brush is as easy as walking through a wall.

❦

The next day, Sunday, Halloween, Ellie told me that she met this cool guy, Nathan Rohr, whom she thought was a genius. Ellie was sure that he would help us find a better place to live. Ellie met Nate at the New Moon Bar where we both worked. Nate's boss, and ours, Hal Maki, owned the restaurant. The restaurant was their meeting room.

I hadn't met him yet, but I would serve Hal and his crew coffee many times when I worked the morning shift. I waitressed in the front cafe and served breakfast till 11:00, with super-size homemade caramel rolls that I was told attracted lines of hungry tourists in the summer. Outside tourist season the rolls mainly stayed in the showcase until their cliff-like edges got too hard to eat. Ellie worked in the back where they sold liquor and served fine food.

Nate didn't work at the restaurant. He built roads and did mechanic work and odd jobs for Hal. He described himself to Ellie as "Nate in Shining Armor." She'd told him how our heat bill was rising as we heated the great outdoors through the wide spaces between the logs and the floor. Nate had a plan to help us, she said, and he was coming over the next day. Nate knew of a cabin for rent at an old resort on the Arrow Trail.

He did come over in his midnight-blue, three-quarter ton Ford dump truck. Nate's hair was curly and dark, and his cuticles were greasy black. He wore coveralls and a lined jean jacket. He was five foot ten inches, one hundred and fifty pounds. I was fascinated with him. He seemed extraordinary.

The first hummingbird I had ever seen was dead. I found him on the brick window ledge in Susan Stone's back yard. I thought I'd discovered something from another world. I had this same feeling looking at Nate.

I felt cautious around him too, but I couldn't tell why—at first I thought it was just because Ellie had told me she thought he was a genius. Who wouldn't be nervous around a genius? He watched me, closely. I could feel him watching me as if I were transparent, and there was something behind my window. I remembered as a child sitting in the bathtub blowing bubbles between my thumb and first finger, enchanted by being able to see through the bubbles. I'd stare and stare at them as if looking for eternity. I longed to see through them, but being seen through myself made me ill at ease.

"So, you girls are looking for a place," he said.

He had a way of telling you what was going to happen in your life now; something peculiar like that happened behind his words.

"Hal owns a resort that will be perfect for you. The resort is for sale, but don't worry about having to move right away; it's been for sale for years. Everything Hal has is for sale. The cabin isn't large enough to share, but one of you could stay in my place. I've got a place just up the road from the resort."

We learned that Nate lived "in town," which meant he lived within the city limits of Alma. He rented an apartment above the co-op. Hal owned the Co-op building. It seemed to me that not only was everything Hal had for sale, but he also owned most of the town, and much of the surrounding land.

"My place on the Arrow Trail is empty," he said. "You could help me out by staying at it, and I could help you out by letting you stay there. It's a perfect arrangement," he said.

I knew we were going to do just what he said. He took us for a ride in his dump truck, up the Arrow Trail. He showed us the "Little Cabin"—also known as *Tupa*—at the resort. Anything past Tupa toward the lakeshore was no longer driveway, and would be considered the yard of Tupa, or the "Big Cabin," Pioneer. We drove about a mile further north to the Silver Lake campground. Nate pumped water into a five-gallon jug. Being with Nate was like being on a tour. I was amazed that he had a five-gallon jug with him. Nate highlighted his good points as if he could read my mind. At that moment he said, "I'm always prepared." He drove back toward town, past the resort, a mile closer to town, and turned into a gravel driveway, and showed us his place. The tour took seconds. At the end of the driveway on one side was Nate's sawmill, and on the other side was his cabin. The cabin was ten feet by twelve feet, with a half loft. He showed us how easy it was to get the ladder to the loft out of the way, by sliding it under the mounts beneath the loft floor. He lit the kerosene lamp and the cook stove and made us coffee with the fresh Silver Lake water. It was the best coffee I've ever had.

For several hours we sat in the lambent light from three kerosene lamps, listening to Nate tell us stories while he kept the fire going in the wood stove. The place was small so it warmed almost instantly. Nate said that he wasn't living at his cabin while he built a road for Hal—it was too far for him to drive every day. We learned that Hal owned the old resort, including Tupa, and most of the land on Turtle Lake. He had owned all of it at one time. It was as I thought: people said that Hal owned everything in Alma, or had owned it at one time.

We learned that Nate was one of the few children born in 1942 just before the baby boom. So many American men were at war that year that the birth rate was low. Nate said he began working for the Makis at age fourteen, when he couldn't get along with his parents. He never actually lived in Hal's house, but at the Crystal Slope Lodge that Hal owned. He was the hired help part of the family. Nate was now thirty-four.

Even though I still had this feeling that we hadn't decided—it was more as if we'd been chosen—we discussed the details of the move. Ellie would stay at Nate's cabin. I would rent Tupa from Hal. He said I could get it for seventy-five dollars per month, and whatever it cost for fuel oil. "Since it's a log cabin, Anna, you shouldn't have to pay much. I've lived in Tupa; those thick logs hold onto heat."

We gave notice the next day: November 1. We told the Graheks we'd be out by December 1.

Sally Lies had a friend with some kittens. I got a kitten: black and white with yellow eyes. I named him Max Wiley. He slept on my Biology book while I studied at the kitchen table. I petted his face and stroked the white whiskers along his solid black cheeks.

❧

On November 30, the day we moved, the leopard Volkswagen didn't start so Nate took extra trips with Hal's truck to help us. We moved all of our things, but I couldn't take my car. I told the Graheks I'd be back to get it as soon as I could.

Now we had cheaper places to live, but no car. Ellie was good at sharing our woes with strangers. The first night we moved, a customer of Ellie's gave us an old Chevy. The way it worked was Ellie paid for gas. My parents paid for the insurance so we had a way to get to school.

Ellie settled into Nate's place. Even though Nate arranged it, I rented a cabin from Hal Maki for seventy-five dollars per month. My mom sent a check every month. I got a lump sum and then wrote my own expense checks from it. I was in a world of adults here, and it was embarrassing to be taken care of by my parents.

My cat, Max, and I moved into the tiny L-shaped cabin named Tupa, which is Finnish for "home." The inner logs were painted in mustard yellow. The cement floor was red, with much of its paint worn away. The front door entry was at the base of the "L" and opened directly to the kitchen. The sink was set in a red linoleum counter. At the edge of the counter, right by the door, an apartment-sized gas stove sat with plenty of space around it, as if someone had thought to leave room for a full-sized stove but only found a half-size one for the spot.

Things of Hal's were like that; mediocre would always do.

From the window over the sink, I could see the aspen-lined driveway leading up to the Arrow Trail. If I looked to the left, I could see the creek running parallel to the driveway. On the other side, above the red wooden kitchen table, stood three large red pines, the outhouse, Pioneer (the big cabin), and the sauna.

᪥

Everyone was saying that this was the coldest winter on record, and it was still only fall. Below-zero temperatures made everything harder to do. It took several weeks before I could arrange to pick up the car. Nate was just going to tow it to the resort for me, so I could "deal with it in the Spring," he said. I tried to get the Volkswagen, and the Graheks, our former landlords, wouldn't let me have it. They thought I should have to pay them rent for storing the car. I think they were mad that we hadn't stayed all winter. They had probably already spent the money they had hoped to get from us. When we walked behind the cabin, where the car was parked, we noticed that someone had shot out the windows, and flattened the tires. I said I wasn't going to pay rent when they had wrecked the car. We left without it.

Nate told me what we would do. He said, "We'll get up early tomorrow morning, just after sunrise. I'll hook my cables to the front of the car, and we'll take it. They can't keep it, the bastards!"

Nate helped me take the car the next morning, just the way he said. It was scary. Of course the Graheks heard us just as we were pulling out, and they called the police. We got pulled over and I showed the officer the flat tires, the broken window. I said, "It doesn't seem to me that I should pay them—they should pay ME for the damage!" He agreed with me and let us drive off. I was grateful to Nate for his help. I felt brave around him.

❧

Dale Adams lived in the big cabin, Pioneer, next door to mine. We shared an outhouse. Dale was a locksmith by trade and worked for Hal, mostly. He carried a business card: Dale Adams, Artist. He made layered cutouts of pictures of animals, surrounded them with birch bark, and mounted them behind glass. He was friends with many of the people for whom Nate did construction work in Alma. He had known Nate since he was a teenager, when he came to work for Hal. Nate considered Hal his second father. Dale was like an uncle.

Chuck and Katie Baxter owned the cabin they lived in, once part of the resort. They lived with their son, Jeff, across the bridge over a stream going into Turtle Lake. The cabin's nameplate was missing; no one could remember its name. Two other buildings on their lot were vacant. Chuck worked for Hal, too. He hauled gravel for Hal's roads in a dump truck that Nate kept running. The roads were made so people could get to and buy the land Hal owned.

By everyone's best guess, most of the resort had been built in the 1930s. The sauna building, where it stood five feet from the shore of the lake, was labeled as the other cabins were, with a wooden sign: SAUNA. I swept off a spot at the front door of the sauna and read "September 5, 1955," cut into the cement. Chuck told me that when the lake started to thaw just at the edge in the spring we could cool off "after sauna" in the water at the shore.

For the first time since I moved to Alma, I set up my bottle collection in my antique display case. I was able to fit it on top of a bookcase to the right of my desk. I carefully washed each bottle, and cleaned the glass shelves, top and bottom, and the front and sides of the case inside and out. I placed the tiny bottles carefully. In order to get it to fit, the spray top of the antique perfume bottle had to be depressed slightly, which bothered me. I put the tiny Avon perfume bottle I had gotten from Susan one birthday right in front of the perfume bottle. I arranged my old marbles carefully in an ashtray. The fish bones from my camping trip with Janice went into the blue enamel toy teacup. I turned it around so the chip in the enamel was away from easy view.

I slept in the other room on the windowless wall in a single bed. The fuel oil stove was attached to the silver-painted brick in the center of the other wall.

Sleeping was like camping. It was cold. The wolves howled across the lake. I could hear the flow of the creek in the spring and during a summer rain, and the water sound of the flattened leaf stems of the quaking aspen in the summer and fall.

I hauled water for drinking and dishes from a hole in Turtle Lake, from the Silver Lake pump up the road, or from town. I used the stove mostly for coffee. I had a popcorn maker for popcorn.

Nate visited regularly. Actually, he made rounds like a hospital nurse checking on his patients. I found out from Ellie that he stopped at her place first. Then he visited me.

I thought he was interested in Ellie because of her pretty smile; that's why he offered her his place. He told me later that he favored me because he noticed that Ellie's birth control pills weren't current. He said he edged himself over to the table to see if I was up to date. He was pleased to note that on a Tuesday both the Monday and the Tuesday pill had been carefully pushed through the foil.

I assumed Ellie and I weren't the only ones on his visiting list, but I enjoyed seeing him. It was lonely in Tupa. Time in the winter moves more slowly—as if it, like everything else, has more trouble moving in the cold.

He made sure I had fuel oil in my stove. The stove's auxiliary fuel tank consisted of a fifty-five gallon drum on two sawhorses with a line running through a hole in one of the logs. Inside the cabin, the line lay on a channel that had been blasted in the concrete, but which had not been filled back in, so the dirt floor was exposed. I filled a five-gallon container with fuel oil in town, and then poured the fuel in the drum outside. In the coldest months, the stove took more than five gallons per day. Sometimes I would awaken cold, knowing the stove was dry. Ellie and I were able to shower in the gym at school. Ellie didn't have electricity at her place; at least Tupa had electricity. On Thursdays we could shower at the Community Center across from the Post Office in Alma. We usually met each other there and rode home together.

Ellie said Jerry Beck took her into a bear den and she got to hold a tiny cub.

"New cubs are almost helpless," she told me. "They can't see, hear, smell, or walk."

"I heard baby bears have blue eyes. Did you see the bear's eyes?" I asked.

"I don't remember noticing the eyes," she said.

One morning when I drove in to pick her up for school, her teacher's car was in the driveway. I didn't knock. It hurt me though: Ellie was better at living than I was.

Chapter 12

Nate had a collection of cars that didn't run. Hal wanted him to get them out of the parking place at the resort before spring; he wanted the place cleaned up so it would be easier to sell. Nate had collected the cars when he lived with Suzy in Pioneer, where Dale lived now. Suzy had been Nate's girlfriend just before Carol. He'd never moved his things out of the resort when Suzy left him. That's the way it was in the first months living at the resort. I found out where people came from, and who used to work where or live where. A lot of the history I learned surrounded Nate's past loves. I barely noticed that I had become next on the list. I realized later that it must have been obvious to others who had known Nate for years: I had moved into the vacancy left by Carol, the girlfriend just before me.

He was chivalrous—playing Nate in shining armor, making sure I had this and that, with his adorable smile. I had just made popcorn in the popcorn maker. He showed up and we sat over the yellow plastic bowl, with wooden chairs from the table placed in front of the stove. He gave me a kiss on the forehead and held the back of my head so sweetly. I began missing him after that, looking for him when he wasn't there. I didn't see that my lonely soul was being put in a trance.

Nate smoked cigarettes and stood around his old—he called them antique—cars and engines, looking at them as though there were some magic in looking. After a while, I stood there with him, merely copying the serious study. I had no idea what I was looking at or why. He had a

GMC four-door that had cloth seats and smelled musty, but he was proud that it had been a luxury car in its time. Nate had an appreciation for what had once been splendid. He found joy in junk.

Nate also loved spontaneous travel. He was always looking for some reason to "go bumming." We sometimes borrowed Chuck Baxter's red '69 Saab, or sometimes we took one of Hal's cars. We frequently found a way to take somebody's car somewhere.

We'd stop at the Minnesota-owned Holiday Station for gas. We could leave town either by traveling southeast on Highway 2 or southwest on Highway 159.

Highway 2 is so remote it could lead to eternity. We stopped at Embarrass, Minnesota, which is exactly on the Laurentian Divide. The Pike River flows north to Hudson Bay, and the Embarrass River flows south to the Atlantic. Hence the divide between water flowing north and water flowing south. Embarrass is also, Nate explained, the coldest spot in the country, where temperatures can drop to sixty below.

"Cold," Nate said. "Damn cold."

We usually didn't plan where we were going. Sometimes we visited his parents, Nate Rohr, Sr., and Mary, who lived in Illia, Minnesota. On our way to see them, we would drop in at one of the many 3.2 bars along the way. (During prohibition, Congress had tried to weasel out of a complete ban on alcohol by declaring that any drink with less than 3.2% alcohol could not be called an "alcoholic beverage" and thus could not be banned.) Nate said you can't drink fast enough to get drunk on 3.2 beer. We drove past logging sites, new-growth forest, and numerous tamarack swamps. Nate showed me a stand of white pine on Highway 2 where, he told me, the oldest trees in the state still grow.

Nate introduced me to his white shepherd, Oden.

"Oden is part shepherd, part wolf," he said, showing me the thick underfur that confirmed his wolf heritage. I didn't think to ask him how he knew. I took his word for it.

"Oden is spelled E—N, not I—N. I named him after the God, O-D-I-N, but I didn't like the spelling, so I changed it. Spelling doesn't make any sense to me. 'Open' is E—N, Oden should be, too."

Nate said he hated rules. He liked to reject them or change them.

"It's a more honest way to live," he said.

After a while he changed his name from Nate to Neight.

He was Nathan David Jude Rohr.

"I picked Jude as my confirmation name, as Jude was the Patron Saint of Lost and Forgotten Souls," he said.

Chapter 13

I visited my parents at their home every holiday. At first I found rides with other students returning to the St. Paul area. When school was out, Nate and I borrowed Chuck and Katie's Saab the first weekend in June, and Nate drove me to visit my parents. We bought French bread, mozzarella cheese, and mild banana peppers at Trapp's groceries, and drove out of town.

This time Nate was driving me to Spring Lake to visit my parents, but since we lived in Alma, we always just said "the cities." "The cities" was all places in St. Paul and Minneapolis, including the suburbs and nearby towns, such as Spring Lake. It was early June 1977. Though I'd known him since the fall of 1976, my parents hadn't met him yet.

"Hey, Charlie," Dad said greeting me at the door.

"Nate, I'd like you to meet my parents, John and Clare. Dad, Mom, this is Nate."

I thought it was funny to hear him call my mom Clare, as I hadn't had adult friends yet. Most of my friends still referred to my parents as Mr. and Mrs. Books, not "John" or "Clare."

At thirty-four he was closer to my parents' age than to mine.

Nate made fun of his gray hair. He said, "Clare, just because there's snow on the roof doesn't mean the fire is out in the basement."

She looked at him and said, "No. But it's a pretty good indication that something's going on." They both laughed.

It wasn't just the adult name that gave me pause. This was one of the times I knew I wasn't all grown up. I didn't quite understand these jokes. Was my mom flirting with my boyfriend?

Everything was always in perfect order at my mom's house. I hadn't even seen dust or cobwebs until I moved out on my own. I remember my mom finding a single hair in the bread drawer. She'd held it up, looked at it, winced, and said "Yuck!" I wondered how she felt about hair while it was still on a head. I wondered how she felt about me.

Nate was impressed with all of my parents' antiques and asked questions about many of them. There were subjects Nate could talk about with my dad. They talked about hunting and sports. My dad mixed me a drink, and I thanked him for it. I praised my dad for everything he did, as he had once told me he didn't think I liked him. I stood at the kitchen sink, under the steamy window, with Mom, peeling carrots, slicing onions, and chopping celery for dinner. She liked Nate.

"He's charming, Anna. He's witty and talented. What more could you want?"

Mom rarely liked my friends. She liked Tommy, at first, until the psychiatrist had called. Before that, if he stopped over to see me and I wasn't home, he talked to my mom. One summer he gave us each an antique Mason jar, stamped "1890" in the glass. My parents said I had bad friends; it was said by way of explanation and condemnation of my choices. Mom's warm compliment helped. It was such a nice feeling between us, and so rare that I knew I would never forget it.

The four of us drank gin and tonics before dinner. Though I had slept with Nate numerous times, Nate and I took separate rooms there because we weren't married. Mom and I made up the bed in Janice's old room for Nate. I slept in my old bedroom, and Mom went downstairs to her bed.

Nate stayed up drinking with Dad. In the morning, I got up,

abruptly, at 6:30 a.m.

It was a beautiful morning. The air had a fresh smell. The wrens were singing and moving about the wren house on the oak at the corner of the house by the dining room window, but I had a terrible feeling. I walked down the hall to his room, but Nate wasn't there. I walked out to the driveway and the Saab wasn't there.

I sat at the kitchen counter watching the small-screen TV that we called the "little" TV, smoking cigarettes, twisting my hair, watching the road, and hoping that Nate would return before Mom and Dad got up.

I was in love with Nate. I enjoyed seeing my parents enjoy themselves around me. When they got up, they were as disturbed as I was that he was gone. They feared that something dire could have, must have, happened. They thought he could have been picked up for drinking and driving. I thought so, too.

Dad told me three times that the last thing Nate told him was that he would "see him over eggs."

"I just know he was planning to be here for breakfast. I hope we didn't make him angry. Would he be upset with us for some reason?" Dad said.

"No. I'm sure that isn't it. You mustn't blame yourselves. He's unpredictable," I said.

I couldn't help but worry that he had been picked up for something as well. I knew Nate had a police record, but I was too nervous to tell my dad. So far, he was relaxed, but I thought at any minute it was going to be my fault that he had to worry about my boyfriend. This is like sucking your stomach in for hours, longer than you could ever do it without a corset. I was always pretending.

We all three looked out the window whenever we heard a car coming. We also talked about other things as we waited.

Janice and Eddie lived in a trailer at the Spring Lake Mobile Home Park. They had been married almost a year and she was trying to get pregnant. Mom said she had some tests to see what was wrong, and if she could do anything about it.

"Susan Stone graduated from high school," Mom said.

"I'm happy for her," I said.

"Yes. I've heard they are having quite a party for her. Mr. Stone has been here a couple of times, borrowing things. They got our forty-cup coffee maker yesterday. Dad took them the folding chairs on Thursday."

"It's nice they're having a party for her," I said. Susan and I were best friends. She was younger than me by one year.

I didn't mention about whether I would go to the party or not, because I didn't know what was going to happen. It felt as if each ticking second on the kitchen clock was a drop of acid filling my stomach. Mom looked up numbers and Dad started calling local jails to see if Nate had been picked up. I knew they were fully prepared to bail him out.

Just after one o'clock in the afternoon, Nate called. He was at Carol's, his old girlfriend, who was pregnant with Nate's child. In about a half an hour, Nate, Nate's dog Oden, and Carol came driving down the road. He brought pregnant Carol into my mom and dad's house. Shamelessly. He didn't even seem the least bit self-conscious. I couldn't believe it.

My parents invited them in. Nate introduced Carol. I sneaked out the window onto the deck and ran next door to Susan's graduation party.

After I had a few drinks, I knew it was time to go home. My parents were entertaining Nate *and* Carol now. Shortly, as if they were waiting for me, the three of us and Oden left for Alma. I sat in the back of the car with Oden, though I had been in the front on the way there, and waved to my parents as we backed down the driveway. What they thought or felt was just another thing we haven't ever discussed.

How could he have left without saying anything? How could he do this in front of my parents? Had this been a whim or a plan? How could I drive down as his girlfriend and return as cargo? Did he get me to buy gas for him so he could visit Carol? Had this been his plan all along?

After several miles, Carol turned her head back to me and said, "Why are you crying? What has happened to you?"

I didn't respond. What had happened to me? I didn't know what had happened to me. My witty boyfriend had turned repugnant right before my approving parents' eyes. That had happened. What's more, Nate had told me he was done with Carol. She was part of the list of past girlfriends: Lynn, Ellen, Suzy, and Carol. A list. Irrelevant. Not real. As children, we feel like time begins with our birth. Nate began at the time I met him. *Carol, what has happened to me is you have become real,* I thought, but didn't say.

Carol stayed in Alma, with Nate, in his apartment. They visited Dale and, I assumed, Katie. Although, Nate left his car in the clearing right across from Tupa. Carol never even looked at Tupa, so she didn't see me staring at them out the window from the shadows.

꩜

Katie told me about the pregnancy. She said that Carol had more abortions than were healthy for her. When she got pregnant this time, the doctors told her if she had another abortion she would likely not be able to have a child.

I stayed alone in my cabin. Each time I entered my home, I took note of the wooden sign, "Tupa." I felt better in a way, at home, taking care of my own business. When I was with Nate, I noticed, we took care of his business.

I got out my copy of Wayne Dyer's *Your Erroneous Zones* and tried to convince myself that I was in charge of my own happiness.

They were fighting the next day, as I had heard they did constantly before Carol left Nate. In a few days, Carol left again.

Nate never apologized to me. He was careful at first, though, just drove down the road and turned around. Next, he stopped by to see if I needed anything in town. He always had a concerned look on his face. Wayne Dyer's book said I could choose to react the way I wanted to and feel what I wanted to feel. But I felt terrible, though I didn't want to. Wayne had a twenty-five-question checklist where "yes" responses indicated personal mastery and effective choice making. I answered mostly no's. This depressed me. I failed at self-help. Wayne said that the notion of my own death was supposed to motivate me to a better life.

Wayne presumed a lot. The notion of my own death gave me peace.

I can't say I didn't have the sense to stay away from Nate. I knew I should stay away from him. I fantasized about staying away from him but didn't, and then suffered guilt. Being with Nate was like wearing plaids and stripes. It didn't match. So when I did it, I didn't match. I also felt weak that I couldn't resist him, and stupid for it. For single moments, I wasn't lonely around Nate and didn't feel like dying. Wayne's words faded in my mind. It was the loneliness that Wayne didn't reach. But something deeper and more mysterious also happened to me with Nate, just like with Larry. I was locked into a relationship not so much with Nate, as with a deep, bloody wound inside him, and I felt as if it were my job to save him.

Chapter 14

I did an odd thing one night. I cleaned up, did the dishes, and turned on all of the lights, especially the lamp on my corner desk that resembled a water pump. The pump handle had the string in the center so it pulled the lamp switch on and off when you pushed it down.

I wrote a letter to Larry Lohmand.

Dear Larry,

I'm glad that it didn't work out between us because I am going to have a hysterectomy, and I'll never be able to have children. I know you would be disappointed about that. If you're not already impotent, it will be too late for us. It's lucky for you that we broke up.

It was a made-up story. Even though I thought I might get a hysterectomy, I didn't know I would, the way I told him.

Nate asked me if I wanted to go for a drive. And we were off again. We started to take regular trips, bumming again. Only now I sucked his cock while he held the steering wheel with one hand and the curve of my hip under his other. We drove from 3.2 bar to 3.2 bar across the north woods.

Chapter 15

I got a job for the United States Forest Service that summer as part of a required internship for school. I cleaned campgrounds. It was 1977, and staining was required in odd-numbered years. I stained every post, sign, and picnic table along the entire twenty-five miles of the Arrow Trail, on both sides of the road. I gave up trying to save my clothes and just wore the same redwood-stained shirts and jeans every day. My hands were permanently redwood. This was training as a Con-Tecker. This was saving the world.

I lived on the same road where I worked, so my partners agreed to pick me up at the top of the driveway to avoid my having to drive to town and then ride back out with them in the official sea-green colored Forest Service truck. The trucks were actually the sea-green crayon color I remembered from the crayon box. The sea-green color clashed with the wilderness.

We prepared for the tourists by cutting brush along trails and campsites. We cleaned up after tourists the rest of the year. We cut grass with scythes at the campsites. Once the sand flies took such chunks out of our skin, Will Salo, my semi-retired partner, and I dropped our scythes and ran down the campground road as fast as we could. Sand flies could make you do things like that.

The worst was when some people from Ohio—you knew that from the license plates—put their pot of spaghetti not in the can on the campsite, or in the dumpster nearby on the campsite road, but upside down on the newly stained picnic table. We had to clean that up.

Except for staining picnic tables, Ohio pig farmers, and for going in outhouses that hadn't been used for a while so you could hear the cobwebs ripping as you pulled open the door, the job was easy. Will told me the group at the office understood that we didn't have enough work: they wanted us to "try not to get caught sleeping."

It reminded me of Jerry Beck's favorite book, assigned to us in school, *The Peter Principle*, which stated that in a hierarchy, such as the U.S. Forest Service, every employee tends to rise to his level of incompetence. Workplaces where people stayed and had opportunities for promotion were riddled with incompetence for this reason: if you got good at your job you got promoted until you were no longer good at your job.

Every week I walked the Stuart River Portage to the river, about three miles, by myself. Checking the portage was legitimate work. It was a long walk, and Will preferred to stay in the truck. Will smoked cigars and put his hat over his face and waited for me. He wore coveralls, the same style as Nate's, only clean. About all I got to know about his life was when he told me, "You could sink a ship in what I drank," with his cigar bobbing up and down on his thick bottom lip like a boat on waves.

I knew there were bear, brush wolves, and moose in the area, but I wasn't scared; I liked walking that portage alone. It gave me time to think.

Many things are dying in the woods in Alma. The rocks hold the grief of centuries and in places you can see where they finally crack from the pressure. It was as if the wind howled a gray sound that painted the rocks and dead wood. Barkless trees stood gray around the living. Alma is a place that can grow things without enough of what they need.

I wasn't feeling well. My stomach hurt all the time. It hurt to have sex. My periods were irregular, even on the pill. I made an appointment with Dr. Beane at the clinic in Alma. He gave me antibiotics and told me not to drink. I took the pills but I still drank. I didn't feel better. I visited Dr. Beane again. He said that vaginas were prime places to grow infections because they were dark and moist. "Think of it as pneumonia in your vagina. You need rest."

I told Katie what the doctor said. I asked her to go to the top of the hill where the Forest Service truck picked me up, to tell Will that I wouldn't be able to work.

I went to her house later that day. Katie looked up from rolling out the thin, table-sized sweet dough for her potica. I'd never seen potica until I came to Alma. Most Slovenians made walnut or apple potica for holidays. She made it routinely, like bread. Katie could make potica herself, although I think most people got help rolling the dough.

"I told him you had pneumonia of the cunt," she said looking up with all her teeth showing, and for just a flash I thought I felt them sink into the soft skin of my belly. I don't know why she embarrassed me this way.

❧

I preferred staying busy. Most of the time I didn't feel settled enough to read or study. When I wasn't active at work, I fantasized about missing something at home. I liked to hang onto Nate. I thought about him when I wasn't with him. I wondered what he was doing.

Nate seemed free. He worked if he wanted to. He had irregular hours. I could join him more while I was out of work, resting. I sat with Nate and the working men in Alma, drinking coffee. I loved to eat toast made from homemade bread at Angelica's Cafe, located one block off Main Street. The sign there read:

If You Are Grouchy, Irritable,
Or Just Plain Mean
There Will Be a $10 Charge
For Putting up With You.

Maybe the sign helped. Nate was usually nice to me at Angelica's. I loved being there. The off-white coffee cups were double thick. Nate thought they kept the coffee warm longer. I liked the way the coffee almost matched the color of the cup when you added milk to it. You could always tell if the coffee was old by the color it turned. It was also real milk, not the evaporated milk we used at home. The rattle, clack, squeak, and sizzle coming from the open door of the kitchen percussed the choir of people in conversation. Breakfast at Angelica's was average, for average people, having average days. I felt average at Angelica's—which, for me, was better than average.

The men at our booth expressed wonderment that I was Nate's girlfriend. Everyone thought it was so lucky for him that he got to sleep with such a young, firm woman. They emphasized "firm" as if older women turned to clouds.

One morning I had breakfast with Nate, Dale, Hal, and a new acquaintance, Wally Whiting.

"How do you do it?" Dale Adams, my neighbor at the resort, said to Nate, looking at me as if I were behind glass and couldn't hear him.

"Charm," Nate said.

"Even if I could attract a young thing, it wouldn't matter. When you get to be my age it's like trying to stuff a marshmallow in a piggy bank!"

They laughed.

I noticed a man in a suit in the booth across from us. "Who is that?" I asked.

"Norman Koivisto," Nate said.

"What does he do?"

"He's the city attorney."

"Is he nice?"

"No. He's an asshole."

This answer didn't surprise me. Nate thought everyone was an asshole.

᪥

We got drunk in town one night with Chuck and Katie. Nate invited us to his apartment above the co-op when the bars closed. Nate gave Katie and me tattoos using a sewing needle and a bottle of India ink. Katie got an outline of a heart shape just above her right breast. I got a scarab-looking bug tattooed on my left wrist bone. Nate dipped the needle in the India ink bottle and then patiently poked my skin in the outline of a bug.

After that we continued to drink. We had sex side by side on the floor. Nate didn't have a bed. We switched partners midway.

Chapter 16

Rudy bought tracts of land in the outskirts of Alma, and then he'd have Nate and other slaves build him a road for peanuts with dump trucks held together with bubble gum, Nate said. Nate resented Hal. He was sure that Hal wouldn't be able to operate without him, as he needed a mechanic to keep his stuff running. People who knew what he knew would never work for what Hal paid. The way I looked at it, they both took advantage of each other.

The roads they made weren't roads the way you think of a road; they were just barely above paths. They cut the trees and hauled enough gravel over the path to fill in the potholes. They put a culvert in here and there. Any big rocks they simply left in the road, and you had to drive slowly over or around them. The people who bought the lots from Hal paid to upgrade the roads. Hal's latest project was a road into some property on Silver Steel Lake so they called it the Silver Steel Road.

Chuck and Nate switched off hauling gravel in dump trucks or pushing it flat with a bulldozer. I slept in a shack, at the beginning of the road where Nate stayed when he worked. He heated it with lots of candles. We lay in bed together in this bright, warm place, smoking up the leftover oxygen and waiting for morning.

"This is copacetic," Nate said.

"What does that mean?"

"It means it's good, completely satisfactory," he said.

I was still sick. When I had intercourse it hurt, but I tried to hide it.

For some reason, I acted as if I liked sex and pretended it didn't hurt.

I was off work to rest. I wandered in boredom along the Silver Steel Road, because being with Nate was my purpose. He was working, so I walked and looked carefully at the miniature pinecone shapes on the hazelnut bushes, and the rocks, the narrow dirt road. Beaver traps were set around so we didn't let Oden run. He usually stayed with Nate. I watched in the woods for the traps. The sun came through the pattern of leaves in a dance, now this position, now that. I listened to the buzz of the meadow and swamps, the swarming sand flies, and watched for an owl or an eagle. I felt the heat coming up off the grasses and smelled the diesel from the equipment.

I heard the rumble of the truck and waited. Nate leaned out over the open window.

"Do you want a ride?" he said. I got up in the truck.

"It's funny, Nate, that I have been walking around here for almost a year and we haven't ever seen a bear. I've never seen a live bear up here. Don't you think that's odd?"

&

Ellie moved to town in August. She said it got to be too much without electricity. She found an apartment in Alma and was looking forward to being able to take regular baths.

After that, Nate moved back to the Arrow Trail. I spent a lot of time at Nate's shack—that's what he called it—even though my cabin was just down the road from his. He would leave me there alone for hours. Max was lucky that I lived near Katie. When I was gone long hours at school, or when I took off with Nate, she allowed him to eat from her cats' bowls. I knew he wouldn't go hungry, but I felt guilty that I neglected him.

Chapter 17

I stayed alone in Tupa one night. Dale Adams knocked on my door the next morning.

"I'm having a party tonight," he said. "I'm going to show some movies. Why don't you and Nate come over about seven o'clock?"

I looked forward all day to movie night at Dale's. I thought, *I wonder what movie an artist would want us to see?*

In the movie, Linda Lovelace screwed a Doberman Pincer. Being grown-up was such a disappointment.

Later, Nate tried to put one of his knickknacks, a crystal doorknob, into my vagina.

"A baby's head fits in there," he said.

The next day I said to Nate, "I don't like sex."

"I know. I can tell," he said, which surprised me, because I thought I had been an effective fake.

For some reason I thought about Susan Stone's outdoor party during high school, when we had walked to the lake to go swimming.

We took off our clothes and jumped in the water and then got dressed and started to walk back to the party. A man, a friend of Susan's, followed me. He took me off the path, knocked me down, pulled down my pants, and began raping me, I guess. He was so pathetic; it was hard to think of it as a rape. He had a shockingly tiny penis. It felt no bigger than a thimble inside my vagina. Yet he squealed and grunted in my wet ear, "I want to make you come. I want to make you come." It was pathetic, even more pathetic than how ineffective I was at protecting myself.

On my way home from that party I got a ride from Marty Farr. He pulled over at a wayside rest and raped me, too. His cock was much bigger, though, as was he. He slammed me into the front seat of his car, with my neck crammed against the seat. Jesus Christ.

I absorbed shame from others by osmosis.

I had told Susan a version of this. I was sleeping over at Susan's house one night. Mrs. Stone had just said that my breasts had grown from mosquito bites to hornet bites.

"Why does your mom say that?" I asked.

"I don't know," she said.

Then I told Susan that during one of my parents' parties a man had come into my bedroom and taken off my underwear. He got in bed with me.

"Do you know who it was?"

"It was dark. I couldn't tell," I lied. "He said, 'You don't mind if I do this to you.' It wasn't a question, and I didn't answer it. I don't know what happened after that."

"Has anything like that ever happened to you?" I asked.

She said, "Yes."

My heart pounded sledgehammers of blood against my sternum. I stared at a piece of skin lifting off Susan's lower lip.

"And you don't like it either?"

"No," she said.

Night after night at Nate's I stayed there having painful, excruciating sex with Nate or one of his friends by kerosene lamp, or by moonlight, or in the darkness.

The first time was with Dale Adams. I knew I shouldn't have seen that movie. He came up there and sat at the table with me while Nate was on the couch. He came over to the chair as if Nate had told him to and unzipped and unsnapped my shorts and pulled me forward on the chair and started licking my pussy. Eventually he turned me around and screwed me from behind. He never said my name or kissed my face. Nate didn't say or do anything but sit on the couch. I didn't either. I was such a stranger to myself, as if I rested on the curved edge of the waning moon and watched my body coolly in the distant and reflected light from the sun.

Bringing people was all a part of his drinking cycle, and I had come to both expect and dread it. Nate brought a perfect stranger back with him one afternoon. Nate met someone new at a bar. They were drinking and became fast friends. Sex became dread. I wondered why, if he knew I didn't like sex, he pressured me for so much of it, and encouraged others to have sex with me. I wondered how he had known that I didn't like it since I pretended that I did. I didn't ask.

Chapter 18

Paula came to visit, another sudden intrusion from Nate's past. Nate brought her over, and I met her in Tupa. I took a chair from the kitchen table into the living area, and Nate sat there. Paula sat on my desk chair, and I sat on my bed. For the first time I learned that Nate built his shack on Paula's land. He had convinced her to let him build the place on her property. In exchange for living there, he was supposed to build her a summer home.

Paula wanted to see what progress Nate was making on her cabin. She was impressed to see the sawmill set up on the property, and she liked Nate's place. She asked him when he would get around to making a building for her. She told him she was impatient.

I stayed at Tupa while she visited, because Paula stayed with Nate. One morning, someone knocked on my door. I stepped outside to greet one of Hal's friends, Wally Whiting.

"I'm just out here to see the resort," he said. "Hal has it for sale."

"I know," I said.

I remembered meeting Wally at breakfast with Hal and Nate. I looked at Wally's white patent leather belt and matching white shoes. And then I looked at his face. He touched my cheek and started leaning forward as if to kiss me. I stepped backward and turned to the driveway and walked across the creek to Katie's house as fast as I could without running. She laughed when I told her that Wally Whiting had just touched my cheek.

"Oh my gosh," she said.

"I can't believe it," I said.

Katie frequently told me about someone who had propositioned her or made a pass at her. One time in the New Moon a tourist offered us each five hundred dollars to spend the weekend with him. We turned him down. Bad manners by middle-aged men were as common as dead branches on a forest trail.

When Paula left, Nate came down for a visit.

"Paula said you look emotionally disturbed," Nate said.

I didn't know what to say to that. Paula worked at the State Hospital in Moose Lake. She wasn't a counselor or anything; I think she worked in the budget department. I guessed that if you've seen one emotionally disturbed person, you've seen them all.

"I liked Paula. Are you telling me that she didn't like me?" I asked.

"No, she just thinks you're screwed up," Nate said.

Chapter 19

Nate and I went to a party at someone's house in Mountain Iron, a town near Illia. I went to sleep; Nate stayed awake. He woke me up in a rage. I usually tried to figure out what made him angry in order to prevent it. What could I have possibly done from a sound sleep to enrage him? He pulled me up off the floor by my arm and said, "We're leaving." I don't know why we left the party when other people were sleeping on the floor; it looked as though it would be just fine to stay. We left. Then we got lost.

Even though I was careful to be helpful, Nate stopped the car.

"You're stupid!" he said, and he hit me on the side of the head, so hard my shoulder bounced off the car door.

"This is all your fault," he screamed, and put both of his blocky hands around my throat and started choking me so that I couldn't do anything but squeak.

I looked out of the car to the moonlit snow. I didn't see a single car or light. I didn't think I could find a place to go even if I could get out of the car. I would either freeze to death or Nate would run me over if I tried to escape. Maybe he read my mind, maybe we both saw my death in that moment, or maybe his demon left him, but he relaxed his hands, and started to drive. I didn't ask him where he was going; I was afraid to. I guessed we were either going to his parents' house or back home.

Nate's parents lived in Illia, Minnesota, about fifty miles from Alma, in a garage apartment, which meant their living space was above a garage. Mary's bedroom was on one end, and Nate, Sr.'s on the other. They met in the kitchen, which was in the middle; if they talked at all, it was there.

I'd first met Nate, Sr. when he visited us in Alma. The first time I met Mary, during one of our car trips to Illia, she sat at her kitchen table smoking. She took a big drag off a Marlboro 100 as she said, "All I do is sit and smoke."

I wondered how to respond, holding my face and my astonishment stiff.

"You must be philosophical," I said.

"No. I hate men. I liked Nate when he was born. That's why the back of his head is flat. I didn't turn him over he was so cute. But he's just like the rest now. Men disgust me," she said.

I managed to stay quiet, recalling these memories, as Nate drove along into the morning. We eventually got to Mary and Nate, Sr.'s house just as the sun was coming up. We stayed in the unfinished bedroom in the back corner of the garage, on the main floor, so we were able to let ourselves in without waking them up. I didn't have to be careful about sinning here, the way I did at my parents' house.

I slept a while and woke up with Nate next to me. We were covered with a white sheet, and a pink polyester blanket with a shiny faux-silk edge sewn on with a wide zigzag. I thought that the edge would be off that blanket long before the blanket wore out. I hadn't even taken off my clothes. A bright light shone through the basement window. I felt as though I were in a spotlight of guilt.

Though the room where we slept was built inside the garage, the toilet was outside the room, in a skeleton of two by fours. A string, weighted with a beer bottle opener, controlled the light, but I didn't turn it on. I sat on the toilet in the cement garage watching the stairway, hoping Nate, Sr. wouldn't come downstairs.

I tried to get back to sleep by rubbing the soft inner part of the arches on my feet together. I still couldn't sleep. I thought about the well-dressed actresses I had seen in TV movies as a child, women with thin waists and pearl necklaces slapping men who misbehaved with a single stinging crack that got the men to see the light.

Nate opened his eyes. I felt horrified, disgusted, hungover, guilty, and ashamed but what I said was, "Do you love me? Nate, do you?"

"I'm not any good for you," he said.

I thought he must have remembered what he'd done to me earlier in the car.

This all happened fast but I knew that I didn't want him to feel guilty. I was angry at him and wanted him to feel terrible. I also hated myself for being with him, and was afraid that if he felt terrible he would hurt me again—or he would leave me. I didn't want either, so I felt I needed to protect him from feeling guilty by reassuring him that it was okay.

Mary sent us home with two cardboard boxes of porn magazines. I couldn't figure out why she did that, and why Nate took them. I couldn't even think about it. You need to have someone to talk to deeply in order to make sense out of your life. In order to talk to someone deeply, you have to be able to speak truthfully to someone who can do the same. It would be years before I could finally say something that was the truth, and it took even longer to find someone who could listen and respond. I adapted to living an illogical life. Living in this condition, I developed a high tolerance for lies, especially my own.

❧

When we got back home, I stayed alone in Tupa for a few days. Katie told me that Carol, Nate's old girlfriend, had a baby girl, but she had given her up for adoption. Nate was glad that he had finally had a girl. Carol wrote to Katie, but she didn't visit again.

I distracted myself from worries about Nate and Carol by studying. I liked to read my Botany text. I enjoyed Botany. The book was thin and green, with delicate hand drawings of plants and diagrams of plant parts. Botany used the practice, first started by Linnaeus in 1753, of binomial nomenclature—that is, describing individual plants using two words: the genus name and the specific name, such as genus: *populus,* specific: *tremuloides*, "quaking aspen." It also made me feel good to study from such a serious-looking book. I felt as though my dad might have studied out of a book like that at the University of Minnesota.

My pelvic pain continued on and off all summer, though I resumed work. As a requirement for graduation, my summer internship for the program had to be completed. I returned to school again in the fall.

Throughout the summer Dr. Beane had been trying to treat my symptoms with sample antibiotics. In the fall, I told him I still wasn't feeling any better.

"I won't be able to handle my classes if I don't feel better than this," I said.

"What classes?"

"I'm a student at VCC, in the Conservation Technician program."

"Does that mean you have insurance?"

"I think so. I think I have insurance as long as I am in school and under age twenty-one. Why do you ask?"

"Well I think we should do a laparoscopy to see what might be going on." He walked me to the scheduling desk, and we set it up that day.

I wondered if I would have gotten something other than free sample antibiotics several months earlier if Dr. Beane had known I had insurance. I wondered why he hadn't asked me sooner.

☙

I had the test at the hospital. They kept me overnight. I waited all morning for Dr. Beane to stop by with the results. He didn't. I finally called him at his office from my hospital room.

"Did you find anything out?" I asked.

"No. Everything looks fine," he said.

A few weeks later my blood pressure went up, so he took me off the pill. He suggested I use an IUD instead. The day I got the IUD inserted I had such a frantic response I couldn't move off the couch. The pain was like labor. Katie told me the body tries at first to give birth to the foreign object.

I felt as if I was getting worse. I spent a week in the Alma Hospital on IV antibiotics and bed rest.

"You've had the treatment for Pelvic Inflammatory Disease. You should be better. If you aren't better, I think you should see a psychiatrist," Dr. Beane said.

Nate told Katie he thought that I was just trying to get attention, so he was determined not to give me any, for my own good.

I searched for information about Pelvic Inflammatory Disease at the Alma College Library. I got lost for a while in the books there. At the same time I learned that women weren't allowed in the art museums in the thirties because it was assumed they couldn't have talent, so the logic followed, how could they have appreciation of art? Less than fifty years ago.

I looked through a book of art, in protest. I saw Goya's painting of Saturn eating his children.

I looked up Pelvic Inflammatory Disease in a medical book. The way it was explained to me was that I didn't have syphilis and I didn't have gonorrhea, though they kept checking. I had P.I.D.; it was nonspecific vaginitis, one of the many bacteria that can affect the female organs. Though I knew that syphilis and gonorrhea were sexually transmitted, it was never explained to me that so was P.I.D. And even if it had been explained it wouldn't have made sense because though all the men I've dated were unfaithful to me, they didn't have any diseases. It would never have explained the problems I had been having since I was about twelve years old. The treatment for P.I.D. was clearly listed: rest and antibiotics. This was just another shock, a puzzle, an event that rested insecurely on the rock of me like lichen.

Chapter 20

It was a cold day in October. I spent the night at Nate's. He left me alone the next day to heat the house with the wood cook stove.

"Keep the fire going," he said.

The wood was so green I could barely get it to burn. The fire required constant attention. I split the wood thinly with the red-handled hatchet by holding it perpendicular to the cabin floor with my left hand and getting a straight hit at the top; then, with the hatchet in both hands, I banged the log down until it split. I did this at least twice to each piece of wood, making extra-thin pieces. Then I set the wood on the top of the cook stove, actually baking the wood dry. When I almost put the fire out by adding too much wet wood at once, I added only one piece at a time to the fire. It took concentration. Green wood burns like wet cotton. Besides being nearly impossible to burn, wet wood gives off virtually no heat. I was cold. I was scared that Nate would be mad. I thought that if I had more skill I wouldn't have so much trouble.

When Nate got home, he saw the pieces of wood lined up on top of the stove, with spaces between them for better drying. He opened the burner on the cook stove and stirred the coals. I thought he'd be mad, but he wasn't. He looked at me kindly and smiled.

"I left you with such a problem," he said. "It's impossible to keep a fire going with green wood. You did a good job, Anna." I nearly relaxed.

☙

Dr. Beane all but told me, "You're not sick; you're crazy." I'd rather be sick than crazy but I didn't have the two so separate. I thought I could be both. The physicians seemed to have it all mixed up, like, if I were crazy, I couldn't be sick, and since I lived in the woods and dated Nate I must be crazy. What more proof did they need?

I tried another specialist in the Twin Cities, a doctor my mom knew, the same doctor who had diagnosed me as too young to be sick seven years before. He said I was too young to have what it seemed like I had so I must not have it and he sent me home. Mom was in the room during the exam this time too.

"Can you please tell us what is happening? Why am I in so much pain? What causes the bleeding?" I asked.

I was getting dressed when the doctor said, "If you wanted to be well you wouldn't be using that IUD," he said.

That was it. I pulled down my pants; got back on the table, and spread my legs.

"Take it out," I said. He took it out. Even without the IUD I didn't get better.

By February I was miserable. When I stood up one morning a storm of blood rushed down my legs.

Dr. Beane couldn't think I imagined this. I called and told him how when I stood up in the morning a quake of blood had rushed from between my legs and formed a pond around my feet. We made a deal that I could see one more specialist and then he was going to recommend psychiatric treatment in an inpatient stay at Miller Dwan Hospital in Duluth. Dr. Beane's referral was at the clinic associated with St. Mary's Hospital on 3rd Street, also in Duluth.

I scheduled an appointment with Tom Hoyt. Dr. Hoyt was a sandy-colored man in his fifties. The expression on his face barely changed as I stared over the sheet on my knees while he examined me.

"I feel two masses," he said. "One on each ovary."

He admitted me to the hospital for an emergency laparoscopy, where they would make an incision in my naval and insert a camera so that they could get a better look.

"I've had one of those already," I said.

"You're about to get another one."

This laparoscopy indicated that scar tissue and a new infection had spread throughout my pelvic organs. The masses were cysts.

It was so strange how the first laparoscopy showed nothing, and three months later I was in this much of a mess. I wondered if Dr. Beane had lied to me. I wondered if the IUD had done something to me. Dr. Hoyt said I was going through menopause, as my ovaries weren't functioning. I would have to have a hysterectomy, but he said they couldn't operate while the infection was so severe; so the surgery couldn't be scheduled for at least a month.

"You mean I'm not crazy?" I said. He didn't answer. Now, finally, modern medicine could think in twos. Now that I was sick, I could also be crazy.

I spent two weeks in the hospital on IV antibiotics, with another shot every four hours. In the past, when I didn't say in so many words that I needed help taking care of Max, I didn't have to face the shame of letting Max down. In this way, I acted as if it weren't actually happening. This time, I asked Katie to take care of Max, instead of doing it behind the shadows of my shame.

I was ordered to rest in bed until April. I hitchhiked back to Alma carrying a dozen roses sent by Mrs. Stone, Susan's mother.

February was Winter Quarter, so I dropped out before completing Winter classes at Alma College.

I waited outside of Jerry Beck's office to speak with him. One of my classmates, I couldn't see which one, said, "I bet she's here to get out of something."

I cried when I told Mr. Beck what was happening.

"I have to have surgery. I don't see how I can finish school."

I saw Sally Lies down the hall when I left Jerry's office, but I didn't speak to her.

The April surgery prevented me from starting Spring Quarter. The courses I had left to complete wouldn't be offered again until the following winter, so I dropped out of school.

Chapter 21

The surgery was scheduled at St. Mary's Hospital in Duluth on April 19, 1978. I took the bus to St. Paul to be with my parents a few days before that.

Nate got a ride from Chuck down to the Spring Lake so he could be with me, too. He stayed overnight at Bill's, Carol's brother. He met me at my mom's house the morning of the eighteenth. Nate rode with us from St. Paul back to Duluth.

It was the day I was going to be admitted to the hospital, one day before I was scheduled for surgery. I was about to have a hysterectomy after years of trying to convince people that something was wrong with me. I had finally convinced them. When you don't know yourself it is difficult to get through a day, let alone a difficult time. I only knew one coping attitude besides drinking: be tough, like a callous.

Mom and Nate were visiting as if it were any other day. We hadn't discussed my surgery or my dropping out of school. I was irritated with the look on Nate's face, as if he understood what was happening. I hated people for seeming as if they understood.

The dining room narrowed and darkened. The sounds of the cups on the table were too loud. I wanted to get away, but I felt as if there were a rule against getting away. I started to get away in spite of myself and couldn't catch up. The room narrowed further. Perhaps I felt the way a golf ball would feel in its core as you made a slice in the shell. In school I learned that there isn't any hope of saving a golf ball once it's got a crack in the shell because the pith is wound so tight and is under so much pressure. Still, even without hope, I stuffed myself all back in after my thin surface had cracked. I was leaking out through my skin. I moved to contain myself even though I had a rule against leaking out through my skin and I was ashamed. I had to go anyway, and I started out the door and moved faster and faster. I kept moving, but I couldn't move fast enough to keep myself from spilling out. I kept moving. Finally I got myself all stuffed back in.

We rode up together to the hospital in Duluth. Nate was in the front seat with Mom.

"It's all right, Clare," he said. "I've already had all the children I want."

While Nate reassured my mother that he was all right, I embroidered the trunk of an oak tree along the side seam of the green army pants I had cut off and made into a skirt. When I pulled the hoop tight, I could hear the needle plunk into the fabric as percussion to the sound of the car tires on Highway 35 North.

❧

I checked in to my hospital room. The psychiatrist that Dr. Tom Hoyt sent to see if I was ready for surgery said he thought "I had my shit together."

"How are you doing with this?" he said, as he sat far forward on a desk chair. I feared that he would fall off of it, as he was quite overweight and the chair was unbalanced.

"I'm happy about this," I said. "It's been so long trying to find out what is wrong with me, and I am simply relieved."

Even I knew this was nonsense. Nonsense. Even as I told him that I was okay—so relieved that my ordeal was over—I couldn't figure out why he believed me.

What was so happy about any of it? About not being believed when I said I was sick and hurting? About not ever having children? Why was it so easy to convince him I was pleased I was sick, when it had been so hard to get taken seriously when I was suffering?

I had surgery April 19, 1978. I was twenty. I remembered the letter I wrote to Larry telling him that I couldn't have children, before I knew it was actually true. Was that letter prophecy or planning? I couldn't decide.

As soon as I could get up and move around, I wheeled my IV down to the end of the hall by the elevators and sat on a low bench where I could smoke, and I began to cry. Dr. Hoyt walked by on his way to the elevator. He sat down next to me. He seemed stiff in his white coat. I didn't feel good to be near him, but still, I wished he would say something kind to me.

He said in a stern tone, "Anna. If you don't change your lifestyle, this will keep happening to you." His well-adjusted self hurt me as if each thread of his neatly-starched white coat was a voice united in a chorus singing a song in a piercing tone: "What's Wrong With You?"

I was quiet as a wall. I didn't know what he meant.

I knew they had looked for a sexually transmitted disease. I'd had numerous syphilis and gonorrhea cultures, which were always negative. They did say that gonorrhea was hard to culture. I heard that at least five times. I'd been sick for years before I had a lifestyle, if what he meant by lifestyle was Nate.

On the other hand, lifestyle implies some level of choice. Even if I understood what he was saying to me, I had no more choice in those days than a snowflake in an avalanche. To have a lifestyle you have to have a life. To have a life you have to have a self.

Chapter 22

I just assumed that if I weren't in school my parents would stop helping me financially. They did stop, but we didn't discuss it.

I bought a car, a bad car—how do you decide when all you have is one hundred dollars? The muffler was loud and leaked exhaust which entered the car at slow speeds through the holes in the floor. Oil smoke trailed out the tail pipe when you started out. The column shift often stuck in second gear. I'd get going in first; if the linkage stuck in second, I'd have to stop, lift up the hood, manually move the shift linkage out of second and start over again. Luckily it didn't happen every time.

I drove up to Alma in my cheap car, with my two-hundred-dollar, blue safety-check faithfully written by my mother. She said this was the last check.

I thought I should get car insurance and drove to town to get some. I had seen the Wally Whiting Auto Insurance sign on Sheridan Street since I had moved to Alma. I stopped there to try to insure my car. Wally looked much like Mr. Wies. I recognized him from Angelica's Cafe, and remembered he touched my cheek. He didn't seem to recognize me.

He gave me a quote for insurance as he flipped through one of his thick three-ring binders. When I gave him my P.O. Box for an address, he asked me where I lived. I told him I lived on the Arrow Trail.

"That changes the situation," he said. He gave me a quote three times the original.

"Why did the price go up?" I asked.

"Because I consider you a moral risk," he said.

I didn't get insurance that day. I was so angry. This was punishment, deep down, for not doing whatever he expected me to do when he touched my cheek that day. But to him, this was just religious racism of a sort—punishment for living on the Arrow Trail, perhaps for living with Nate, though I didn't think he could have known that yet— even in the lightning-speed gossip of Alma. People judged you not for your merits but for their assumptions. It was that reputation my mom had warned me about. "You don't want to get a reputation," she said. She was right. It didn't matter what you were as long as you didn't have a reputation. I was lost and abandoned and in much need of care; it must have been obvious to at least one alert adult, but the reputation of the road where I lived was what mattered. I couldn't believe there was a policy that read "Arrow Trail address: three times the price."

Living on the Arrow Trail was a reputation ruiner because we were thought of as drug addicts with loose sexual morals. In a way it was true. Many of us were on drugs or drank too much, and many had loose sexual morals. On the side of it being unfair, even if true, was that on the Arrow people were also hardworking, talented, and kindhearted. Arrow Trailers were also honest about what they were doing. It wasn't all hidden the way it was in so many people's homes without the burden of a reputation. For example, I could cause Mr. Whiting some problems by asking him if he'd mind if I told his wife that he was over at my house touching my face. Some of us were good people who were lost; events were occurring outside of our control. We were young.

Nate said I could move in with him, so I did. I was recovering, so I slowly moved my belongings from Tupa up the road to his ten-by-twelve-foot cabin made of rough-cut lumber.

Chapter 23

The morning of the day I had officially moved out of Tupa and in with Nate, he gave me a ride in his wheelbarrow. The wheelbarrow was traveling fast and the wind passed over me softly in the way of a wedding veil. I laughed as if on a carnival ride. The sky rose as a giant balloon before my horizontal face. I was a star that day. I looked up and could see Nate's flat nose, and his reflectionless brown eyes as he leaned over the moving vehicle, and that too made me laugh. At the end of the driveway he stopped, stopped abruptly, and then gently propped the wheelbarrow on its front so the wooden handles reached upward the way the wings of an owl ascend to capture a rabbit. It was a deep wheelbarrow, so I could stay contained there, now cross-legged.

I sat there in a wheelbarrow with an "I'm a hooker" button that came with Nate's new Hooker CB radio pinned to my pink and white hospital robe. My hair was wild and uncombed, but tame compared with Nate's. He only combed his hair after his weekly shower or sauna. I was jealous of his ability to look weird naturally. I worked at it.

I wasn't thinking forward. It was my first day at Nate's following my surgery, so this wasn't just any day; it was a celebration. Nate was sweet-tempered that day. I was in love, and love brought me simplicity.

Before taking a ride in the wheelbarrow, I had been in bed, holding a heated brick wrapped in a towel over my incision. It had been two weeks since I'd had a hysterectomy, but I was only nineteen and healing fast. I stopped this fine Alma, Minnesota, afternoon with my

Hooker button, my almost wild enough hair, in the wheelbarrow throne, with nothing else to do except sit at the end of the driveway and watch tourists drive by. The Arrow Trail wound past the Soaprock National Forest and through the edge of the Bending Tree Canoe Area. It was a seldom-used road in a remote area, except in tourist season.

I waved at the pre-May fifteenth fisherman on their way to catch fish. This day, they caught a glimpse of me. This is where I found myself. I realize now I was like a tree frog in that I turned to the color of my environment, and it took me a while to absorb a place. That was it: I didn't believe in it, or perceive it, but rather *absorbed* the place where I found myself.

Some tourists drove by on their way to a Soaprock National Forest Lake, or BTCA lake. Some people in town liked to drive by; the rumors made them curious. I think some of them expected to see us having sex on the road. People assumed we were counter-culture, Arrow Trail hippies. Middle-aged men from town befriended the women on the Arrow readily, thinking they'd "get lucky."

At the end of the driveway, Nate left me in front of the tree-sized driftwood trunk with two branches planted upside down and a sawmill sawblade hanging in the crotch of it, along with an oversized crowbar attached to a branch. The way Nate envisioned it, the crowbar was supposed to be used to beat the saw blade for a prehistoric sort of doorbell. Nate could envision unusual household goods. The nonsense of it just made it more valuable to Nate. It didn't matter to him, for example, that the doorbell wasn't on the door. He could think of the end of the driveway as a door. The huge doorbell was amusing compared with the tiny home it rang. It was probably the doorbell, and not my smiling face, but some people actually stopped. True tourists: true "don't want to miss a thing, save this for the neighbors, can't wait to tell their wives about what we saw up north" tourists. That morning two cars stopped, about ten minutes apart, and took pictures of Nate and me in front of the strange doorbell.

The driveway went straight in about thirty yards, and ended right between the front door of the cabin, and the dog kennel. Nate had cleared trees just east of the house on both sides of the driveway. Nate set up the sawmill parallel to and on the south side of the driveway. He stacked the logs to the north. The sawmill was operating. Nate cut up logs for other people, in exchange for some of the lumber he would collect to build Paula's cabin. That was the plan.

Nate had visited Bill again, Carol's brother, while I was in the hospital, looking for sawmill parts. He scrounged three garbage cans of junk from the truck yard. I sorted all three cans, which were filled to the rim with dentist drills, wheat-back pennies, nuts, bolts, screws and items I couldn't identify that I carefully made a pile for anyway, an "unidentifiable" pile. After three days of recovering from surgery, sitting in the late-spring sun in the rock driveway, listening as the sawmill carved flat pieces from white wet wood, I got bored.

"I'm bored," I said.

Nate said, "I work on a sawmill; I never get bored."

I decided to clean up the place. We didn't have a lawn mower. I cut the grass on the sides of the cabin, which wasn't grass at all, but seedling popple trees. I chopped their skinny trunks in the fresh-smelling air with dull, soon duller, scissors. My cutting thumb was numb for a month after that. Following the lawn-cutting, I raked. I pulled the rake, and the rake pulled my guts. I spent the next day in our loft bed, inside the "postage stamp" cabin, affectionately called that by Nate for its small size, only crawling down the ladder from the loft in order to heat the brick in the three burner gas oven. Without electricity, the brick was my heating pad. My mom told me how as children they had taken hot bricks with them to their feather beds to keep warm in the winter nights. That's what gave me the idea to use the brick.

c&ƎƆ

Katie came to visit. She saw me moving slowly. She said, "I don't understand what the big deal is. I've had cats spayed and they seem fine the same day."

Nate was in and out on projects at his convenience. Nate cut a load of logs for himself, and then he returned to working on the Silver Steel Road for Hal. Chuck worked steadily. Nate thought he was too smart for that.

Nate knew somebody who worked at a shampoo plant. He got several empty fifty-five gallon, blue plastic barrels used to store shampoo. Our shower was made from one, our rain barrel from another, and he cut one in half and put a toilet seat over the opened top for our toilet. Two more blue barrels awaited reinvention at the back of the property, where Paula's cabin would be one day.

Nate left in the morning. I had chores to do, and felt better. I fed Oden, who was in the doghouse, enclosed with a chicken wire fence. I took the plastic watering can and dipped it deep into the blue chemical tub converted to a rain barrel, and watered the tomato plants. Next I watered the planter Nate had made for me. It was a hollowed-out log of white pine cut lengthwise and mounted between two large round trunk slabs that supported it the way wheels hold an axle. I planted it with pansies because there was so much shade in the woods.

As the water poured from the spout, I was reminded of an image from childhood. A pile of unfolded, unstacked paper bags had lain on the counter of Mr. Orbeck's fifth-grade classroom. I folded the bags, bent them in the corners, and flattened their mouths, folded them again, and made a neat orderly stack. I did this slowly, intent on catching the attention of Lane, who sat clear across the room. I hoped Lane would notice. I imagined that he was totally focused on me. When he saw the skill with which I folded those bags I imagined he would think, "Now, she would make a good wife. Look at how she flattens those bags."

I didn't care about bags; I was just imitating, imitating my mother, most likely, who performed duties in the way of a good wife, as if the act of living with a man, made me into a wife.

My life and my body were separate from my sense of myself, as if what was happening to them was different from what was happening to me. That me had stepped out, left, disappeared, and wouldn't help. All I could do was imitate others. I was guessing how to be a person. Each day I made myself up. By that time, I had expanded my skills from bag-folding to washing. I knew how to wash dishes and clothes, countertops and windows, and I could wash out my will without any evidence at all.

❧

Chuck and Katie were having a party. I wasn't fond of baking, so it was likely more imitating, but I baked some cookies for it while Nate was at work. I ground some of Nate's marijuana, rubbed it in the bottom of the strainer, and pushed it through repeatedly until it was fine. I kept pushing the moist green leaves through the strainer until I had a cup of dust. I added some flour, peanut butter, extra oil, sugar, and one more egg for moist, sweet, hardly-at-all-like-pot peanut-butter cookies.

When Nate got home from work he brought wild flowers and wine, red wine in a big green bottle with a maroon cap over the cork, replaceable, reusable.

"After you're done with the wine, you can use the bottle for your pennies."

"Here, Nate, have a cookie," I said.

"I've got something special for you, Anna," he said.

"What is it?"

He reached in his pocket, and took out a nickel-silver suspender hook that he had found in the dirt.

"I found it exactly where I had placed the jack I used to change a tire, as if it had been waiting for me. Look! Anna! It's not even tarnished; I uncovered it this way, shiny as ever. That's the way nickel-silver is—nice."

"Thank you! Wow! I think I have a piece of leather I could use to make it into a belt."

I praised Nate the way I had praised my father, praise with fear added in. I was troubled around him, but at the same time I loved him and wanted something, longed for something from him. It was as if I took it as my responsibility to prevent his outbursts by anticipating what might set him off, and I praised him as I sensed his inadequacy was part of his danger. But I was furious with him too, for being dangerous, and for my accidental attachment to him. I tried to make him feel better without arousing suspicion, in order to have some chance he'd fulfill this mysterious longing.

I felt sorry for Nate, and this was also similar to how I felt for my dad. I remember being sick with remorse that Dad suffered so much. Though I didn't understand what bothered him so, I wanted to help my dad, too. I remembered D.H. Lawrence's story "The Rocking Horse Winner" where a boy is compelled to ride his rocking horse in order to get visions of winning bets on horses in order to provide money for his mother. He was so in tune to her needs that he heard the walls speaking, "There must be more money." There was something mysterious like that for me. If I got too close to certain people, I got pulled into a voracious need of theirs. It became an against-my-will job to fill it. Whatever it was, Nate and my dad shared it.

My father and I used to swim to the middle of Lake Elizabeth to a big raft, built by my dad and Mr. Stone. He'd swim in an inner tube alongside of me. He'd let me hold the inner tube on the way back. I wanted to please him. I'd swim and then I'd dive off the board.

I didn't have any control over the depth of my dive, not knowing to pick the angle, and I dove too deeply before I turned around. I kept swimming up and up and up. I swam and still no surface, up and up, and then I burst through, just in time. I didn't tell my dad it happened. He wouldn't have liked it. He would have said I should have known not to do it that way. My dad thought you should have skills before you possibly could.

I gave up that thinking, handed Nate another cookie, and put the rest of them in a zip-lock baggie. We walked to Chuck and Katie's house at the old resort. Tupa was empty, for rent again. I felt lonely walking by there. It turned out that I was the last person to rent Tupa. No one ever lived there after I did.

The Baxters knew how to throw a party. I felt redeemed in my shabby domestic reputation when everyone loved the cookies. I didn't try one. I hated pot and peanut-butter cookies.

Wes showed up. He lived right next to us on the Arrow Trail. Nate hated Wes because Wes had helped Suzy escape from Nate. Suzy was the girlfriend before Carol. I could tell Nate wasn't glad to see Wes, and we rarely saw him after that, socially, even though he lived in the woods right next to us. I only rarely saw him from a distance in town, or on the road to or from town. He must not have known that Nate was coming to the party, or he wouldn't have.

Something took a bite out of the fun when Katie's four-year-old boy, Jeff, discovered the cookie bag. All the praise I got for the cookies turned to fear. What if Jeff had eaten a pot cookie? What if we hadn't been paying attention?

Katie was trying to explain to him the concept of an adult cookie, when Nate whispered to me.

"I have to get home, too many cookies," he said.

When we got home, Nate escorted me around the yard, as an artist, as a photographer, making me look at each frame.

Anyone would look at our house and yard as a junkyard. But Nate had a different perspective.

"Look; study this," he said. "Look at the sawmill," run by a 1948 Waukesha, thirty-years-old-this-year engine. I had sent a card to Waukesha, Wisconsin, in honor of the machine's birthday a few days before. I sent a picture of Nate cutting a log, and let them know the engine was still running. I had done that to please Nate.

We took a walk down the series of rough-cut boards, which Nate called the boardwalk, to the outhouse.

"Is there a better place anywhere to take a shit?" he asked. "Look at the '52 Chevy." He pointed at my manual transmission training car, which had a three-speed column shift. We had already fucked in it, "Carefully," he said, even though I was supposed to wait four more weeks.

"Look at that cabin! That barber pole works. You'll see just as soon as we get electricity."

Nate offered it to me, offered it all to me, because the moon was full, and he had eaten too many cookies, and because he realized how rich we were. He offered me the contents of the semi-cab-sized culvert filled with years of collections. He spun me around and pointed to the stack of car batteries waiting to be used to power our CB radio.

"Why right there, my dear, is a fortune in car battries."

"Batt-er-ies," I said.

"Don't you see, do you see, how rich we are? Don't you see what we have here? If we took a picture of the yard, of the house, without the CB radio antenna, it would be impossible to tell what year the picture was taken, some time after 1950, but not 1979."

"Show me where you plan to put Paula's house," I said.

He pointed to the back of the property, just behind the culvert. We walked to the house. I clutched the red-rusty door handle with my palm and pushed down on the latch tongue with my thumb until it clicked (following previous instructions from Nate: "Clutch it till it clicks," he said).

We climbed the ladder made of two by fours to our loft bed. Our moonlit faces were bluish green. Nate looked as if he were a boy. I could see the baseball cap on his head. He showed me once again that the back of his head was flat because he had been so cute his mom never turned him as a baby. I saw the moon in his dark eyes. We lay down together on top of the mattress. It was too warm to get under my grandmother's wool quilt, a gift from my mother.

Naked, Nate clutched me, and started to whimper, as he might have sounded in 1950. He seemed to be a child in need of comfort. He started to shake, as if he were an old Chevy engine whining.

He said, "I think I ate too many cookies—just hang on." I hung on, hung on for him as if hanging on to the rope of a big bag swing: afraid, afraid to swing out into the air over the black dirt woods, into the forest of darkened branches, of trees and roots, into the forest of my own childhood. He shook and let me comfort him. His hot tears fell onto my face and shoulders.

"Thank you for holding me," he whispered.

"All right," I said, but I knew I was the one being held.

Eventually in the moonlight that singed my skin, the hot-quiet, can't-tell-what-year-it-is night, we fell asleep together.

Chapter 24

Chuck and Nate were walking on the back of the property, and found a fawn. They didn't know if they or someone else startled the predator that was about to kill her, but her baby neck was still wet from the saliva of whatever had come close to doing so. They brought the long-legged thing home, and we took her in the house. This was definitely a good thing about living in an unfinished house: we did not have to be fussy about bringing wildlife into it. Her legs slipped all over the plywood as she was unsteady on the flat floor. Deer are better on uneven ground. So at first I held her in my lap on the couch. Katie gave me some baby bottles and I fed her cow's milk. All night she cried out "Maaahm! Maaahm!" with her heartbreaking call.

In the morning, Nate got up for work and left. I realized she was barely drinking the milk. I put bigger holes in the bottle and it still didn't work. I got on the CB to ask if anyone knew what to feed a fawn.

In forty-five minutes, the game warden was at our house. He took the fawn away to a wildlife refuge. It was legal to kill wildlife in season, but it was not legal to capture them. I said we weren't capturing her; we were saving her. When you look in the eyes of a fawn, it obligates you to protect it, like a spell. I'm sure of it. He didn't see it that way.

I didn't want to keep her anyway. If I got her to grow up, someone would just shoot her, probably someone from my own neighborhood.

I was still trying to play house. That afternoon, I found some potatoes in the bag that hadn't come to life and put them in the oven to bake. It seemed a meager dinner, potatoes. I wondered what Katie was cooking. Chuck and Katie always had food. Chuck worked steadily for Hal. But they had Jeff to feed. I supposed feeding Jeff kept them motivated.

Chuck also got a charge account at Trapp's, the local grocery store, as part of his pay for working for Hal. Chuck charged, and Hal paid. That helped. Hal probably got a discount from Trapp's by doing it that way, or a tax write-off. At least with the benefit to Chuck of the charge account, Hal wouldn't have to pay him as much money per hour. That's how Hal was.

Nate didn't get a charge account at Trapp's. Hal said that Nate wouldn't work if he wasn't hungry, and even that didn't help much. Nate bragged about that, too. Meager living was a virtue for Nate. He told people he lived the entire last winter on mustard sandwiches, white bread, and beer. I had been with him for a lot of it.

Potatoes were all we had, so I put them in the gas oven with the white enamel front, and put a match to the burner.

My stomach usually reacted to Nate, as if it knew something about him that I didn't. When I heard him drive in, my stomach dropped the way it feels when you take a fast elevator down. He opened the door.

"What the hell? It's so hot!" He pulled open the oven and shut if off. "What the hell? You dumb bitch! It's ninety degrees—I don't believe it—Jesus Christ, you!" he slammed the door of the house and the door of the truck and backed out of my evening.

The voice in my head got too loud—I needed to walk but I couldn't stop the internal lecture: *You dumb bitch how could you be so dumb he's right you know who ever thought of having baked potatoes on a hot summer day? Why did I even try to make whoever heard of potatoes for dinner some dinner it's not my fault we don't have any food, is it?*

I had planned to leave Nate when I graduated and instead here I was, an idiot, a dropout, baking potatoes on hot summer days.

I walked down the driveway and turned left toward town, thus beginning the first of my many attempts at "Fuck you, I'm leaving."

I didn't want to be there. I hadn't intended to move in with him. He asked me to live with him after my surgery, and my parents didn't. Before I got sick, I had planned to finish school and then my imagination planted me in Montana, far away from him. I had aspirations, but no connections, and no idea how many obstacles were in my way. I had no place to go and no way to go there.

But I imagined myself much more independent, not sloppily hooked to some whimsically moody man. I wondered if a ship resented the wind before it mastered it. That's where I was: moving but going nowhere.

❧

I looked down when I walked, not from bad posture but from years of hunting agates, though I never found one in Alma. I didn't think agates could be found north of the Laurentian Divide, yet I couldn't stop the habit of looking. The sound of the wind moving through dry balsams and the ancient fragrance of sweet fern breaking through weighty iron rocks changed my mood by pulling me into the present.

I looked up and about a hundred feet in front of me, traveling in the same direction was a brown bear. Black bears can be brown, black or other colors, a detail I remembered from school. So this was a black bear with a brown color.

I stopped walking as if to more thoroughly consider the bear's plans. At that moment, a truck came out of the logging road directly to my left. I pointed at the bear and looked at the truck. Then I looked back at the bear, but he was gone. The two men, tourists—the same tourists who had photographed me in my wheelbarrow throne—didn't see the bear. They saw me standing perfectly still, with my hand in the air pointing east, like a loser. I suppose their memory of me in the wheelbarrow with my robe on prevented them from stopping.

When I got to the third curve, about a mile east from where I started, I saw the clear-cut area with trees growing all around, with no larger ones to protect them. I decided to turn around. I never got far before I realized that I had nowhere to go.

On the curve where I had first spotted the bear, I raised my head to avoid being taken by surprise. There he was, also turned around now, again with his back to me. I walked slowly behind him, and watched as he crossed the road. Then I lost interest in him, because he was traveling away from the house.

When I turned in the driveway, I could hear Oden barking. He usually didn't bark at me, and I was musing about this when another brown-colored black bear stood up from behind the pick-up, the Chevy with the column shift, and the '52 Olds. If you come face to face with a bear, don't run. I had just read that the worst thing you can do is run.

We faced each other, both of us standing. He was just a tad taller than I. He must not have liked rules either because we both took off running: I ran into the house, he ran to the woods. Moments later he was back. I started banging pans inside to scare him off. Strangely the sound brought him closer—as if the pans banging were a dinner bell to him. He approached the window and looked in. His stiff, Mickey Mouse ears were listening for another invitation, and his black nose made puffing noises on the screen. Bears use their noses the way people use their eyes, to get information. I was so excited! I had never been this close to a bear.

Oden barked wildly. The bear didn't acknowledge his genetic relationship to dogs by greeting Oden. He pawed at the door of the cabin. My teeth started to chatter the way they used to when I swam too long as a child. I remember that Nate said that the door opened out and had that great hinge and handle for this reason, to keep a bear out, but still I took up the CB mic; luckily the car battery that powered it wasn't dead.

"Break one nine for Star Trek, Star Trek are you out there?"

"Ten four, this is Star Trek; is that you Charlie?"

I was using Charlie, my dad's nickname for me, as my CB handle. I was Charlie Brown, and Nate was Pig Pen. I quickly decided to call DeeDee, a.k.a. Star Trek, on the CB. DeeDee was a friend of Nate's, married to Will Salo's grandson. Will Salo had been my forest service colleague.

"Star Trek! God! There is a bear in my yard!"

"Shoot him!"

"No! No. That's not it at all. He's not hurting anything. I think he's sort of tame, might be from the campground. I'd like to be friends with him, not kill him."

"I'll come over and shoot him for you."

"No. That's all right; Star Trek. I just wanted to tell somebody. I got excited. You know."

"Where's the Pig Pen?"

"He must be at Katie's. I thought he might have been with you. Thanks. Thanks. I'll let you know what happens."

The bear left, darkness fell, and I was alone in the loft with my brick and a three-year old *Reader's Digest*, a cast-off from Nate's mom. I continued to read by candlelight, long past the time when the pinkish haze came through the two triangular windows that formed a square as I looked out from the loft. I listened to the night. I heard the early movement of the invisible nightlife. I heard the grouse drumming without rhythm late in the season, the wolf spider leaping in the cupboard downstairs. A wolf spider can leap so fast it might as well fly.

I thought of the screaming creature I had heard on my first night in Alma. Perhaps it was because it was difficult to see, but I couldn't submerge myself into the *Reader's Digest* enough to force the worries and memories from my mind.

I thought about a trip I had taken a few years before with Lane and other friends from high school to a cabin in northwestern Wisconsin. Each of us swallowed some window pane—salty glass panes of LSD— as we got out of the two cars that carried us there. We surveyed our quiescent surroundings; the lake was smooth as a lollipop and before long we were all high.

On LSD the world turns to a fairy tale, with all its beauty and horror. I left for the woods and listened to the moss tell me its life story as I sat in the dark. I thought I was too ugly to be around people, my face felt as if it were dripping blisters.

Later I saw Lane sitting at a table in the cabin. He wasn't paying attention to my qualities as a wife. He held his head between both hands and shook it back and forth.

"Oh no!" he said.

I saw what was happening to him. This was the bad trip we were warned about in health class, but I couldn't let it into my mind. I couldn't say to myself: Lane is having a bad trip. That would have been as if I were having a bad trip and I couldn't be having one because I wouldn't know what to do.

I couldn't quite tell what was happening to me in Alma, either. It was as if my life had not begun because I couldn't admit to having the life I was having.

Chapter 25

We visited my parents again the second weekend in June. If they liked Nate less since they met Carol or since I moved in with him, they didn't say. My parents were skilled at staying out of my business. They were friendly. Mom made chicken and wild rice casserole, with a salad. Dad poured us drinks. Nate had a beer with a glass. I had a gin and tonic. Dad still poured liqueur after dinner. We never had liqueur unless we visited my parents.

Nate slept down the hall where Janice used to sleep, as he usually did. I slept in my old room. In the middle of the night, I went into his room. We started fighting. At first we whispered our disagreements with each other, but eventually we got loud.

I couldn't sleep. We usually left Sunday, and Nate wanted to stay another day. I told Nate that I didn't feel right being at my parents' house and I wanted to leave the next day.

"Nate, we should leave tomorrow. I have to get back to Alma. I feel like I need work. I'm going crazy here with nothing to do."

"Don't tell me what to do. I've got my reasons for being down here."

"I'm not trying to tell you what to do, Nate. Can't you think of me? I bounced a bunch of checks to get us down here. I feel afraid. I want to get back to get some money."

"Well listen here, can't you just relax? You're always on such a work trip. You think too much."

"Think too much! That's absurd. I'm not thinking too much, I'm hungry. I don't want to keep bouncing checks. I feel embarrassed here at my parents' house. They're judging me."

"Oh God, Anna. Give it a break," Nate said.

Mom must have finally got sick of it and she called out for us to shut up. I had imagined shouting to them to shut up as a child. I never had the courage to say it when they kept me up all night. The unspoken "SHUT UP" carved a wide path within me but the two words never came out my mouth. That unspoken urge to speak was acting as a fallen log in the stream of my life. Here my mother was telling me to shut up after just an hour of fighting.

Many times, after they were done fighting and got quiet, I sneaked down the stairs, and listened at the bottom until I could hear my mom's breathing above the sounds of the house. And then I could go back to sleep. Once I went downstairs and they were still awake. My dad saw me; he made me walk out of the stairway and into the room.

"What do you want? What are you doing?" he said.

I don't remember what I said. But he shoved me against the wall. He took me by the hair as if my head were an ear of corn and he hauled me back up the stairs and into bed.

"Don't ever do that again," he said.

This memory was in the background of the fight I was having now. In the present, my mom was not afraid of *me*. She called from the bottom of the stairway so her voice carried clearly into the room interrupting our fight.

"If you two had anything going in your lives, you wouldn't have so much time to argue. Dad and I have responsibilities and would like to get some sleep."

The shame stung me like sunburn. She was right. I hadn't got a thing going in my life and I needed to get something going. I needed to find some direction. That's what I had been arguing about.

Chapter 26

I saw Dr. Hoyt for my six-week checkup. I drove the hundred-dollar Chevy with the leaky exhaust and sticky linkage to Duluth by myself. I should have asked for someone to come with me, but I was trying to be brave. I equated isolation with bravery.

All Dr. Hoyt said when he examined me was, "Ah, isn't youth wonderful?" I guessed that meant I was healing, but I didn't ask.

I walked around Duluth, bought gas, did some window shopping. I meant to get going before dark, but I wandered too long. I could have left, I just didn't. Suddenly I was leaving Duluth at dusk, exactly what I hadn't wanted to do.

I drove up the Central Entrance toward the Miller Hill Mall. By the time I reached the highway, it was dark. The light that illuminates most dashboards was burned out so I couldn't see my speedometer. In this clangorous, smoky car I got pulled over.

"Do you realize you were going seventy miles per hour?" the officer said.

"No. I didn't. I was in a mild hurry because I realized it was dark. I didn't mean to stay in Duluth so long. I would have never driven this car, but I had a doctor appointment here."

"Where do you live?"

"Alma," I said.

"Do you have a driver's license?" he said.

"Yes." I handed it to him.

I turned the ignition off as the exhaust smoke from underneath the car surrounded the officer's head.

"Why does your license say you live in Spring Lake?"

"I'm a student at Alma Community College. The license still shows my permanent address."

"I'm not going to give you a ticket, but I want you to go directly home."

"Thank you, Officer. I will. I'll be going right home."

I tried to drive away, but as I got just a few feet ahead, the linkage stuck going into second gear. I pulled over, lifted the hood, moved the gearshift lever from second and back into first, and started over, all with the officer watching me. I only had to do this once, and the officer didn't change his mind about giving me a ticket. When I got home, I never drove that car again.

Chapter 27

"Need anything in town, Nate?'

"Fill up the gas cans. How about a case of beer?"

"Got it. I'll see you in a while."

The truck was a 1953 version of the Chevy Luv, with rounded side windows in the rear corners of the cab. I paid seventy-five dollars for it, and Nate got it running. It was compact and practical: easy to stuff with laundry, empty beer cases, dogs, and gas cans in the truck bed, out of the way. The truck was designed for short people. Even with short legs, my feet reached the clutch and the brake with ease. The engine made a bugle sound when I pressed my foot on the starter button to the right of the gas pedal. It was even insured, no thanks to Wally Whiting.

I traveled on Highway 53, and noticed the sign for Old Highway 53. When Highway 53 gets old, maybe the sign will be changed to Very Old Highway 53.

I parked the truck in the Midway Waters Bank parking lot and walked up to the post office. It was so pleasant to approach this brick building, with its inscriptions honoring the Postmaster, architects, and engineers.

The inflow and outflow of information, the rhythm of communication, like waves on the water or seasons, comforted me as I walked up the cement steps to the entrance. I was glad, walking into the post office; I proudly held my post office box key in my hand, as if this act connected me to history and to life. I glanced at the pictures of the Nation's Most Wanted list in case I knew any of them, though I never did. I read a few local announcements about pancake breakfasts at the Moose Club, and Bingo at the VFW, and I felt good for a moment. I must have carried this joy with me as I left because when I was walking by the employment service, for no particular reason, I went in and filled out an application.

"Can you type?" the clerk asked.

"Yes," I said.

"It's light typing, and I haven't a clue about the hours, but they just called this morning from the *Northern Messenger*. Here, take this card with you. It's right next door to Salo's Store. Do you know where that is?"

"Yes. My friends Lee and DeeDee own that store. Thanks. I know where it is." I wasn't dressed for a job interview, but I was clean. I'd had a sauna the night before.

I didn't type *well*, but the woman at the employment office hadn't asked if I could.

As I drove the few blocks to the *Messenger* office, I remembered how I learned to type. I had been sleeping over at Susan's the night my mom broke her collarbone. I was ten. They said my mom had tumbled down the stairs. I felt uneasy about that. I thought my dad had thrown her down. I don't know why I thought that, but even Susan asked me if I thought my dad pushed her.

Mom needed to go into the hospital to get the bone set. I had taught myself to type, because I wanted to write my mom a letter while she was away. I thought it would be extra special for her if it were typed. The only other typing I had done was for my dad when I helped Christina.

Now I walked into the building, the one closest to the alley and Salo's Meat and Grocery. A woman stood behind the counter, near the cash register. Four other women stood around a big table in the back, handing each other stacks of paper.

"Are you the boss?" I asked.

"No," said the woman behind the counter. "He's the boss." She pointed to a man seated at a desk.

He didn't move or acknowledge me.

I said, "I'm here to apply for a job."

The man moved toward me from behind the wood and glass barrier and whispered, "Let's go outside; these women, you know."

I was wearing my "smile anyway because you want the job" face. I followed him even though I had no idea what he meant.

His car was parked in the middle of the alley, running, with the driver's door swung open. He was ahead of me, and walked around to the passenger's side and motioned me to get in his car. I thought it was unusual to get in the driver's seat of a car with a man you have just met, but this wasn't any man—this was a prospect, an employer, so I did it anyway.

I handed him the "MY NAME IS" introduction card from the employment office. He moved the card close and then an arm's length away from his face. I leaned over closer to him, and he smelled of Saturday night; the card was upside down and he was drunk. Here it was again, that strange split between what was happening and what I felt about it. Something in me was saying why would you want to have this life? Why would you want to have this job?

"My name is Anna Books," I offered.

"Dave, Dave Chelesnik. I own the *Messenger*. That was my sister in there, Emma. She's sort of bossy. I'm the boss, though. Ah . . . ah . . ." He struggled reading the card again. "What is it?"

"Anna."

"Anna. Can you type?"

"Yes. I haven't done a lot of typing, but I know where the keys are. I learn quickly."

"I think it'll work. I've got a feel for this you know. I ah . . . ah . . . When could you start?"

"When would you like me to start?"

"How about Thursday? Thursday, around nine. Those women will be gone then. They yak, yak, yak. I always stay away from here on Tuesdays. I just stopped in for a minute today. You're lucky you found me; I'm all over the place. I can't stand all those women talking. Come Thursday."

I got out of the car and he moved over and drove slowly down the alley.

As long as I was so close to Salo's store, I picked up potatoes, Velveeta cheese, two loaves of Taystee White Bread, and Skippy Creamy Style peanut butter. Nate ate peanut butter sandwiches on white bread and dunked them in his coffee. He thought he had stumbled onto a candy bar sensation: sweet coffee, with Carnation evaporated milk, and peanut butter. I bought enough sauerkraut, pork chops and kidney beans to make a pot of *Kupus en Gra*. (Translated from Slovenian: sauerkraut and kidney beans. Nate's mother, Mary, had given me the recipe.) I bought four of the five-ounce cans of Carnation evaporated milk for Nate's coffee and a carton of Marlboro cigarettes. I picked up two blocks of ice and one case of Pfeiffer beer at Bear Paw Liquor on the north side of town.

Finally, using up the rest of the money Nate had given me, I pumped gas into the two five-gallon gas cans for the sawmill. I had seven dollars left. I put seven dollar's worth of gas in the truck. If Nate needed more gas he could use his Georgia credit card—a siphon-hose-and-a-suck-easy-gas-transfer. I couldn't wait to tell him I had a job.

Chapter 28

I caught on fast enough at the *Messenger*. I started during the last week of May and felt as if I knew what I was doing by the fourth of July. Dave told me later that his sister Emma had been worried at first. The *Messenger* was a weekly shopping guide, mimeographed, stapled, and wrapped in grocery ads put together on Tuesdays, and delivered by neighborhood kids on Wednesdays. My job was to stencil and type the mimeographed ads, including the want ads. Want ads were one dollar per issue no matter how many lines. Some businesses had a running ad in the want ads, and, I learned later, only had an eighth- or quarter-page ad for Christmas. I interacted with the walk-in customers, got the pages ready for printing, and helped the women collate it all when they gathered on Tuesdays.

I stopped at the Tippy Canoe for a beer after work one night and found my neighbor, Chuck Baxter, in there.

"I come here every night for a beer after work," he said.

Part of having a regular job was having a regular routine. He asked me if I wanted to ride to work with him. I only worked Monday through Thursday, but I thought that was a terrific idea. So beginning the next week I rode to work and back with Chuck on Mondays and Wednesdays. I drove on Tuesday because that was the day we put the *Messenger* together and it was always a long day, and on Thursday I usually got off early.

I looked forward to those wondrous rides with Chuck. We sang

"There's a Hole in My Bucket" and other folk songs. I didn't feel chaotic around Chuck when Katie wasn't there. He was never mean, but it was more than that. Chuck was kind. He let me know that he liked me. He both regretted and cherished our drunken sex together he said.

"I've only been to bed with three people in my life," he said. I was surprised considering our crowd. "My first girlfriend, Katie, and you."

If I overslept and wasn't ready, Chuck just sat in his car, waiting for me. He didn't yell at me when I got in. If I forgot anything so that we had to go back, he didn't act impatient. He just waited. He was polite. In the cold weather, I wasn't afraid riding with Chuck, the way I sometimes was driving home alone. In Alma, in the winter, there is no chance someone wouldn't help you if they saw you broken down on the road. Even people with different minds or morals would stop, but there was a chance that you could freeze to death before someone came by. Cars were infrequent on the Arrow Trail in the winter months, especially at night.

Chuck talked to me about Nate. On the ride home sometimes I was able to cry and tell him about what was happening. I didn't share all of it with him. If he judged me for anything, I couldn't tell.

I felt loved during our trips back and forth down the winding Arrow Trail. The scenery was beautiful. Sometimes we just rode without talking. The silence whispered possibilities. I enjoyed watching the clouds and the progression of the seasons in the trees and yards of the homes and cabins we passed. The road went right along the shore on the east arm of Burntside Lake, the largest lake in the area. Alma was known as the end of the Earth. Around the bend every day at the east arm, one could get a graceful glimpse of eternity.

On Wednesdays, we stopped at Trapp's. They did the butchering Wednesday morning, so we could get bones in the afternoon if we got there soon enough. Some people made soup with them, but we gave the bones to the dogs. One Wednesday, Nate wanted me to go for a ride with him. He was in a hurry, so I just stuck the bag of bones in the house and forgot about them.

That night, I awakened. From the loft, I could see the full moon through the triangle windows, and at first I thought that's what woke me up. I felt alarmed about something and looked down to the main floor of the cabin. I saw a glowing light through the bag of bones that I had forgotten on the floor. Was it on fire?

I got up and looked in the bag.

"MY GOD NATE THESE BONES ARE GLOWING!" I said from the doorway, waking him. We couldn't believe it. Were people eating the cows from these glowing bones? Were they radioactive? Was it the Russians? Nate thought it was the Russians, something they had put in the food.

The next day I took a paper bag carrying a single bone to Alma Community College. I saw Sally Lies there. She was just walking down the slope of the front yard and she didn't speak to me.

I felt I had something special—it might have been top secret! I could have been an agent for the CIA when I found Jerry Beck in his office and showed him the one bone I had with me. The others were refrigerated at Katie's house. We shut the door of his office, and turned off the light. The single bone glowed bright enough that we could see each other's faces in the dark room.

Mr. Beck said that they glowed because of naturally occurring phosphorous in the process of decay. The light of the moon charged the phosphorous. It usually happens to rotting logs. People come across this in the woods.

"It's called foxfire," he said.

Chapter 29

Some of this time passed in a blur of humiliation. One extremely hot fourth of July, we traveled in Nate's unplanned way to Woody's, a friend of Nate's, who lived in an unincorporated town in Wisconsin. That's what the small towns in Wisconsin were called: small town, unincorporated. I asked Nate why they were called that and he didn't know. It seemed to be a way of diminishing the town and the people in it.

"Are those your real boobs?" Woody asked me.

"Would you like to touch them?" Nate said.

And Woody did. He reached out and touched my breast as though Nate could give him permission. I felt like an unincorporated body.

Once Nate and I passed out on Katie's bed at a party for Chuck. Nate got up and pissed on the floor, and she said I just looked at him, and then collapsed on the bed. I mean what was I doing? What was Nate doing getting so drunk that he didn't know where he was pissing? And how could I watch him do it, and not do anything? God! I rolled that over and over in my mind.

Once when I was trying to get away from Nate, I slept at the *Messenger*. I put my coat on the floor behind the boxes of paper near the back of the shop, farthest away from the window. I awoke when a mouse crawled over my leg. I thought about that for months, too. If the mouse crawled over my leg while I was awake, where else did he crawl? Were there others? I'd get to that point in the thought, and then shudder inside, until the original memory would return, and it started over. All of these loops of memory that couldn't be understood, forgiven, or forgotten disturbed me so.

After the time that the mouse crawled on me, when Nate and I were fighting I'd get a room at the Alma Hotel for eight dollars a night. It was just a room with a bed. The guests shared a bathroom with a deep bathtub. If there weren't too many guests, and there usually weren't, I could bathe in the deep tub without running out of hot water, and sit there for a long time.

I got to know the place. Nate didn't know where I was. I never told any of our friends that I stayed there. The owner was an old woman, and she didn't know me or Nate. He couldn't get upstairs without paying, and he couldn't bother me without disturbing other people, too. Since Nate abhorred witnesses, I was reasonably safe.

Nate must have thought I was at work one night that I wasn't home. When I got to work the next day the front door of the *Messenger* was smashed. I never told anyone that I knew who probably did it, but I was sure it was Nate. I felt guilty, as though I should tell Dave and pay for the door. Nothing had been stolen. Nothing else was broken except the door. Who else would it have been? Nate never said he did it, and I never asked him.

Later Lee told me they had heard some knocking one night and looked out from their apartment above their store and saw Nate's car parked across the street. The next day he saw the *Messenger's* door was smashed. So then I knew for sure, but I knew for sure anyway. Nate's crimes had a certain feel about them.

My life was good in between hotel stays. I lived on in spite of Nate, or between him. I made a wide seed bead belt on a loom. I read as many books as I could without arousing suspicion. *My Mother, My Self*; *The World According to Garp*; *The Martian Chronicles*; *Animal Farm*.

Nate didn't like it that I read books. He teased me for it.

I joined the Book-Of-The-Month club. I got four copies of *Our Bodies, Our Selves* for the welcome kit, and passed them out. A woman was not a full human being, but property first of her father then of her husband, the book said. I was against that idea. I wanted to be free.

Nate said, "What do you think you're going to get out of that? You always have your nose stuck in a book. Do you think you're a professor? I wish you paid half as much attention to *me* as you do to those books."

Chapter 30

I bought a Husqvarna chain saw for Nate at Sawmill Sales, because he wanted one. I had a savings account at the Midway Waters State Bank, and Nate found out about it. He couldn't stand that I had money. Even *my* money burned a hole in his pocket. So he started working me about that chainsaw.

"I'll be able to get our wood ready for winter," he said. "How do you think that's going to get done, Anna? Are you going to do it?"

I didn't want to use my savings. I was trying to save money to leave him, but because I had the savings, I was able to get a loan to buy the chainsaw. I came home with it, and set it on the floor of the cabin. Nate wasn't home. He came in late. Though it had been just what Nate wanted, he didn't comment on it.

"Aren't you going to look at the chainsaw?" I said.

"It's here. I'll look at it tomorrow," he said, flatly, without looking up.

"Do you want to see the passbook for the loan? That Midway Waters bank has such a pretty logo," I asked.

"Why don't you get out of here?"

"Why? I just got home. I just got the chainsaw, for you, so you can cut the wood for us, like you said."

"Get out!" Nate said. "Just get out of here."

I picked up the chainsaw as I left. He took it from me, and then threw it at me and knocked me over. The handle on the saw got bent. It hadn't even been started yet. I ran through the woods to Wes's property. I got in the back seat of one of Wes's old junk cars. By the time my eyes adjusted to the dark and I could see from the light of the moon I realized the back seat was filled with garbage. I thought of myself as a dead junkyard bear as I fell asleep.

The next day when I saw Nate, he didn't say anything about the bent handle on the chainsaw. He didn't ask me where I had stayed or why I was back.

Chapter 31

Tourists were coming in for deer season. I listened to the CB.

"Did you get anything?" a radio voice said. I eavesdropped.

"No, buddy. I heard something in the bush. I shot at it but I didn't get anything that I know of."

I told Nate about this conversation when he got home. We hadn't ever heard of anyone getting shot, but we heard a lot of shots in the nearby woods. It was scary to hear people talking about how they would shoot at noises. We all tried to stay inside during hunting season.

We took another road trip to Wisconsin, and showed up at Woody's house. I listened to the sky before we went inside. Going in, my stomach hurt in a way I associated with being too far away from home.

I was relieved when Nate announced we had to leave. I didn't want to stay the night, though I didn't tell him that. Nate said that he liked to drive at night. We were both watching the billions of stars in this incredible sky, deep as the divine. We were sober. We hadn't smoked any pot.

I felt them waiting for us as we turned the corner. I could feel it before I saw it. Sure enough, around the bend, there it was. A UFO. Finally. I thought I might have seen one so many times before. This one was there without question.

Huge. Hovering. An enormous disc—with flat sides flashing squares of light in a rhythmic sequence—floated above us. Nate pulled over to the side of the road and we waited. It was as if we *had* to wait, as if we were receiving orders from the heavy, floating craft. We had to wait, as if commanded to see and to be seen. It was incredible how this huge craft hovered above us and didn't make a sound. When the car was off, we couldn't hear a thing in unincorporated Wisconsin, in the middle of January. The twinkling stars in the frozen night made more noise than this UFO. We watched, speechless and still, the way you are if you see a moose or a bear in the woods.

And changed, too. Once you've seen a bear or a UFO, you have seen and been seen by something you don't understand. You are everlastingly distinct, though we haven't a word to describe this change.

We told Chuck and Katie about it and they were amazed. They didn't even consider disbelieving us. People on the Arrow Trail could tell one another about unusual experiences. We were already considered odd, outcast, undesirable by the good people, who lived in town. We didn't have reputations to protect with each other. Once that's the case, there isn't any reason not to talk about certain subjects, though I still had some secrets. You could tell anybody on the Arrow things that in other circles would be disgraceful, or suspicious. No one on the Arrow Trail would stare at you in disbelief, ridicule you, or hold it against you later. We didn't try to convince anyone, and we didn't tell anyone we didn't think would believe us.

That's an odd thing about seeing a UFO, too. It's curious how you go on after that as if nothing has changed on the outside. It's something like this: well, here you are thinking you're living in a world where the most that happens is you run into bears, or save fawns from foxes, or try to escape mean boyfriends before they kill you. But then you see a UFO, a craft that appears to know you're there before you know they're there. It's as if it isn't possible for the things one worries about to be the only things to worry about, and that was comforting to me for some reason. It made my worries shrink. It brought eternity and mystery to me, and I was relieved for it. It was as if because a mysterious, inexplicable UFO could be seen, perhaps it wasn't so terrible that I was such a mystery to myself.

Chapter 32

I embroidered a skull with flowers in the brain cavity onto the back of a denim shirt for Nate. Next I embroidered a round circle of pansies on the back of a denim vest for myself. I enjoyed the colored thread.

I sat at the table while Nate was out. It was dark except for the kerosene lamp. I used the light from a modern style, square-based lamp I got from Janice for Christmas. The lamp from Janice didn't have a mantle, so though it wasn't as bright as one that did, it didn't give off a hissing sound; I didn't have to keep turning it down as it got hotter. Using this lamp created no risk of being disrupted by a smoking mantle.

I was almost done with the work. I decided to add some clusters of baby's-breath to accent the beautiful pansies. I made them with ecru thread using French knots that I wound with patience around the needle. A pleasure grew as if from the floor and I had an orgasm without masturbating.

I made it through the long winter embroidering by kerosene lamp and listening to the CB radio, sometimes with Nate home talking on it, sometimes just listening by myself in the cabin alone while he was out somewhere.

I have a job, it's quiet, I'm working on art, and I'm warm. It's peaceful with nothing to worry about. I'm glad that Nate is gone. I now have four things in life I dearly love: the sky, silence, suffering, and time to ponder the three other loves.

Chapter 33

May 1979 brought a fierce outbreak of forest tent caterpillars, also known as army worms. Army worms caused almost complete defoliation of aspen trees and many hardwoods in the area. We filled a three-pound coffee can with the worms in less than an hour by pulling them off the side of our house. Katie put a couple of pounds of them in her blender, and sprayed the mixture on her garden to save it. Apparently army worms aren't meat eaters, so the smell of the blended worms kept them away.

You couldn't drive down the road without squishing worms. The anti-environmentalist sentiment was active in Alma. Someone put up a sign on Main Street:

SAVE THE ARMY WORMS

Not a single *populus tremuloides* had a leaf left by June when the worms began their journey to moths in July.

I ran into Ellie at the New Moon. She had finished her program and was going on to UMD in the fall to continue studying biology.

She told me about a job opening as a waitress trainer for Crane's Family Restaurants. The team of trainers was flown to various United States locations to train the new staff of the brand new Crane's stores opening across the country. On average, teams were out three weeks and home one week, depending on whether it was a corporate or a franchise store. The franchise stores sometimes chose not to have certain optional parts of the training, and so a team could get done sooner. The idea of a job like that started to take hold.

When I got home, Nate was busy building an enclosure for the Waukesha engine that ran the sawmill. He showed me how to build a wall. I pounded the slab wood, green rough lumber, into the two-by-four frame.

"Hold it up tight, as tightly as you can. That way when the wood dries out, the gap won't get too large," Nate said. If people usually used dry wood to make a wall he didn't say.

Sometimes Nate and I had rational conversations. We'd talk and disagree, sometimes without it getting ugly. Sometimes Nate quit drinking and he'd become funny and thoughtful. Since Nate and I occasionally got along well, just not often, the job at Crane's sounded perfect.

"Nate," I said. "I saw Ellie in town today, and she told me about a job in the cities for Crane's Family Restaurants. You know Crane's don't you? They're open and serve breakfast twenty-four hours. I'm thinking of applying for the job. Do you care? Would you mind if I did?"

"I doubt if you can get a job in the cities," he said. I didn't say any more.

⚜

I was driving myself to work because Chuck was on vacation. I slept in because I didn't have to start work as early as Chuck did. I was on my way out of our house, with my thumb on the handle on the inside, when Katie pulled the door open from the outside. We were both startled. She was all dressed up. She was wearing a hat and a flowered sundress. I knew immediately what was going on.

"Nate's still asleep," I said, and left.

I was mad all the way to work. So Katie was coming over to screw Nate when I was at work, and sympathizing with me in my plight and bad relationship with him at the same time. Oh I had such mixed-up feelings. What did I care anyway? I didn't like Nate, but I did love him.

And Katie. She was sweet otherwise. She took care of Max. She could make dinner. How many times had I fed myself on her good cooking? She knew how to take care of her family a lot better than I did. She was always baking bread or baking potica. She was sort of a neighborhood example of the one to turn to; she worked hard and did many things right. That was a good part about Katie. She did everything right—and she slept with my boyfriend.

Then, going pro-Katie again in my head, I thought about how she helped others. You never saw Katie sleeping in the afternoon the way I did. Yet, back against Katie, she's probably going to sleep with Nate all day. She was bad at that, notorious for having affairs.

I *was* surprised she was interested in Nate. I thought she had many others to choose from. This must have driven Chuck crazy. I wonder if he knew about it?

I didn't say anything to him about Katie, but when I got home I told Nate about the job opening at Crane's again.

"It sounds fun," I said. "The pay is probably better than what I can make here."

"Do you know how long you're gone at a time?"

"No. But I'll find all that out. I probably won't get it. But Ellie said they were hiring, and I think it would be worth it to try to get the job."

❦

I drove the Chevy truck by myself to Spring Lake. I couldn't help but imagine that maybe I'd get this job, and maybe I'd get away from

Nate. The more I was away from Nate, the better it was for me. I stayed by myself at my parents' house, and didn't feel so guilty and ashamed.

I was so nervous that my mouth was dry as I walked across the corporate office parking lot in plastic high heels I'd bought at Target. The sun was so hot that in places the plastic heels were sinking into the tar. I thought I might fall.

The interviewer was young, like me. I had lots of experience waitressing, though no experience training people. They had trouble finding people who were able and willing to travel.

To my absolute surprise, I got hired.

❧

"Nate, this will be great for us. You won't have to put up with me, but we can still be together."

"You're young; you don't know anything. When I was your age I wanted to see the world, too."

"Because you've changed your mind about what you thought was important, I'm supposed to follow your lead? Haven't you always said to 'grab the gusto?' Is only *your* gusto worth grabbing? I want to work. Look at the bright side: you won't have to be around me too much."

"It's just that you don't know what I know. You can't see it."

"See what? I can't live through your life. You're older. If I had lied to you about my age, I could see rubbing it in, but you've known from the start how old I am."

"Young people are starstruck with the glamour of travel, but it's all fluff."

"That's not it. I have a dead end job here. You're mad at me ninety-percent of the time. It wouldn't hurt to try it. I could always quit. If it doesn't work out, I could quit. Besides, I fear my future. I can hear people ask me already: 'What did you do in your twenties? I was intimidated by a man into acting fifteen years older, frozen, because I didn't know as much as he did.' Can't you let me be young and dumb? Weren't you dumb once?"

"You think you're so smart. You'll know what I'm talking about when you get to be my age."

It was hard to know which was more appealing: escaping the terror of living with Nate, or escaping the shame of it. He was right, though, that I couldn't see what I was doing. But I couldn't tell him that. And I did know something: the job was more of a choice than living with him had been. Perhaps nothing else made sense, but that did.

"Are you mad that I'm not you?" I said.

"You don't know anything about life," Nate said.

"I want to be myself, whatever that is."

"People know me for my talents. There isn't a mechanic in Alma who wouldn't want to know what I know. You don't know anything."

"You keep saying I don't know anything, as if my youth traps me into doing nothing. How am I ever going to learn something? Most of the time you act as if you hate me. It doesn't make any sense that you're against the idea. I'm taking the job."

I thought he wasn't really worried about me making mistakes. He just wanted to find a way to feel better about his own, and telling me I didn't know anything about what I was getting myself into was his way of doing that.

Of course I felt guilty about living with Nate, and afraid of it, too. Neither of us were ready to face how much I was trying to solve the problem of living with him. I'm sure that was part of why I wanted to take the job, and why he didn't want me to. For my own part, I finally realized I had a goal: I was not going to be perpetually vengeful about all the things that hadn't gone my way. I decided no matter what I was not going to turn bitter. More than that, I had the problem of my life knotted up within me. Inexplicably one of those knots released into a decision.

"I'm taking the job," I said.

It was no secret that Dave, my boss and the owner of the *Northern Messenger* (the *Messenger* for short), had a drinking problem. It was equally well known that Jim Weeks wanted to find a way into the *Messenger*, for a job at first, but eventually to own it. He worked for one of the enemy papers, the *Alma Excavator*. The *Alma Voice* and the *Alma Excavator* were both jealous of the *Messenger* because it had a larger circulation than the other two combined, making it easier to sell ads in the *Messenger*.

My vulnerabilities were not well known to me. I didn't know that Jim Weeks saw in me a way into the *Messenger*. I wouldn't know for a long time how good he was at getting what he wanted.

The worst thing about my taking a job at Crane's was that Jim found out I was leaving. This told Jim Weeks's cat's mind that it was time to pounce. Jim knew that Dave listened to me. Dave couldn't run the business without someone watching out for him; if I quit, then Dave would need some help.

"Dave is a guy with one foot in the grave and the other one on a banana peel, and Jim knows it," Nate said.

I met Jim and Dave for lunch at the Habit Asylum Bar and Steakhouse, just one block up from the *Messenger* office on Main Street. Dave ordered a Brandy Manhattan. Jim had his proposal to work for Dave only if he got to buy the business should it ever come up for sale. The proposal was typed. He'd seen an attorney. He had thought this out for a long time. That surprised me. I didn't expect it. It's always shocking to see your ideas about a person confirmed. He said he wanted to work for Dave with the option to buy the *Messenger* at the end of Dave's life. It was a take it or leave it deal.

"Do your kids want the *Messenger*?" I asked.

"No. They don't want anything to do with it," Dave said.

"Is it okay?" Dave slurred as he looked at me and then at the papers that Jim had handed him. I thought of the time I had handed him my namecard from the employment office. I wondered if he was sober enough to understand what was going on.

"I think it's okay," I said. I had the feeling that if I had said it wasn't okay he wouldn't have signed the papers. I know that Dave trusted me. In that strange way he had trusted me when we first met, I think he had a feel for this, as he had said back then. But how would *I* know if it was okay?

Dave was disappointed I was leaving. He said I could continue to help him to put out the *Messenger* whenever I was in town. I knew he was going to miss me.

Chapter 34

During my last week of work at the *Messenger* full-time, Janice called me at work.

"Hi," she said. I've got something to tell you."

"You're pregnant."

"How did you know?"

"You never call me, so it must be important."

"I wanted to call sooner, but I was afraid. I was afraid about the way you might react."

"What do you mean by that?" I said.

"I just thought you might be sad. You hear about people who feel jealous when—"

I interrupted her. "Janice. So I can be sad for myself and happy for you. Why would I be jealous?" I said.

"I had conjured up all kinds of horror stories about the jealous sister who couldn't have children, who sneaked in the house at night, up the stairs to the baby's room and cut it, cut him, with a knife, an ivory-handled knife with a big flat blade."

I laughed. "Jan, you and Eddie are still seeing too many drive-ins. I'm not bitter. I'm happy for you. Why should I care that you have children just because I can't?"

Chapter 35

After I got hired at Crane's, I visited my parents again by myself. I rode the Greyhound bus from Alma to St. Paul. Mom took me shopping for clothes at Hazelwood Mall, near her house. I bought dresses. Most of the time at Crane's I would have to wear a waitress uniform, but before the restaurant opened, we were required to wear dresses.

When I got back to Alma, I modeled for Chuck and Nate while they worked on the sawmill. I changed clothes inside the cabin, then stood outside the front door, and showed them each new outfit. I was excited about my new job. They had smirks on their faces, and it seemed as if they didn't take me seriously, as if I were playing house.

I got a pimple on my face that week and Chuck said, "I see you've got your 'I'm starting at Crane's' pimple." Nate drove me to the bus stop in town. Once again, I took the bus from Alma to the Cities. The next day, Mom and Dad drove me to the airport. I thought I saw happiness in their faces, and I relaxed just a tiny bit.

While I waited for the plane to board, I saw tall, beautiful women with long necks. They looked as if they had never had a bad experience. I stared at them as though they couldn't possibly be real, the way one might look and look at a large diamond. I was headed for Janesville, Wisconsin. I was going to train waitresses to be good Crane's corporate soldiers—to serve food in the Crane's way. But first I was going to be trained by watching a trainer in Janesville. The other trainers on the team were cooks. They trained the cooks to make food in recognizable tastes and portions. Chain stores were looking to make uniform experiences for clientele, so that you would have the same basic Crane's experience in Wisconsin or New Mexico, Florida or Washington. I think they got the idea from McDonald's.

I checked into the hotel, got up to my room, unpacked my bag, organized my toiletries in the bathroom, and Nate called. He started the conversation by singing me all four verses to Shel Silverstein's song, "The Things I Didn't Say."

"That's sweet, Nate," I said.

"I want you to come home," he said.

"No. I'm not coming. I'll be back when this is over, " I told him.

"Haven't you got it out of your system yet?" he said.

"Nate! I haven't even got it into my system," I said.

He called the next day.

"When will it be over?" he asked.

"They never know," I told him. "As soon as the new managers feel ready to run the restaurant without help from the corporate office, we can leave. They've told me it's usually about three weeks."

"I don't like living without you. I want you to come home," he repeated.

"I'm not doing this *to* you—I'm doing it *for* myself, Nate. You didn't like me when I lived there all of the time. I can't understand why you like me now. You've been blaming me for everything. I'm surprised you want me home. But I can't come. They're counting on me here."

He called me all night. We didn't have a phone at home. I was afraid to ask where he was calling from. We would hang up, and in about an hour, he'd call again. I didn't ask the desk to stop the calls because I was scared he would drive the five hundred miles to Janesville.

I was so tired the next day. The first part of the training, before the restaurant opened, consisted of watching slideshows of corporate policies, learning proper waiting techniques, and then showing similar slide shows to the management, and then to the new wait staff. They had every detail down. It was at Crane's that I learned you should always serve a water glass by holding it at the bottom, rather than the top, of the glass. Since then, I can't be at a restaurant without noticing where the waitress or waiter is holding the water glass when he or she sets it down. I sometimes feel like saying, "Would you want to drink from a glass with my dirty fingerprints on it?"

The next phase of the training had three parts: a full shift as a trial run—with staff as customers—followed by a special opening for a few invited people from the community, and then the official opening to the public. After the official opening day, we would stay for two weeks for a franchise, or three (or longer) for a corporate store. The franchises paid for the training, and it was included in the price of a corporate store. That's why the franchises would always send us away sooner— they only took the amount of training that was required by the corporate office.

Nate was partly right. To stay at a hotel was much more fun than to live in one. It was lonely, and boring. Many people drank after dinner. I didn't enjoy the bar. I swam in the pool a few times, but I was self-conscious.

But my work was exciting and scary. Once the store was open, I worked nights, twelve-hour shifts. I was coaching people how to waitress the Crane's way, though I feared most of them knew more about waitressing than I did. I was sure I'd be found out. For several nights, my shift consisted of waiting on the counter, while I checked the waitress's food before they took it out to the floor, answered questions, and took a table here and there when someone couldn't keep up.

The head-trainer cook, who worked the night shift with me, was nice. His arms were so long he could reach down two grills without even moving his feet.

A man of about fifty started coming into the restaurant each night at about 11:00 p.m. The restaurant was quiet before bar rush. He was dressed in a suit, wore a diamond ring, and drank regular coffee, black, no sugar.

"Where are you from?" he asked.

"I live in Alma, Minnesota," I said.

"What brings you here?"

I explained about the training team as I put some packets of jelly on the plate a waitress carried as she walked by.

Many times I noticed him watching me as I brought hot plates out on the floor for waitresses, or stopped by to warm his coffee.

One night, as I filled his coffee cup, he set his Playboy Club Key, a flat gold credit card with the Playboy insignia, face up, by his saucer. I recognized it because my dad had Playboy paraphernalia at home. My parents had been to different Playboy Clubs while traveling.

"Would you like a job?" he said.

"No. Thanks."

"It's just what you are doing here," he said.

"No. I like my job. I already have a job," I said.

I felt myself nearly vanish, as if I were almost extinct.

❧

Nate was bothering me so much that I asked the main office if I could get a transfer to another store instead of going home after the Janesville stint finished. They needed somebody in Orlando. I left the next day.

The heat built to such intensity in July in Orlando that each day a huge thunderstorm sizzled on the pavement in the late afternoon. Then the temperature cooled to a more reasonable ninety degrees. I still had the night shift. I tried a few times to sit out by the hotel pool in the morning; but it was too hot even at eight or nine a.m. It was unbearable by ten. Mainly I sat in my hotel room and put quarters in the wall slot that said "Magic Fingers," which made the entire bed rumble softly and vibrate along the surface of the mattress. It didn't seem like magic or like fingers, but the sound was relaxing. I read Ayn Rand's *Atlas Shrugged*, the book I'd heard Jim Weeks was reading. I talked to Chuck about the book from my hotel room. I didn't like it as much as he did, but I sure knew what it was like to feel as if I were living in a world with no sense.

When Nate couldn't reach me, he began writing letters, in a notebook—an unsent collection. I talked to Chuck one night. He said Nate was pale and shaking and he wanted me back. He told me that he was writing letters to me every day.

"He's been practicing playing the spoons, to get his mind off everything," Chuck said.

"On top of your new job, Paula, the woman who owns the land where he lives, sent a lawyer after him to force him off her land, or to follow through with building the cabin he promised her. My buddy's in a bad way," Chuck said.

Chapter 36

I came home and Nate had transformed. The house was spotless—at least, it was as clean as you can get a cabin with rough lumber walls and plywood floors and no electricity. Nate was clean too; he had combed his hair. The only thing out of place in the tiny house was the spiral notebook he had used to write to me while I was away. He sat quietly while I read his letters. It was a clash for me reading them. He was writing these tender letters to me just after threatening to kill me if I didn't come home, and calling me thirty or forty times per night while I begged him to please let me sleep. That's why I had gone to Orlando without telling him where I was. And there he was writing tender letters to me when he thought I was gone and not coming back.

Dear Anna,

I woke up this morning and drove to town to check the post. Now it is evening and I am lonely again. I visited Chuck and Katie. Katie fed me spaghetti. I thought when I got home there might have been a note from Lee that you called saying when you will be home.

I love you,

Neight

Anna,

Thunder and lightning tonight. I have a favor to ask if this letter ever finds its way to you. I am living in a broken dream. I don't use the word "sorry" because it doesn't fix the hurt people go through. Anna you left with nothing of mine but a memory and have removed yourself from all that would remind you of me. I live with two fears: one of having your things around me as a constant reminder of my love for you. Knowing how I have treated you, I haven't given you much reason to want to be here.

The other fear is to move your things away from me so I am not reminded of you day in and day out. I don't want to do that for I fear you will think I don't want you and don't love you. I have a choice to remove myself and I may have done that in a moment of weakness.

I pray you do come home. My only hope at this time is that you will decide as soon as possible and let me know in black and white what you think.

I do know the lessons I have learned in our relationship have brought me closer to the gift of giving one's self and now all I want is to give to you. I hope you don't get upset with my letters like you did my calls. I feel better when I write to you.

I checked the bus for a week and only got more upset. I have never been as close to another person in my life. I won't bother you until you let me in OK.

Goodnight honey,

Neight

Dear Anna,

I think it's unfair you won't give me your address so I can write to you. I too have things to express and share. I am insecure and unstable. Please let me know if you aren't coming home. I have to know so I can adjust.

I look around now at thirty-six years old and know I have more to give than ever. There are so many things I could have shared with you and I didn't even know I wasn't sharing. I have a broken heart that you won't let me write or call. You know one of the things I wanted you to be is independent.

You are blind to knowing how much happiness you have given me. Your loving me and being with me when you were here brought tears to my eyes. I see as my hand clings to this pen some of why you are gone and understand it. I'm having trouble living with my conscience. I made you feel that I wasn't a part of your life. I am sure most of the time you didn't know which way to go. I did this because I feared losing you. Because of my fears, you are gone. I didn't mean to make you feel responsible for my failures, as you said. Come home when you get done there, and we can take a long look at each other with as much honesty as we have in our hearts.

Max and Oden are fine. I have about half of Chuck's lumber cut up and hope to finish soon. I have had lots of trouble with the mill, but I think it's working out. We hauled the logs from the Silver Steel road, and the pile is so big you can't see the house.

Chuck and I finished hauling the logs from up the Arrow, cut them all, and sold the lumber. I'm going to sell my share of Chuck's, too. I have to sell a lot of things to stay on top of this.

The flower and tomato plants are growing like the wind. The army worms are gone but before they left they ate all the leaves off the trees. I haven't cut the grass; I have been too busy. The house is clean, dishes are done, now laundry again. I think I'll get a washer or make one. I stay home with a cable across the driveway and pray for us.

Love,

Neight

Anna,

Here I am again writing down what I feel and no place to send it. Being unable to get in touch with you is a terrible hardship. If and when you come home, if you care, you can read all of these letters.

It's hard to have my neighbors tell me what you are doing when I want to be the most important thing in your life as you are in mine. Not knowing for sure is Hell. Every car that goes by I think is you and my heart stops, only to leave an empty feeling in the pit of my stomach when it isn't.

I know you have said to Katie that you won't be home later than July twenty-fifth, but I still hope you care enough to be home sooner. I guess we think differently because if I were you the way I feel I would walk home on broken glass to be by your side. Absence does make the heart grow fonder.

I even scrubbed the floor so I could keep my hands and head moving. If I sit still I think too much. I have asked Lee to check the post office every day, but you don't write, so I just put that out of my mind as much as I can. I moved the couch out to the culvert.

Now we have lots more room to move about and the house is easier to clean.

I love you Anna.

Neight

P.S. Just saw Lee and no letter from you—so sad.

Dear Anna,

I can't sleep. Every song I hear these days is about lost love or broken hearts. It must be my weakness. Tonight I have been thinking that you may be with another man. I just get shivers thinking about it, and I know that if you were or are I would deserve to feel what I have done to you.

I even flash on killing myself. It may sound stupid to you, but to me what is going on is so much a part of my past life that it is unbearable at times. At times it just doesn't make a difference whether I live or die because I have thrown much of my life away already. I have even stopped drinking going on two weeks now. I have to, for myself, so I can take an honest look at myself. I don't like what I see in myself, and if I am drunk it is worse. I pray a lot these days. I have let God down before, too; I hope this time I don't.

I begin to accept myself slowly, and gain some direction. Every day I mark off the days, and feel as if I am back in jail, without a release date. Life has become as lonely as jail. I guess my saying about all of us doing "life without parole" is true.

Earlier I walked down the Arrow and I thought I could hear your footsteps beside me. When I stopped I was alone. I came home and tried to sleep but couldn't. I walk around talking to you, hoping you can tune in and write me a letter that answers some of my fears. I think of selling the Olds for a plane ticket to Orlando just to see you. The thing that stops me is I believe you don't want to see me.

Well Anna I think I will try to sleep once more, please take care and I hope to see you soon.

Pleasant dreams.

Neight

Anna,

I drank with Lee today. I am sloppy drunk. I thought it only proper to see what I am like and I don't like it. I know in only three hours, I am not the same. I just had to unwind. OK. You see, Anna, I love you. I don't like being in an empty home without you. Now more than ever I wish I could snuggle up to you as if I had eaten five cookies.

The nights you are restless because of your own dreams and mind are Hell for you, I know. But please don't take me wrong. I only hope to help you, not make it worse, as I have. I love you, and I've been fighting it. I had never felt so comfortable and in love, so I didn't understand what it was. I didn't understand. I'm sure my lack of wisdom doesn't make it easier for you. I have treated you badly.

I saw the picture you sent to Chuck and Katie and it made my body tingle and be light. I almost could not handle it. You are beautiful. I feel lost without you. I am going to try to sleep, please God.

Neight

Anna,

Here I am again. Hope you don't mind. I visited my parents. It rained like Hell this morning so I figured I would take a ride. I helped Dad with a few projects, ate, and came home. I timed it so I would get to Alma in time to meet the bus. I just keep hoping that you will come home.

I fought hard not to love you. I wasn't even aware of it. I am afraid of being hurt or hurting you, and at the same time I'm scared to death of losing you and being alone. I never thought I'd feel this way again, but I'd like to marry you. I'm going to do the dishes and go to sleep tonight. I will be anxious until I hold you in my arms.

Neight

Anna,

I was just in town to see about parts for the mill and check the post—all junk mail for you. I sure wish you could give as much energy to a letter for me as you do for that junk mail.

I looked through the picture albums this morning. I think you can figure out what I am feeling. I just can't figure out how you can be cold and say you love me. But I do know, it's because of how I act toward you.

Lee was over wondering about the road to his cabin. He bought the saw rig, and the stove Chuck used last winter. He wants me to start August sixth, when he has his vacation. He also bought all my radios: CBs and antennas. I guess none of it makes sense to me anymore, and I just want to get out from under it.

Paula served me with papers. She wants her cabin or she wants me off her land. I can't believe she wouldn't have talked to me first. Talk to me. That's all it would have taken.

Mom and Dad came over today to visit. Dad brought some carb parts for the Ford Tractor and a bearing for the truck. It was hard to be around them. It was Mom's birthday, and I didn't have anything for her. I gave her one of those green enamel pans you got from Janice. I hope you won't mind.

I love you,

Neight

Anna,

It's 1:30 in the morning and again I can't sleep. Now you're coming home and I'm not sure I deserve to have you. I smoke two or three packs a day, can't sit still, can't sleep, can't eat. You see, Anna, my talent has no value without direction. I am jealous of a person like you to the point of feeling inferior. When it comes to your jobs, you just go to it no matter what.

I can't wait to see you,

Neight

Anna,

The strange part of it all is that when we first started to get together you were the one who was emotional, and now it seems as if I am and you're not. I sure hope that your scars will heal, especially the ones that came from me.

Love to you,

Neight

He wanted me to sit near him, and he held my hand while we went for a drive. I ached from the sensitivity in his letters. I wanted him to mean what he said the way a broken bone wants to mend.

The next day, my twenty-first birthday, he left without saying a word. I spent the day at home alone, and fell asleep. It was staggering how quickly the old Nate returned.

Chapter 37

Since I took two Crane's assignments in a row, I got over a month off. I worked a few shifts at the *Messenger*. I left for my third assignment, to Fort Dodge, Iowa, on August twenty-seventh. When I got there, Nate had already called—I got the message as I checked in at the hotel. He had promised he'd be reasonable, so I told him where I was going. He called every night again. I tried to stop the calls, but he left persistent, angry messages. He called the restaurant. Though I refused to speak with him at work, I could tell that the staff was irritated by his calls. I was jumpy, irritable, afraid of what he might do, and ashamed of what people thought of me. I finished my assignment, and I was pretty sure I would quit.

I called the main Crane's office from Alma and told them not to send me out again. I was done on September fifteenth. My parents needed to know I was quitting because they had been involved in taking me to the airports and the bus depots. Dad said that I was missing a great opportunity and that I should stop being an underachiever.

I didn't tell him I was quitting because Nate was harassing me so much I couldn't take it anymore. I told my dad that you had to work too many hours, that the hourly rate was low. Crane's wasn't planning to open any more stores so the team would stop soon anyway. Most of the people would take jobs as cooks and waitresses at the stores at the close of their roles as trainers. No Crane's awaited me in Alma. All of this was true, but I knew it didn't change his opinion of me. I could feel it.

The house wasn't quite as clean this time when I got home. I read Nate's new letters in the spiral notebook.

Anna,

I am awful nervous without you being around. It's the end of the summer and I haven't done shit. I had front wheel trouble with my dump truck today. The front right wheel bearing almost flew off. My truck was down all day and I finally had to borrow parts from Hal's truck. I fixed our stove and put on a new stovepipe. At least I got that done.

Love,

Neight

Hi Anna,

It's too bad we had a fight. I thought, if it's not too late, I would say it this way and not try to make you feel as though you were being asked to be a ping-pong ball. If you would like to keep your job, please do. I will write the blank check that you sent to me out for a million dollars and hope it doesn't bounce.

I love you.

Neight

Anna,

I know I upset you by my phone calls last night. I guess I just feel lonely. I haven't cut the firewood because I don't have the drive. I get depressed when things go the way they do between us. Winter is just around the corner and I didn't get shit done this year—depressed, depressed, depressed.

I love you.

Neight

Chapter 38

I was feeling defeated. Escaping was hopeless, and yet I still tried. For now, I had Nate.

"My dad hates me, Nate. He always has. I can't do anything right for him," I said.

I thought about Janice's twelfth birthday. The memory of it came up in my throat and stuck like a plugged drain. I couldn't keep it down. Injustice must stick in the throat like a sliver in the hand and work its way out in the same slow fashion.

Janice turned twelve in July, 1967. My dad's parents, our grandparents, came to the party as they always did. We had hamburgers and hot dogs, potato salad, corn on the cob, iced tea, milk and coffee outside on the deck on top of the garage. Dad cooked the burgers on the grill.

My grandparents gave Janice a savings bond. Grandma had bought the bond years before to help get my dad through college but he had never used it. I was jealous. I felt left out. This was the most important gift I had ever seen. Everybody oohed and ahhed.

I said, "Do I get a bond?" My dad was furious. He came into the kitchen where I was stacking dishes and he yelled at me.

"You selfish brat! Your grandmother and grandfather don't have to give you anything." He leaned down close to my face and said, "You're worthless! You don't deserve anything." My grandparents didn't hear what he said to me.

Of course, increasing my guilt, for my birthday—the twenty-seventh, just fifteen days away, when I turned ten—I got a bond, another bond, the same as Janice's.

This was a time Nate and I could just talk. He didn't say he didn't believe me or that I was imagining my dad to be like that. He didn't feel overly sorry for me either. Though it was intermittent, I felt accepted by Nate.

Chapter 39

"So do you still have that bond, Anna?" Nate said one day.

"Yes. I guess so. My parents have it."

"How much is it worth?"

"It was worth five-hundred dollars at maturity. It's over thirty years old. It's probably worth about double that."

"Hal says he'll sell me the backhoe for a thousand down, plus three-hundred-fifty dollars a month. It's just the thing I need to get out on my own. I'll be able to make enough to get Paula's house built. I'll be free of Hal. I won't have to work for him."

I called my dad and asked him for the bond. Dad sent me a check. He didn't say a thing about it. He just sent me the money. And I gave the thousand to Hal. He gave Nate the backhoe keys.

It was easy to get rehired at the *Messenger*. Dave had told me that he'd take me back anytime. He was glad to see me. "I missed you," he said. "I'm glad you're back."

❦

Nate's backhoe business slowed late in the fall of 1979, and he took a trip with Carol's brother, Bill. They took Bill's truck for some reason—I didn't listen—to Texas. I didn't know or care and didn't hear from him while he was gone. I was still mad that he hadn't let me keep my job at Crane's. It was a relief that he left.

He came home on Monday, just short of three weeks out. I

remembered Nate's stories of trucking, how the prostitutes approach the trucks in truck stops. I assumed this trip was his revenge for Crane's.

Chapter 40

Taking the curves on the Arrow Trail in my truck, I saw a tourist hitchhiking, perhaps one of the men who had seen me pointing at the bear. The tourist was a common summer creature, with a camouflage hunting cap, jeans, red plaid flannel shirt, and a large, green back-pack. This one reminded me of my old neighbor, Lane, so I stopped.

"Thanks for the ride. I've been in the woods. Just got out. Been in there three days."

"I've been living in the woods for three years," I said.

"Oh. You have? Really?"

Alma had a competition for ruggedness: leathery skin, calluses on the palms and fingertips, and dirty outdoor clothing were status symbols. Nate demonstrated that he could pick up a cigarette coal between his fingers and not even feel it. This was winning the competition.

Tourists only looked the part. Their trips varied in length, but mine was one relentless adventure. My fight contained no status and it made me grumpy to see this sweet and smooth person trying to look tough. I didn't tell him that though. We rode to town, and I dropped him off outside the Suds-Yer-Duds Laundromat, where I would be after I put in my day at the *Messenger*.

When I got to work I read in the *Alma Voice* that Sigurd Olson got an honorary doctorate of philosophy on October fifth. I never did find out what past events made him great, and I'd never met him again. I know that the locals didn't like him much. The 2,000 square miles of BTCA had been designated as a wilderness without much input from the locals, and it made people mad. One year, Sigurd was hanged in effigy by protesters on Main Street. He was blamed as one of the people who got it all started—saving the wilderness that is. Crystal Slope lodge had closed its doors in February of that year, blaming the restricted use of motors for the decline in business. I hadn't heard much about it because Hal Maki hadn't owned the Crystal Slope in years.

I stayed with the bad mood I was in since I picked up the tourist. He didn't cause it, though. When I thought about it, all I could pinpoint as a cause was that it was laundry day. I had forced myself to make Thursday my laundry day. Thursday I worked a short day to make up for the long days Monday and Tuesday, and Friday I didn't work at all.

Though I had forced myself to follow through, it felt great to be home Thursday night and have three days off with clean clothes. This Thursday, Nate showed up at work during lunch and took the truck. He was sweet, smiled, kissed me. He saw me stamping letters and he showed me how to take the roll, lick one stamp, put my thumb on it at the corner of the envelope, then tear the stamp from the roll leaving it pasted to the letter.

"It's more efficient, Anna. Employers are impressed when you're efficient."

That remark made me cross. A part of me looked at Nate sideways and thought, *You're giving* me *employment advice? Are you kidding? You're acting like you care what happens to me at work after forcing me to quit a perfectly good job?*

Of course I was too frightened to say it. I acted even more politely and gratefully to him now. I knew I was caught in a dangerous web.

"Nate, remember I want to do laundry after work," I said.

"I'll be back. I'll wait for you to do the clothes."

"Promise?" I said.

"Promise," he said. "I'll wait at the New Moon Bar and drink beer while you wash the clothes."

At one o'clock, Dad called.

"Janice had her baby. It's a boy. She had trouble in delivery but she and the baby are doing fine."

I hung up. I felt hurried, frantic. Isn't it wonderful, isn't the baby cute, isn't it beautiful?

This was wonderful news. Wasn't it? I was in such a hurry, such a hurry, all of the time to get whatever I was doing over with, to get everything done.

I wondered if I had any feelings underneath all these shoulds and becauses. I should do the laundry. I should send a gift. I should have been there. Oh, I needed my pillow, with the cool, sky-blue pillowcase, and the worn fibers about as long and as soft as the hairs on my face. I wished I could lie down and rub those fibers and feel better. I longed to lift the pillow straight off my face and feel the tingle as my facial hairs returned to their natural state. I turned the pillow over when one side got warm from my body heat—the other side was still cool—and sank my face into the fabric until it warmed again. I was like one of Harry Harlow's rhesus monkeys—preferring my pillow, the cloth mother, especially when I was scared.

I was anxious for Nate to arrive, and the laundry to be done. I left my body and had a fantasy: the new aunt will go home. Her thoughts will skim the surface of the still red bikini-style incision and try to make sense of her life, but no help will come. She won't know what to make of it.

Nate bounced into the office. His hair was a dark halo, skin the color of a Pfeiffer. Nate thought of himself as a one hundred and fifty pound bottle of beer.

"Nate, Janice had her baby. It's a boy. Alex. Nate, you know what? When I was about ten, I figured out that my father was an only child and the father of two girls. I realized our family had no namesake and it bothered me because I thought it bothered my dad. It kept me awake at night. Before women's lib, before I had given any thought to having a family, or love, I got the idea that there would be no one to carry on his name. I talked to him with sincere tears in my eyes, and I said, I won't call myself my husband's name. We will have a baby. My husband will have brothers and it won't matter to him. We will agree, I will keep the Books name and the baby will, too. Don't worry, Dad, I told him. Your name will carry on. I was worried for him that the Books name would die out. I told him we won't be the last of the Books. You know what, Nate? You'll never guess what the baby's name is. Alex Books Stubler. Alex Books. The name of my dad's dead dad. I just don't know how to feel. That's the only hard part. It's not the baby; it's watching my sister carry out a dream of mine. I'm not sure how to feel about it."

"Oh, yeah, come on let's get going," Nate said.

I felt vacant. I realized much later that I felt way down deep as if I needed to be swaddled in cool cotton and held by some huge hands. I wished someone would see how sad I was. Why couldn't I be picked up like the fawn and carried off to a wildlife refuge, where someone would make sure I wouldn't get hurt or killed until I could grow up?

"Are we going to do the laundry?" I asked.

"Yeah. Come on."

We got in the truck. Nate drove. I felt insecure and worthless just then. I know why I admired him: he had skills. He was a mechanic. If his car was broken he could fix it. If a wind blew down a wall of his house, he could repair it. I hadn't even taken "Car Care for Girls" in high school, though it was offered, so I had driven for five years before

I had any idea why a car needed gas. "Gas, oil, water," Nate taught me. I knew less; therefore, I was worth less than he.

I thought through his point of view again, as if what he thought was important was the only thing that was. *Yes Nate you're good. You know how to work and I don't. You know how to put stamps on the envelopes. You have wasted all of your children so it doesn't matter that mine will be trapped forever in my bones with no uterus to free them.*

We drove past Suds-Yer-Duds.

"Where are we going?" I asked, feeling panic.

"Lee and DeeDee have asked us over for dinner. I saw them at lunch. I'm just going to pick up some beer."

Nate had different fad friends. Lately it was all Lee and DeeDee. "Oh. Nate. God. I just want to go home, please. I have a headache and I'm tired. Couldn't . . ."

"You know, Anna, you're a drag. These two have been cooking all afternoon. They invited us to dinner. You bitch! You should be grateful."

I should be grateful for that, too. I should want to go to Lee's, and I shouldn't care how I'm feeling the way he doesn't care how I'm feeling. I hate trivia, I hate parties, I hate roast beef. I just want to go home. He stopped in at Bear Paw Liquor, and came out with a case of Miller bottles. He headed back toward, not away, from town, so I knew we weren't going home.

❧

"Oh! DeeDee! Your place is cute," I pretended after we arrived. I was jealous of the running water in her kitchen and the indoor toilet. She had curtains—white fluffy curtains, with ruffles, and a row of strawberries along the edge.

We ate, and drank. I sat politely for a while. Assertiveness. I'd read in one of those old *Reader's Digests* in the loft at home. Yes. Yes. Assertiveness. Just state what you want to happen and if they give you any shit about it, state it again.

"Nate, I want to go home."

"Bitch." His thick hands pushed me out the door.

Assertiveness works. I am getting what I want, aren't I?

"I'll be right back you guys," he called to them. "Have to take the bitch home."

I started to cry, mostly from embarrassment. But I didn't care, did I? Why did everyone seem as if their lives made sense?

"You're a cunt. You take it all seriously. Who gives a shit about what you want? These guys have been nice. They just want to have a party. They just want to have fun. You—why do I ever take you anywhere? You want to be included—HA! You always say you want to join me, and then when you do, you're a real drag."

I don't care I don't care I don't care I don't care he makes me sick. Being home alone will be much better than any dumb beer party.

I put my concentration on the tears; he hated tears.

He stopped the truck at the front door. Before I had both feet on the ground he was in reverse.

I fed Max, split some kindling, and made a fire because the night was cool. I heated water and made coffee. I walked down the boardwalk, to the outhouse. I left the door open and looked out into the yard. I watched the night come.

I liked to drink coffee in the outhouse. I wasn't in a hurry there. I drank a lot of alcohol, but not as much as Nate. I enjoyed being alone and sober. It was a pleasant October evening, perfectly still. The sky was clear. When there wasn't a wind in the woods, listening was unopposed.

It was just a matter of time before Nate came home, and I expected him to be drunk.

Inside, I tried to read but couldn't. I blew out the lamp, tried to sleep, and couldn't. I sat up every time I heard a car to see if it was Nate. Then the two headlights shone through the windows. The hump of gravel made the two beams point upward to the stars and then down to the ground. When they leveled off, one headlight per eye froze me the way a rabbit freezes. My feet felt hot and cold at the same time. Bubbles of fear formed in my neck.

Nate climbed up the ladder and sat on the trunk. His smile didn't stop my fear.

"I have taken ten hits of acid. Do you hear me? Ten hits of acid, and I am drunk! Move—MOVE—get out of bed—I want to—lie down, have to lie down."

I moved around him sideways like a spider moves. I wished I could leap like a wolf spider. He wrapped himself in the blankets. I took his place on the trunk. He started to moan, "God, I'm so high, high, hi-ahh-ahh-ahh."

I was scared for myself and now scared for him, too. I had never taken ten hits of acid—at most, two. Despite the mind-expanding possibility of LSD, my vision had been of the world as a huge pile of Right Guard anti-perspirant. The life that people were living, the one that I couldn't reach and didn't seem to belong to, seemed nonsensical. I couldn't figure out why anyone ever did anything. I couldn't see any reason to live. I became passively suicidal.

As an antidote to my LSD despair, I concluded that the only possible reason for living was to write history books. In my vision, wave after wave of the same patterns were recorded in books. That was the purpose of life: to record patterns.

How high would you be on ten hits of acid? What would he do? What would he do to me? I was trembling, and my eyes stuck to his writhing body as if it were mine. I felt his hatred.

"Get me my gun!"

"Why the gun?" I tried to stall; I knew it would be worse for me to refuse.

"Get me my gun; it's in the car!"

I moved slowly down the ladder. I opened the door to the moonless night. I needed to move slowly in order to get out of there. If Nate raised his head he could see me out the window, so I needed to be careful. I opened the door on the driver's side. Pretending to reach across to get the gun, I locked the door on the passenger's side. Still standing, I pushed in the clutch and the starter button with my right foot, and turned the key, thinking *please start*—it did—then put it in gear. I knew Nate could hear the car start. I was halfway down the driveway before I shut the door, with my shivering, pounding heart.

"Oh, don't come after me," I said as my heart kept pounding. I tried to think, but I was too scared so I talked to myself instead.

"Nate needs somebody, can't be that high by himself, I'm not who he needs. I can't let him do God knows what to me—to himself." I saw a light at Chuck's. I drove in the driveway. Chuck was walking to his door, just home, too, from a bar.

I stopped the car, opened the window and said, "Chuck. I need your help. Nate has taken ten hits of acid. He's mad at me. I had to get out of there. I don't think he should be alone. Will you talk to him?"

"Sure," he said.

"He wanted me to get his gun out of the car and I just left."

"Where's the gun?" Chuck asked.

"In the glove box."

Chuck took the clip from the pistol, and slid it under the seat. He put the gun back in the glove box. A kerosene lamp glowed through the side window of the house. I turned the truck around for a fast getaway.

I could see Nate through the window. Chuck entered first, I followed. Nate was making a sandwich, a peanut butter sandwich; the stove was lit. He was heating coffee. He was calm, quite sober. Another trick, a chameleon trick. I shook my head.

Chuck said, "Anna told me you were in a bad way, buddy."

Nate looked straight at me, "She's a stupid cunt; get her out of here." He pushed me out of the way, left the house, and came back with his gun.

"Where's the clip?" He slapped me.

"Hey! Don't do that," Chuck said.

"Just give me my clip and both of you get out of here," Nate yelled.

I moved to the car and got in the passenger's side. Chuck picked up the clip, started the engine, walked back to the front door and handed it to Nate.

To my right I saw a flash of red, and then the noise cracked the night.

"God, Chuck, he's shooting at us." I heard four more shots before we reached the end of the driveway.

I slept at Chuck and Katie's.

Chapter 41

I awakened thinking about how painful lies are. The mind works through a lie the way a body gets through barbed wire fence, with lots of scratches. My mind was trying to find a way to sneak through these barbs without getting hurt too badly. I needed to find a way out.

You always think you're going to leave, and then you don't leave. That's one fantasy you have when you're living with someone like Nate. If I wanted to, I could leave this guy. Just like that, you tell yourself.

You also think, "Starting right now, my life could be charmingly simple and serene, if I could just get rid of this guy."

But your fantasies about who you are laugh at you as soon as you put your hand on the door handle.

The next day I returned and opened the door to the cabin as I always had. It was so disappointing. Nate acted as though nothing out of the ordinary had happened. Apologies never burdened his lips. The only time I realized he even knew the language of remorse was when I read the letters he had written when I worked for Crane's.

Nate handed me a roll of money and told me to buy us some groceries. I stopped at a roadside stand out of town and bought a pumpkin with Nate's money. Somehow I lost one hundred dollars. In the past, he accused me of being careless with money, so I was afraid to tell him I lost some of his. Katie lent me the money so Nate wouldn't find out. I paid her twenty dollars per week until my debt was paid.

Nate never knew.

⚜

Northern Electric Co-op expanded service up the Arrow Trail. All summer they had been adding power on the road. It was finally our turn.

When easements got cut, and poles were placed, the phone service could be added. So we got electric and phone service in the same week.

Nate plugged in the barber pole and had it running. The antique outside light in the eaves over the front door worked. We listened to albums. Nate loved Nilsson's "The Point."

"You see what you want to see, you hear what you want to hear," Nate sang to me.

I bought an Electrolux vacuum from the salesman at the *Messenger* when he placed his advertisement. I got a payment book: eighteen payments of eleven dollars each. The Electrolux vacuum was exceptionally quiet. It had a plastic seal in the special bag to stop the dust from going right back out in the air. I loved it. DeeDee bought one the week after I did. In all, I sold four vacuums with my enthusiasm, and without commission.

Vacuuming was great. The dusty, rough lumber took the vacuum well. Katie and I watched *Rocky* on the ten-inch black-and-white TV, which had sat blank-faced in the loft until we got power.

Katie told me Hal's daughter, Shirley, was admitted to the College of St. Catherine in St. Paul. I'd never met Shirley. I noticed Hal wasn't cheap with his children the way he was with his employees.

One weekend I was sick. Nate knew I was sick and trying to rest, but he still invited three friends inside during the day to drink, part of the long celebration of having electricity. I didn't know these people. I don't think he did either. I think he found them at a bar and had them over for the "Nate Show." He was an expert at making his weaknesses sound admirable to strangers. I thought of the first night I met him with Ellie. I saw that all differently now. He showed us what he had made, how self-sufficient, and smart, and scrappy, he was. He left out the part about how he was living on someone else's land, not paying them, and not doing what he had promised to do in order to live there for nothing. He left out the part about how he had mostly lived off the women in his life, when he wasn't in prison for terrorizing them. Yes. He left all that out.

The people who liked Nate called him "a character." This was a polite, charitable way of describing him. They didn't see that Nate didn't want to be the way he was, and that he wasn't the way he seemed. The people who knew him well often feared him.

I stayed up in the loft, just a few feet above the party. I didn't know what I wanted, but I knew it wasn't what I had.

I heard him defending some mistake he had made to his new friends. "Hey! So what? My pencil has got an eraser."

His pencil is the only one with an eraser, I thought, still trying to sleep. A few days before he had sent me to town for kerosene. I stopped at all three gas stations and they didn't have it. When I came home empty-handed, he threw a fit. He said that number one fuel oil would have worked.

I said, "But you told me kerosene!"

I didn't know number one fuel oil could substitute for kerosene, and I was afraid to do something I wasn't told to do. If I had brought home fuel oil, he would have said I had failed, and given me a lecture about following instructions. But since I followed directions this time, he thought I should have known what fuel to substitute. There were no excuses worthy of Nate, and only rarely could one feel forgiven. Nate despised mistakes in others. It's often the people who most need forgiveness who are the least forgiving.

I felt angry at him for talking about that eraser. If only the rest of us were allowed to make mistakes and erase them neatly from our pages with our pencils, it would be a sweet, merciful world. The way he was talking, it was pure hypocrisy.

The Nate Show continued.

"I take the new pill by Geritol—'no-ass-at-all.' Take a look at this ass, not bad for nearly forty, huh?" he said.

I knew, without peering my head over the loft, that he was just now posing and spinning in the way of ninety-seven pound Charles Atlas turned body builder, turned Modern Day Hercules, turned "The World's Most Perfectly Developed Man." I didn't need to look down to see it. I had this memorized. I heard his friends laugh. They hadn't yet heard it over and over again.

One of them asked, "Don't you have running water?"

"My girlfriend is my running water," Nate bragged.

Oh they loved that.

We got our drinking water from the U.S. Forest Service pump at Silver Lake. The well was over four hundred feet deep, and the water as clear and fresh as any I have ever tasted. Nate bragged about me, too, as I did eventually learn to serve him better. The faithful girlfriend travels two miles north and milks two five-gallon jugs of fresh water every week from the Silver Lake pump.

I made his coffee as he liked it, filling the top of the drip coffee pot with fresh, nearly boiling (you could tell by the sound—it quiets down at boiling so you have about thirty seconds to pull it from the flame at the loudest point) Silver Lake water all the way to the top of the drip container, and an inch more when that dripped through. He liked his coffee mug handles big enough to wrap his large fingers through, and his coffee with a splash of Carnation evaporated milk from a five-ounce can. He needed to ring his spoon like a bell as he stirred in the two teaspoons of sugar per cup.

Nate had wide, mechanic's fingers with oil-blackened calluses and rounded light-bulb tips from years of nail biting. He bragged that he didn't take care of his teeth, and bragged that his nails grew when he lost his teeth and before he had his plate made. He bragged about his prison number, tattooed to his inside left ankle, 36759, and an outline of his prison key tattooed over his heart.

I was attracted to sincerity. I knew Nate was sincere, but couldn't decide what was sincere about him. Nate was also cruel. I couldn't patch this together. I felt I needed to decide which side of him I believed, which side of him was real, so I could design a way to respond to him, so I could decide how to feel about him. It seemed he had to be either/or. I couldn't accept that he was both. He'd begged me to quit my job at Crane's and stay by his side. That lasted one day. I started to see that he always played tricks. Even his bragging was a trick, even his kindness. One could never tell what cruelty he meant, if any, and what he did for effect, for the drama of it, with the cruelty as a mere side effect, or ploy. The same ambiguity surrounded his kindness. Was he kind for what you would notice or not notice about him, or was it genuine, spontaneous, inner? Why did I want to trust one way and not the other? Eventually I would see how this was the same wondering I had about my parents and Janice.

"I'll leave you home to rest," is what he said, which sounded kind, but didn't feel that way. Nate wasn't kind from someone else's need, so it scared rather than comforted me to hear him say that. One was always off balance with Nate. The one way Nate had follow-through: he meant to keep you that way, off balance.

I was so sick and tired. Thinking this way made me cry, as I knew I wouldn't be able to stand it much longer. I needed to find a way out.

Nate must have heard me thinking, taking his attention from the party, he moved part way up the ladder to the loft, so I could see his face. It was just a peek, but he saw me crying. He moved back down the ladder.

It had been a tender look, with a slight wrinkle between his eyebrows; I knew he loved me in that look, and I also knew that he knew I was going to leave him.

❧

I watched the *Phil Donohue Show* before work Monday morning, November 5, 1979. I learned about the U.S. Embassy in Tehran being overrun by Iranian militants who took over fifty hostages. At that time I tuned in daily before work as *Good Morning America* or *Phil Donohue* counted the days of the hostage crisis, as it was called, and described President Carter's strategies to free them. I was a hostage, too, and counting my days.

Chapter 42

I awoke the way a guard dog would to the sound of the car in the driveway. My mind had been tuned to noises. Who could it be? Someone knocked at the door.

I said, "Come in."

DeeDee appeared.

"Hi, Anna. Where's the party? I was with Nate in town. He said he was having a party."

I climbed down the ladder, turned on the light, still marveling at the miracle of it, and took my clothes off the chair. I noticed the clock: two a.m.

"There isn't a party here." I took a beer from the refrigerator outside the door, and noticed how cold and civilized it was. Electricity was terrific.

She thanked me and sat down, gulping her beer, "grabbing up all the gusto," as Nate would say, misquoting the Schlitz beer campaign.

DeeDee was pretty. She had dark hair and a fiery personality. I'd heard she'd been in a few fistfights. People in town were afraid of her, but I wasn't. She liked me.

"I had some asshole drop me off here because Nate said there was a party. I thought I could get a ride home from someone here."

"You can stay here tonight. I'll give you a ride tomorrow, or when Nate gets home with the truck."

I moved one of the chairs from the kitchen table to the rocking chair where she sat. I pulled her drunken legs up and rested them on the chair, covered her with an afghan, and went back up to the loft to sleep.

Five minutes later, Nate was home. I trembled. I turned over in bed to face outside and hugged my knees to keep them still. I heard him on the ladder. I heard him undressing in the dark. I didn't move. I slowed my breathing. Nate slid under the covers and rested his hand on the curve of my hip. I didn't respond.

"Cunt!"

I left my eyes closed because I didn't want to see. I could smell the death on his breath. I heard shaking metal. The inside of my head flamed in the way of an unstable mantle in a kerosene lamp. I sat up. He was out the door.

It took me that long to figure out what happened.

I had a three-pound coffee can with a plastic cover up in the loft to empty ashtrays. The sealed cover trapped the smell, and the metal of the can lowered the risk of fire. He had thrown it at me; it had hit me in the forehead, right side. I felt the blood. I descended the ladder facing forward, turned on the antique chandelier, which hung in the peak of the roof. DeeDee's face glowed close to mine.

"Jesus Christ!" she said.

She opened the door, and yelled to Nate.

"You come back here! Aren't you even going to see if she's all right?"

It surprised me that he returned. He and DeeDee looked in my eyes, and examined the wound. They talked and wiped off the blood, talked about whether to bring me in for stitches. Nate didn't think so, because, "Head wounds always bleed a lot," he said. They both got close to my face. They were flat. They were like photographs, not people. This is a magazine, I thought, not my life. I had a scratch 'n' sniff t-shirt with pictures of bananas on the front. If you scratched and sniffed the shirt, you could smell banana. That is what they were, photographs of people. If I scratched them, they would smell of alcohol, as my boss, as my father smelled, as my grandfather smelled to my mother. Life is pictures and smells. They were scratch n' sniff booze bottle people. They taped a piece of gauze over my head, and I slept. It smelled of sleep anyway.

Chapter 43

Nate's birthday was Saturday, November tenth. It was a weekend of celebration. He drank all day, both days. I was at home sleeping Sunday night. I got up to check the wood stove. I put in more wood, left the damper open, and got back in bed. I heard a car in the driveway, rustling, and voices. I rushed down the ladder to shut the damper, and hurried back to the loft. If Nate had seen me in bed while the stove damper was open, I would have been in trouble. Nate said if I fell asleep with the stove that way, the place would burn to the ground.

He might not have noticed though, because he opened the door to the house and said, to no one in particular, "I've got to get my gun; I'm going to kill him."

He was fighting with Chuck, which gave me a weak sense of relief. Being angry with people was an avocation for Nate. He put so much focus on his rage that he was unable to be angry with two people at once. I was terrified that my luck wouldn't hold. I didn't look outside, but it sounded as if they were driving in and out of the driveway. I could hear them hollering at each other.

Finally, Nate opened the door. I heard him put his clothes on the chair. He moved up the ladder. He brought the loaded gun upstairs with him and said, "If he comes back, I'll kill him."

Then he said to me, "If you don't watch out, I'll kill you too."

I hadn't said a word to him. I didn't sleep that night. I had been waiting to get ready to leave on the inside, to be able to do it, to have a way. Something changed in me, as I lay awake, watching each troubled second go by.

I wondered whether Nate's problem was through and through, in his core. I figured that if I could tell he was totally evil, my decision would be easy. When I saw goodness in Nate, I was drawn to stay.

Whether it was through and through, I couldn't tell, but a lot of Nate was a fist-tight, bone-broken, dream-crushing monster of a conniving, mean man, deliberate in all ways. Whatever he was, I felt pathetic for staying with him.

I was ready to go. In the new light of morning, I knew it was time. At last it was time! My long guilt had been wasted. I couldn't leave until I was ready. I could see that too in this unusual morning.

I could see that one can't always *be* ready, at least not on a wish or a demand. I realized I needn't have been angry with myself for staying as long as I did. It had just become time, as if the bread were doubled in size just now—and it was time just now to punch it down.

I quietly packed a week's clothes in a grocery bag from Trapp's. I coiled the belt I'd made from the nickel-silver suspender Nate had given me into the bag. I took my toothbrush and my hormones from the kitchen sink. I was careful not to wake Nate. I was prepared to leave the bag if he said anything to me about the rustling noise; I didn't want him to know I was leaving before I got out the door.

I rubbed my hand on the two by fours around the doorjamb inside the cabin before I left. It hurt my body to pull away from that wood. It was as though I were a tree, having my branches severed with a saw. Perhaps all those nights embroidering in the dark I had accidentally sewn myself to the place. Something in me was being ripped by leaving. Even though I felt as if I belonged there, I couldn't stay.

On the walk to the outhouse, the smell of fresh-cut wood was particularly strong. I went back in the cabin and absorbed one more look at the loft, the wood stove, the sink with the five-gallon bucket right under the unconnected drain pipe. It all looked lovely to me.

"Good-bye," I said, quietly.

I opened the door and gripped the heavy handle until I heard the snap of the latch as though it were my own bone breaking.

Chapter 44

I parked right in front of the office, and left the door to the truck open a minute while I breathed the air of the quiet morning. It was so quiet in Alma sometimes, even in town. I could hear a melody as if a distant symphony played on the morning frost. Some moments in life are sweet.

I got right to work, the day progressing like all the rest. My first task was typing the want ads.

"I'm so glad you're still working on the ads. I wanted to get this in for this week. This apartment is for rent," Emma said, as she set the hand-written advertisement in the typing bin next to my desk.

I read the ad. "For Rent: One bedroom apartment on Harvey Street, Alma. $150."

"Emma. This is great timing. Is this your place?"

The apartment owner was Emma's uncle, though he lived in the Minneapolis. "When the apartment is empty, I just put in the ad. Then I can show the place, you know," she said.

"How far is it?"

"Two blocks up Central, and one block over on Harvey. Just three blocks from here."

"Do you have a key? Could I see it over my lunch hour today?"

"I'll show it to you at lunch," she said.

I cashed my check at lunch and gave one-hundred-fifty of the one-hundred-seventy-three dollars to Emma. She handed me the key to the door and told me the Minneapolis address to where I should send the rent, beginning in December. I told myself it was the low rent and the bathroom that made the decision for me, but I would have taken anything. It was the only apartment I considered. I would have rented it without seeing it. I did look forward to bathing in a sunny bathroom, and a flush toilet sure beat a chemical barrel over a hole.

Chapter 45

I stayed at the Alma Hotel for the last time Monday night.

It was Tuesday, my long day at work. Every Tuesday we put the paper together because it had to be printed first thing Wednesday morning, and completed before the kids got off school and came for their routes.

I was at work about eight minutes on Tuesday morning when Nate called. He didn't mention that I hadn't been home the night before.

"Hi. Will you bring home a six-pack?"

"No. I won't."

"Why not?"

"I'm not coming home, not anymore. I rented an apartment."

"You had better come home tonight. I'll throw all of your shit in the driveway. I'll burn it all if you don't come home tonight."

I knew he would carry through on his threat. I was done waiting for a way to leave so that he wouldn't retaliate. I would need to face whatever it was that he would do.

"Go ahead and burn it. I won't be there until tomorrow. If you haven't had your fire, I'll pick up my things then."

"Why? What's the problem, Anna?"

"I can't take it any more, Nate."

❦

Nate was home when I arrived, and my things were packed. He had them in the dump truck. I had expected an ugly scene, but true to Nate's commitment to being unpredictable, I got help instead. He was calm, almost cheerful. I suspected that he simply wanted to find out where I was going to live. The decision to leave took so much of my attention, I hadn't thought anything through. I was only picking up my things because he had threatened to burn them. It was eerie how calm he was, but I was grateful; I wouldn't have been able to move alone.

After helping me unload, he didn't stay.

It hurt hearing him drive off. It seemed I could feel the truck getting farther and farther away. I sobbed. It didn't seem I would ever stop crying. The tears appeared with the force of a flood. Not even my pillow helped. I didn't know what I was going to do.

Chapter 46

The apartment was the second floor of a house. The living room, bedroom and kitchen all had closets, because they had originally been bedrooms, before the house became two apartments. You entered the apartment from the main floor porch. Inside the door was a tiny landing just big enough to open the door, without knocking into the stairway, which went up to foyer. All of the rooms, including the bathroom, opened into a foyer.

Each room had a window; there was even one high up in the corner of the bathroom. The bathroom was painted entirely, including the floor, with white paint. The rest of the floors were varnished wood. The bathtub was large and deep, with claw feet, but was smaller than the Alma Hotel tub. The floor of the front porch was the same pale turquoise color as the walls in the foyer, and it leaned forward toward Harvey Street so that my potter's wheel—which Nate had dumped there, the last thing, right outside the front door—looked sadly off balance.

The second day I walked the three blocks from work to my new home. I pulled down the yellowed and cracked shades on the double windows in the living room. Each time I pulled them closed, the shade on the right made a delicate tearing noise. I sat on the mattress on the floor in the bedroom, leaning forward over my crossed legs. I sat for an unknown amount of time before I began to unpack. I wondered if I looked emotionally disturbed sitting there, then got up to put some more things away.

❧

On my way home from work Friday, my third day at the apartment, I met the young married couple, Doug and Diane, who lived in the apartment downstairs. They were both blond with pink cheeks. Doug was a student at the college in the Water Conservation program. Diane worked at J.C. Penney.

Nate arrived on Saturday night, uninvited, with a six-pack of beer. He had been drinking. I didn't lock the door. Nate just walked in. Chuck was there. He was asleep on the floor in the living room because he had a job in town. A friend with an apartment was an asset to people who lived in the woods.

Nate was confused, unconvincingly, about what it meant that I left him. He said he couldn't get it. He showed up as if I hadn't left him, as if our relationship was the same as it had always been, as if I hadn't lived with him so I couldn't have left him and we were still lovers as we always had been and he was entitled to know everything about me. He wouldn't leave me alone.

I told him I couldn't take his drinking and violence. I couldn't take it that he acted as if he hated me most of the time. I was afraid of him, though I didn't say outright, "Stay away from me. "

I didn't know what to do. He wasn't going to leave me alone. I was lost without him, too, and sad. I missed his smell, oddly, more than his companionship, but I didn't understand why he had to be so mean.

He attacked my character for leaving him.

"So you're on your high horse, Miss Independent Alma now? What? Do you think you're perfect? Do you think you were easy to live with?"

Genuine independent thought was a threat to Nate. His words burned like a new tattoo.

I was in my nightclothes on my mattress, trying to sleep. Generally I would ignore his harassment and hope he would leave. He broke a six-pack bottle by bottle on the wall over my bed. He grabbed my arm, flung me as if I were another bottle. I got frightened and moved into the living room to find safety near Chuck. Nate dumped a box of seed beads on the floor.

Chuck woke up.

"Hey, I am friends with both of you," he said. "I don't want to take sides."

Chuck packed up his things and left.

As Nate broke up the place, he said, "I'm going to continue until you call the police."

At the time I didn't have a phone, so I called from the neighbors' place. I stayed in the downstairs apartment with Doug and Diane until the police arrived. I followed the officers up the stairs. I was in my pajamas, crying.

Nate was at the top of the stairs with a calm smile on his face, drinking a cup of my coffee.

"Is this your apartment?" Officer Crayon asked Nate. "Do the things belong to you?"

I looked in Officer Crayon's beautiful eyes; they were brown and shaped like flower petals. His auburn eyelashes were soft as though they were made of oil paint. But something was wrong. His head sat on his shoulders as if it were a knick-knack on a lawyer's table.

I told him it was *my* place. I told him what Nate had done and said. Nate looked so calm.

"Did you ask him to leave?" Officer Crayon said.

Anyone who knew him, including anyone at the police department, was afraid of Nate, but they didn't hesitate to insinuate that there was something wrong with me when I wasn't able to control him simply by asking him politely to leave me alone. Nate and the officer left without having to be told.

Chapter 47

I was trying to distract myself from my loneliness and guilt. I spent time at home rocking in the brown, mostly stuffed—there were a few holes—recliner. I worked for money and to get away from Nate. I didn't lock my door because I couldn't afford to fix it if Nate broke it down, as I knew he would.

He stopped by and cried some more. He told me about his feelings, the reason he did things. I saw the boy in him again. I had waited for three years to awaken that child in Nate, the way I had the night I made pot-cookies for him. I had thought that the child was asleep in him; in me, the child had died.

I let him talk, and I rocked. I wasn't reconsidering my decision to leave him, but I didn't tell him that.

Chapter 48

One day I arrived home. Nate was sitting in the brown rocker looking sweet, his mouth was drawn flat, as if pinched and pulled at the corners, just slightly. I noticed he was clean. His hair was shiny and combed. He had shaved. His clothes were clean. His shirt was tucked into his jeans. I noticed even the tips of his fingers were free of grease. He'd made himself a cup of coffee, and was holding the cup on his leg. I wasn't afraid.

"I want you to leave town," he said.

"Nate. I'm not going to go. I have friends here, and work. I like living in a town where you can have conversations with people by yelling across the street, where you can leave your car running with the keys in it in the winter. I want to stay."

"It's simple then. I'll have to make you leave, Anna." He got up out of the chair, took a gulp from his coffee cup, and set the cup on the stove in the kitchen.

I thought I saw him stumble over my name the way a parent with lots of children goes through the list before getting it right. I'm the fifth woman he's chased out of town, I thought, so quickly it surprised me. I was one of Nate's ex-girlfriends now, so the pattern was set. Now I was supposed to sneak out of town in fear, sever ties with friends, and disappear, only to be added to the list of Nate lore: Lynn, Ellen, Suzy, Carol, and Anna. None of his wives or girlfriends lived in Alma, I realized with a chill.

❧

It was payday, mid-December. I stopped for a drink at the Tippy Canoe Saloon with Jim Weeks from the *Messenger*. We found Ellie already there.

I was upset. I wanted to tell them that my mom had just sent a notice of Susan Stone's murder. I had just opened the letter in the afternoon and found out. I was shocked by the news. It didn't seem real at first, the way death never does. I had the eerie feeling I was going to be murdered, too. The murder of a friend of mine made it more real.

After having one drink at the Tippy Canoe the three of us walked up the alley to the New Moon. I was wearing shoes with smooth soles and I needed help getting up the slippery hill. Ellie was on one side of me; Jim was on the other. We were laughing because it was so hard for me to walk, and because we'd smoked a joint.

Nate turned down the alley coming from First Avenue driving the old truck I'd left behind when I moved. I felt frightened, as if being seen was equal to being stabbed. We waved and continued walking.

We sat at the bar and ordered.

"Moosehead, three," we said, and drank up. The bar was full for a Friday night, even in Alma.

I didn't get to tell them about Susan, because Nate came in and stood about two feet from me. I could feel him. I didn't have to look. Nate slid into my space like braked tires on ice; he could barely stop, but he did. He stopped about three inches from my face. He spoke, loudly; I listened to the strange color of his face, which seemed more frightening to me than his words. Slick rage opened his pores wider even in the dark room. When you're afraid you can see people's skin better. At least I could.

"You're a cunt," he said in a loud voice.

I could see Wally Whiting across the bar. Nate walked to the other end, out of my sight.

None of us moved. The bar smoothed like a twilight lake. Then he walked back over and just stood behind me.

He said, "I'm going to get you. I'm going to give you a scar to match the other one, because I don't give a fuck."

Ellie took me by the elbow, and I lifted up so my legs dropped, and walked out of the bar. I was making myself shorter the way you do when you know the baseball will hit you, too late to catch it. Jim followed behind us. Nate yelled to Jim as we were leaving about how he hoped I was a good fuck. We stayed shoulder to shoulder and walked two blocks up and two blocks down to the police station.

"Here's a piece of gum," Ellie said, "to hide the smell of the joint."

"What can I do for you?" the sergeant said.

"I've been threatened, in the New Moon by Nate, Nate Rohr. I'm afraid to go home."

"You wasted that piece of gum, Miss; I can still smell the booze."

He irritated me. "I'm not driving. I'm of age, twenty-one. I don't care if you can smell the booze. I had one beer. Didn't you hear what I said?"

"Just go home. I can't arrest him until he does something."

"What do you mean *does* something? He's been after me for months. He just threatened to kill me in front of thirty people."

"If you have any more trouble, call us."

"I don't have a phone."

"There is nothing I can do."

"Can I stay here?"

"I suppose, the cell, it's not nice; we don't have many women here."

"I don't care. Don't you understand? If I go home, he'll kill me."

"You'll have to get a blanket and pillow; we don't supply for guests, I mean. Officer Crayon will give you a ride home to get your things."

Officer Crayon had been to my apartment before. He followed me up the stairs. He looked around. Officer Crayon's uniform seemed to weigh more than he did. I found something hollow about this type of protection. His radio kept hissing the way they do. Finally he shut it down.

I saw Officer Crayon staring at the articles on my bulletin board. "Young Woman Found Murdered." The article didn't say much, only that she had been found murdered in her apartment. There were no suspects yet in her murder, but I had one. I knew her father didn't kill her, but he did kick her out of the house. I remember how she told me that her dad kicked her in the crotch, so that she jumped several feet in the air, and called her a cunt. She was gone weeks after that, as she was afraid to go home. She never did go home after that for long, and now she was murdered. It's hard to love life when your dad kicks you in the crotch and calls you a cunt. And when you don't love life, it's hard to be safe in it. I felt sad, and missed her, but her death was still suspended in me with all of my other grief.

The other article said that Lane had been robbed at the store where he worked. These were my childhood neighbors. Friends. Their parents were friends of my parents. Mom had sent me the articles because she thought I would want to know.

Officer Crayon broke my thoughts again by questioning me about the articles. "Who are these people? Why do you have these articles?"

I was irritated that he was questioning me. After all, I had invited him into my apartment. It was absurd for him to think that I would post newspaper clippings of my illegal activities on my own bulletin board, neatly, with colored thumbtacks, and then invite a police officer to my house.

I told Officer Crayon that I had lived in the same neighborhood with these people for eighteen years. "My mom sent me the articles. These are people from my neighborhood," I said.

I picked up my pillow, and the quilt my grandmother had made from scrap pieces of wool. It was mostly black with blues and yellows and tied with red yarn. He drove me to the police station.

"When I shut this, it will lock, so if you need anything or if you want out you'll have to knock."

The foot-thick cell door shut with a thud.

I spread the blanket on the narrow concrete bed and got under it. It occurred to me that the quilt I was wrapped in also covered my mother while her father threatened her mother as a child. That was the blanket I happened to take with me to jail.

As I lay on my jail cell bed I thought of swimming on Lake Elizabeth with Susan for hours and hours when we were kids. I couldn't believe Susan was dead. We swam until our skin was wrinkled. It was wonderful. We'd sing as Mrs. Stone had taught us:

> Rye whiskey, rye whiskey, rye whiskey I cry
> If a tree don't fall on me, I'll live till I die.
> If the ocean were whiskey and I were a duck
> I'd dive to the bottom and never come—hiccup,
> I meant to say up.

We'd laugh even though we'd sung the song hundreds of times. We swam out to the raft and under it and over it, off of it. The air was clean. The water was clean. We had enough to eat. We had everything. I would wrap myself in a towel and come running up to shower, wash my feet off at the cold hose, and come in the house. Life was fun! It was lovely. I had affection for salamanders, snakes, tree frogs, praying mantises. There were owls, and raccoons, loons, and wood ducks on Lake Elizabeth. My mom still loved me. I'd never taken any drugs or disappointed anyone.

Susan and I had stood shoulder-deep in the lake with our heads down making cages around our faces with our wet hair. Susan got the idea to fold our hair up from the wet cage, which made a nice round roll of hair around our faces. We praised each other for looking like George Washington. We played this game many times.

One day, Susan said to me as we had our heads in our hair cages so that her voice echoed, "I always thought it was your dad who got in your bed with you."

"And I thought it was your dad who came into yours," I said as we pulled our hair up and looked like George Washington again, and then dunked our heads.

Chapter 49

In the morning, I knocked on the cell door from the inside, and they let me out. From jail I walked to Angelica's for coffee and toast. I met Jim Weeks at the office around 9:00 a.m. I was afraid to go home.

I worked Saturdays in December with Jim, putting together the ads for the Christmas *Messenger*, a special issue. People bought large ads at Christmas, not to sell anything but to say Merry Christmas and Happy New Year to the town. Quarter-page people went up to a half or larger. People who only bought a recurring classified-sized ad during the year bought a quarter page. Businesses who never advertised during the year bought an ad. The issue was twice as thick as any other issue of the year.

I didn't stop at home in the morning. We worked until about noon. I went home to take a bath, and to eat lunch. When I got to the apartment, my stereo was in the middle of the floor, smashed, along with about fifteen borrowed albums, destroyed. Many of the albums belonged to Jim. All of his were ruined. Some of my albums were intact.

At work Jim said I didn't have to tell him what happened. He already knew. While I'd been gone, Jim said Nate had called the office several times to talk to me. He called again before Jim and I had a chance to talk about it. Nate insisted he talk to me or he would come in and make us both sorry. That was the threat. So I talked to him. His voice changed and he began to cry. He said he wished he could stay away from me. He told me that he might do something so terrible that he wouldn't be able to see me any more. Sounds all right to me, I thought.

I called the police and reported the broken stereo. They said they had no evidence proving that Nate did the damage and told me they wouldn't even question him about it.

"No evidence? He admitted he did it to me and to Jim Weeks," I said.

"We're still not clear why you have a murder notice on your bulletin board," Officer Crayon said.

When I went home again after work, I sadly swept up the broken pieces of albums and threw out the stereo that my parents had given me for my seventeenth birthday. It seemed as though the broom were a violin. I could hear a melancholic melody as I swept. As I found the volume knob in the kitchen, and held it in my hand, I decided I wasn't going to leave town. Nate could kill me if that is what he would do, but I couldn't leave town just because he threatened me. How could I leave and call myself free?

Chapter 50

In the days ahead, when I came home from work, I found notes from Nate on the counter by the sink. Another day, Nate left me a clamorous prayer asking God for mercy for himself and help with his "monster," as he called his bad deeds.

I spent much time gazing in the mirror as if I couldn't stop looking at myself. I didn't know until later that Nate was across the street and up the hill gazing at me through the window gazing at myself in the mirror. I had a version of the thing kids have when they play peek-a-boo: If I don't see you, you don't exist. Except I had a twist: If you don't see me, then I don't exist. I spent hours looking in the mirror to see if I could make myself appear.

It was Tuesday, again. The pages of the *Messenger* had to be pasted up before early morning Wednesday. Nate arrived at the office about eight p.m.

"Anna. I want to talk to you."

"I'm not done working."

"I'll meet you at the Tippy Canoe."

When we finished working, Jim and I walked across the street to the bar after discussing whether or not I should go.

"He'll come to my house if I don't go," I told Jim.

I decided I would rather meet with Nate in a public place. Nate sat at the bar with me. After a beer, I said I was tired and I was going home. He calmly said he would wipe me around the bar if I did. I tried to get up and walk away. He slapped my face. He said he'd kill me if I left.

No one tried to stop him. The people in the bar sat or stood around. It's a myth that men protect damsels in distress. For the most part, they are as coolly indifferent to a man's cruelty to a woman as they are to the scaling and filleting of a fish. After about a half hour, Nate let me go.

I walked home. It was a cloudy, moonless night. If it hadn't been for the single light on Harvey Street it might have been as dark even in town as it had been my first night in Alma. I got under the covers in my bed without taking off my clothes or doing any other preparation for sleep.

Nate showed up in the dark. I could see the shadowy silhouette of his body on a chair by my bed. I heard him breathing. I was afraid to tell him to leave.

He was ordering me: "Tell me to stay out of your life, Anna; tell me you love me, Anna; tell me I'm a jerk. You'll have to tell me to leave. If you tell me to leave you alone, then I will."

For certain his request was a trick. I had moved out: I left him. He hadn't left me alone, and wouldn't leave me alone. I was afraid if I made it clear what I wanted, he'd kill me. Still, I thought leaving him was clear enough.

"Nate, please. I'm tired. I want to go to sleep. I have to work tomorrow."

He continued talking and finally he stood up. I thought he was leaving. Without warning, he attacked me. He pulled off the covers, jumped on the bed on top of me. Next he took a pocket knife from his pocket, opened it, and placed the sharp side on my throat.

He said, "If the neighbors call the police you're dead." With this he threw me off the bed and tore off my clothes. He pinned me to the floor. I hit him and tried to get away. I was lying on my back naked and I thought he was going to rape me. I tried to get away and he placed his fingers on my eye sockets and threatened to tear my eyes out. He calmed then, and I got on the bed; I was crying. I was stretched thin from the long upset.

He sat back in the desk chair. He had the knife. He prevented me from leaving the bed even to go to the bathroom. I heard a voice saying, "This is serious; this could be the end of your life."

I expected to be killed. My soul retreated to a high place in the corner of the room, while a flimsy version of me sat on the bed listening and talking, re-explaining why I was in town, how I felt, why I had left. I heard her talking like a poor quality recording. He stayed until four a.m.

As soon as he was gone, I ran downstairs. I locked my door. I watched out the window as he circled around the block. I had just enough time to run upstairs and he was back at the door.

He told me to open the door. When I would not, he broke the window off the first door, and then he broke the doorknob completely out of the second storm door. As he was breaking in, I pounded my feet on the floor, a prearranged signal to Doug and Diane, the neighbors, to call the police. I didn't have a phone yet. He said he would kill me if they called the police, but I assumed he was going to kill me anyway.

As he started up the stairs, he yelled, "Anna, I just can't stop! You'll have to call the police. I want to go to jail."

He didn't stop me from going downstairs to Doug and Diane's. They had already called. I waited in their apartment for the police.

The officers arrived. They asked me if I was going to press charges. Officer Hitch said that they wouldn't come back the next time they were called if I didn't. I started writing out the statement, exhausted and hysterical.

Nate kicked at me and one of the officers so they decided to bring him in while I finished writing the statement. I felt a cavern of guilt wrap around me. I didn't want him to go to jail; I just wanted him to leave me alone. I finished writing the statement in tears.

I crawled in bed just as the sun was coming up. The police were gone. I hoped Nate was in jail. I fell asleep for just a few minutes. I didn't hear Nate walk up the stairs.

I awakened to his voice.

"Take that," he said as he threw lighted matches on my bed. He smiled as he watched me put them out.

I remember waking up in a panic. I thought he was still there and I would be in trouble for sure for falling asleep, but he was gone. Had I just fallen asleep while he tormented me? How could I have fallen asleep? After a few moments, I remembered he had left the bedroom. I realized I was so exhausted I must have fallen asleep before he left the apartment.

Aware he could be back, I slept for another hour or so before work. The officer's words played in my mind. I had signed the statement and they took him away. But they hadn't even kept him until eight o'clock in the morning. I hadn't told them about the knife or the threats to my life. I was too afraid. He was fined one hundred dollars for breaking the door.

I remembered that Nate had gone to jail for stalking his first wife, Lynn. I remembered how unimportant that had seemed when I first heard it a few years before.

Chapter 51

Christmas, 1979, was first-rate. I visited my parents for the Christmas holiday from Saturday, December 22 to Wednesday, December 26. I had asked them for new things for my apartment. I got some T-Fal non-stick bread pans, a baking dish, and fry pan. I got an iron, and an ironing board. I ordered it from the local J.C. Penney store and my mom paid me for it. She thought it would be too awkward to carry on the bus.

When I returned to Alma, Nate had redecorated my apartment. My door had been repaired, everything but the lock. My cement block bookshelves had been replaced with large popple logs. And I now had a wood stove, one I had bought for us when we were together, not hooked up, in my living room, as a knick-knack. Also, left on the stovetop, a new Chapter of letters from Nate for my collection. He admitted and lamented his inadequacies, proclaimed his love for me, again.

December 1979

Dear Anna,

Not that I mean to use the word sorry, and expect things to be well, but from whatever warped heart I have, I regret the way I am. I looked for you and hoped to see you and tell you. I pray now I will be able to leave you alone. I know how you feel and don't like to see you hide from me. I wish you the best. I don't know how to deal with it.

I love you.

Neight

Hi Anna,

I'm just sitting around waiting for the glue to dry on the door. I couldn't find the lock so I will have to come back to finish. I hope you don't mind my Christmas present of popple logs for your bookshelves. I think after they dry out they will be lighter than the cement blocks were. I hope things went well at home for you.

I do love you, yes I do.

Neight

December 24, 1979

Hi Anna,

I came over with the stove, and now I have to wait for Max. When I was carrying it up he went out. I sure hope he comes back soon. I think the stove will come in handy to set things on. It sure is strange how things get twisted up. When I first met you I lived in town and you were confused. Now it is the opposite.

Tomorrow I am going to make an appointment with a shrink. I have to do something to get back some self-respect. Being able to help you helps me, but it also hurts, and I don't understand. I hope and pray I'm not being a pest. I hope you let me know what is going on with you.

You were wrong about one thing though: if you were gone I would not do any better at getting over you because I love you. Max is at the door so it will shine when it shines.

Love,

Neight

Anna,

I just came back from Illia and thought you would be on the bus. Hope you didn't break down.

Neight

Anna,

Well I did get drunk yesterday and I didn't like it at all. There wasn't much of a change in me that I could see other than the obvious. I still felt helpless about us. I keep hoping and praying that we can get along. I try to compromise and then I fear that you will take advantage of me. But the last person I should feel that with is you. I feel as though you don't want me because you don't encourage me. I know what happens is not worth encouraging along. Now I can add more to my list of wrong doings. I ruined your weekend and mine and I don't know why.

I don't want you to feel bad about my weak mind and lack of will power. I know I can't run from myself. I see more and more that I am ruining what is left. I know what must go through your mind because of the way I act, but please remember that I am aware of things, and try as hard as I can to be the person I know is in me.

I wish you could be home to enjoy your own home. I shy away from my home because it reminds me of my failures. Because of the life I have led there are things I can't have or expect from others. I fear trying with strangers because of my monster. At least you know my monster and with you at times I can relax.

Bye love,

Neight

The high temperature on January 1, 1980 was eight below zero; the low was thirty-three below. Sometimes it was so cold I imagined I could feel the moist air in my lungs crystallize, as though my lungs were snowing.

I waited eleven days until the cold snap broke before going into Penney's to pick up the ironing board. I saw my neighbor Diane there. She told me that they were moving. Doug was quitting school. He got a job with the Forest Service and they were moving to Duluth. She asked me to come over to preview the items they had for sale.

I was sad that they were moving. I bought a maroon couch with a wooden frame and a large old buffet made of walnut from them. They helped me carry both pieces up the stairs.

I bought an electric sander and smoothed the two slabs of four-inch-thick white pine I got as payment for helping Nate on the sawmill. The white pine was easy to sand, as the wood was soft. I added two coats of varnish. Then I placed the mirror image slabs of wood on top of the steamer trunk I'd had for years, and used it as a coffee table. I picked out a remnant of brown shag carpet from the local rug store and had it delivered. I used a double mattress, without a box spring, for a bed, but I got some sheets for it. I found a wood-look vinyl corner desk at the used furniture store in Alma, and set it up in my bedroom. I thought I might even get to sew, as the corner desk would work as a sewing table. I bought myself a set of old Homer Laughlin eggshell flower pattern dishes at The Cobweb Antiques for seventy dollars. I loved getting some of my own things; I began to feel as if I were in charge of my life.

The porch that led to my front door sagged, but it was partially enclosed with half walls and a roof. The door in the bedroom led to a balcony, too small to use, but I could easily crawl out on the roof and sun myself, which I looked forward to doing in the summer.

❧

Jim was adding more sophisticated typesetting equipment. He changed the *Northern Messenger* from mimeograph to the more efficient offset printing, so my hours got cut. I needed more money. After Christmas, I got two new jobs: at the New Moon, Hal's place, as a waitress, two shifts on the weekends, and worked over the lunch hour during the week; and I took a job doing print layouts at Ben Tweten's Print Shop. I was allowed to leave either the *Messenger* or Ben's over lunch to waitress at the New Moon.

January was a busy time at Ben's, which was good. I was working on an American Legion World Series booklet. The Series was going to be held in Alma from August 24 to September 1, 1980. The booklet consisted of ads welcoming the teams, game schedules, and photos of team members. We even got a letter from President Carter, with the official seal. What's more, Ben let me work on a map at home. I pasted the names of every lake in the BTCA Wilderness large enough to label with six-point type. I typed the names, cut them with an x-acto knife, and then I used a tweezers and rubber cement to place the names by the lakes. The entire map would be reduced from full-size for various printing projects at Ben's. The photo-reduction hid some of the flaws, but still I tried to be careful.

I'd heard that some people in town wouldn't go to the New Moon restaurant because the building used to be a morgue. My situation had changed only slightly from the hospital where I learned how to kill myself. With Nate I was learning in how many ways and places I could be killed. I imagined that I would be murdered at work in the old morgue. This is what occupied my mind.

One day, Nate sat in my section for lunch at the Moon. I poured coffee, and watched him put in his two spoons of sugar. I knew not to refill his cup until it was completely empty, so he didn't have to tell me. I didn't know if he saw my hand shake while I poured.

Nate had been to Moose Lake for a psychiatric evaluation. If he'd seen Paula there he didn't say. He blustered on about how he wasn't in the normal range in a single scale on the MMPI.

He showed up at the restaurant occasionally, after the lunch-rush, usually crying. I was afraid not to listen, and numb. He was remorseful, asking forgiveness, again. He told me that he hadn't been able to make his payments to Hal for the backhoe, and Hal had taken it from him. The next time I saw Hal I asked him if I could have my thousand dollar down payment back.

"No," he said.

"But you got my money, a few payments from Nate, and the backhoe."

"Tough luck," he said.

⚜

It wasn't all domestic bliss at my apartment. The logs Nate had used for the bookcases were still wet and they marked up the floor. Before long there were bugs hatching out of them.

About once a week I tried to quit smoking. I'd usually make it out the door of my apartment and then until I had my first craving when I got to Ben's in the morning. I'd have to leave and get some cigarettes out of the machine at Angelica's, right next door.

One morning, Ben was on the fourth run of fifteen thousand two-sided brochures when he noticed that a paragraph read "free gas with boat rental." It was 1980 and gas prices had never been higher. I had set the type and proofed the copy. The sentence was supposed to read: free gas CAN with boat rental. Quite a difference. Ben had to start the job over completely. He never told me what it cost him. It cost him less than it would have if he hadn't noticed, but it was the worst mistake I ever made while working for Ben. His kindness deserved perfect work. I felt sad and disappointed in myself. I didn't quit smoking that morning. I was afraid that Ben would do something to me, maybe fire me; I walked around the block after I got my cigarettes.

Ben never shamed me or acted angrily toward me. He simply asked me to change the layout to read properly. So many people want to help the world. Kindness helps.

Ben would be quiet for hours and days, working on his books, in the darkroom, or at the printing press. And then all of the sudden he'd say something. It left me with the impression that he'd been thinking deeply in all that quiet time. He'd say things such as, "With new advances in science, we've missed living forever by one hundred years."

His wife, Wendy, had been relieved that I started working there, she said, because the woman before me had been exceptionally pretty and fashionable; she worried about her in the darkroom with Ben. She said she wasn't worried about me.

I listened to WEBX, the local radio station, and Paul Harvey regularly.

"Does Paul ever come here?" I said once.

"Paul Harvey isn't local," my coworker and press operator Joe Weir said. He laughed.

"It's a local station; I just assumed the people on it were local," I said. But oh my gosh, I couldn't believe how out of it I was. I didn't know a thing about the world I lived in.

Chapter 52

A week later I drank a lot of beer at the bar after work. I met Andy Dolan. He was smart. A writer. With the logic of beer, I accepted his invitation to his cabin with him and a few of his friends from Minneapolis. It was a musty-smelling cabin. The moon was low and barely visible through the black lacy silhouette of leafless popple and frozen balsams. Andy and I went up in his loft to sleep. The big dipper is barely visible in the winter sky. I couldn't see it from the window in the loft. His friends stayed below and slept in sleeping bags on the floor. No one would be going home at that hour, and I nestled in next to Andy.

His skin smelled sweet, a contrast to the damp old blankets. I began caressing him. I felt desire. I could feel Andy's erection, a small penis which delighted me, not much bigger, erect, than a large man's thumb. I could feel the pressure of my inner self calling. Andy's lack of interest surprised me. Certainly he would want to have sex? I think he did.

He told me he'd been a priest. He left the church to marry. He'd divorced three years ago, and he'd moved to Alma to write and to be alone. He'd not slept with anyone since his divorce.

After this, I felt hatred and disgust for men. No one had paid attention to me and what I wanted for years; they hadn't even noticed my indifference, discomfort, or gall as they thrust, licked and whispered, "I want to make you come," not for me, but for them, for what it would mean about them. And now, in a surprising accident, I was feeling the first genuine desire of my life, and the man was still focused on himself.

Chapter 53

On the second Friday night of the New Year, I decided to stay home. I had been at the bar enough lately, and it was a particularly cold night.

I jumped stiff when I heard the knock, afraid it might be Nate. I moved out of the living room and looked around the corner first before starting down the stairs.

"Nate!" I said while I opened the door, sounding happier to see him than I felt. It was Nate's father, also named Nate—Nate, Sr. I saw his Gold Ford F250 pick-up truck parked right in front of my porch.

"How did you know where I live?" I said.

"Nate told me."

Nate, Sr. raised a kidney bean can up to his mouth and spit his wad outside, and I took a step up to make room for him. I remembered how Nate had always made him leave his snuff can outside. I closed the door from the stairs in order to avoid crowding him in the landing at the base of the steps.

"Come on up!" I said, moving quickly up the stairs. I noticed I was smiling.

"I'll make some coffee," I said.

Nate, Sr. had no response. He was quieter than I remembered him, but we had never been alone together. I always made him coffee when he came to visit Nate.

That's it, I thought. *I'm acting the way I would have acted at Nate's. I'm acting.*

"Would you like some coffee, Nate?"

He nodded. "Yes I would," he said.

I turned my back to Nate, Sr., who leaned against the doorway into the kitchen. I rinsed out and filled the clear Pyrex coffee pot at the deep single-basin sink. I didn't immediately notice that Nate's father was watching my body. My jeans hung loosely over my hips, and as I leaned over the sink my shirt came up, leaving a few inches of my back bare. I was self-conscious, but at first I thought this was only because I was trying to make a good impression.

I moved to the stove, which was next to the doorway, turned the electric burner on high, and set the pot of water on it. I looked at Nate, Sr.'s thick, wavy, pure-white hair. He boasted about his hair the way his son boasted about his youthful physique. Nate, Sr. stared at my stomach.

I took out a can of Folgers from the pantry. "I'm flattered you came to visit me," I said. My hands trembled as I set the coffee can on the stove. "I thought I'd probably never see you again. I thought I'd move in here and join the ranks all of Nate's exes! But I would have missed you. I always enjoyed our visits." I opened the coffee can. "You're not mad at me, for leaving Nate, I mean?"

Nate, Sr.'s expression didn't change. He didn't answer.

"How's Mary?" I asked.

"She's at the lake. She said she wanted to be by herself, so I left her there. I've been staying at the house in Illia."

There were no cupboards or drawers in this kitchen. The kitchen pantry was formerly a bedroom closet where all things kitchen had to fit. I went back to the closet and took the flowered Homer Laughlin sugar bowl from the shelf, a can of evaporated milk, and a knife with a wooden handle and a stiff short blade. I set the sugar and milk on the kitchen table. With the knife perpendicular to the top of the can, I hit the handle with my palm creating two holes in it, the way Nate did it.

"So you're not mad at me for leaving him?" I moved back to the stove and stood ready to scoop the coffee into the hot water. Just as the water began to boil, Nate, Sr. reached out and touched my breast, then moved his hand back as if he'd burned it on the stove. This time his mouth widened, accentuating the tobacco stains in the deep wrinkles around his toothless mouth.

Shit, I thought. *Did that just happen?* I took a step back and kept moving backward toward the sink drainer for two clean cups. I pulled the coffee pot to the side of the stove and heaped eight teaspoons of coffee into the water and stirred it.

"Why don't you go in the living room?" I pointed to the other doorway. "I'll be right in." I took a breath.

My God! I thought. The weight of emotion in my chest made it hard to breathe. Even Nate, Sr., an old man, my boyfriend's father. I couldn't stop yet to be sad, or disappointed. I carried the milk, a hot pad, and the sugar out to the living room and set them on the coffee table. After returning to the kitchen for the coffee and cups, I leaned over the table and poured, staying away from Nate, Sr.'s chair. When I set the pot down, Nate, Sr. leaned forward and encircled me with both hands around the waist, pulling me into his lap. His callused hands reached into my shirt and cupped my breasts. I pushed him away, my feet off balance; the recliner rocker moved backward.

"Nate! Nate! LET ME GO!" I yelled.

Nate, Sr. pushed me down hard on this lap. "I've been waiting for this," he said.

We both heard a knock at the door. He released me. I tripped as I moved across the living room, and caught my balance in the foyer at the top of the stairs.

Andy was smiling through the window. I motioned for him to come in.

"Hi. I was in the neighborhood. I thought you might like to see what I bought at the Alma Bookshop tonight."

"Oh great, " I said with a big smile. "Come upstairs. There's someone I'd like you to meet."

"Who?" Andy said.

"Nate's dad," I whispered.

"No. I'm leaving."

"Please," I said, raising my eyebrows.

Andy followed me up the stairs into the living room. Nate Sr. sipped some coffee, still sitting in my brown, overstuffed chair.

"Nate. This is Andy. Andy lives on the Arrow Trail, too, near Nate." I noticed that Nate acted more the way I had seen him in the past, a friend, a nice man, with beautiful white hair, whose age had mellowed his temper, unlike his wild son.

"Time to go," Nate, Sr. said. He left his full coffee cup on the white pine table. "I've got to meet Mary at the lake."

I left Andy in the living room and followed Nate down the stairs.

Nate, Sr. looked at me, as I prepared to slam the door on his body. He pushed his head back inside the nearly closed door.

"Don't tell my son about this," he said, his wide eyes stretching his gray skin.

Andy was looking at my bookshelves when I got upstairs. He noticed in particular *Silent Spring* by Rachel Carson, and was holding it.

"Have you read these books?" he said.

"Many of them. I like to read," I said.

I started to tell him what almost happened, how fortunate it was that he arrived when he did. But I thought better of it. We talked about books for a while, and he left.

Chapter 54

Andy and Joe worked together at the paper, and Joe and I worked together at Ben's. The three of us decided to go winter camping. We picked the second Sunday in February because it was a slow time at work for me and for Joe.

Andy wrote me a poem about our camping trip and left it with a thimble-sized bottle with a cover for my collection on my desk at work.

> Dear Anna:
>
>   Bear Lake awaits
>
> a shore of white
>
> a shallow valley
>
> the moon rising
>
> and the wolves
>
>   howling free
>
>   See you Sunday—Andy

It was the first poem anyone had ever written for me. I carefully tacked it with four silver thumbtacks on my bulletin board. I was looking forward to the trip. I gave the bottle a prominent place in my display case.

I had food from Lee and DeeDee's store. I made gorp, great

camping food. with coconut, peanuts, M&M's, and raisins. I had hot chocolate packed for sitting around the campfire. I couldn't wait. I hadn't been winter camping before. People who lived in Alma rarely vacationed in Alma. We were going to snowshoe onto the lake and camp in the woods near the shore.

Sunday morning, I was packed and waiting for Andy and Joe to pick me up. They were coming any minute. I heard a noise at the bottom of the stairs, instead of a knock. He had fixed my door over Christmas, but he never replaced the lock he had destroyed. Nate walked into my apartment and came right up the stairs.

"Hi, Anna," he said, as if I had been expecting him.

"Hi, Nate," I answered.

"What are you doing?" he said, looking at the camping gear at the top of the stairs.

"I'm about to go winter camping with Andy and Joe," I said.

He lunged at me from the living room door. I was sitting on the chair and he smashed it and me against the wall.

As he was choking me he said, "I am going to kill you and then I am going to kill myself; it just doesn't matter any more."

Now he stopped. I was so weak I could hardly stand, so I crawled to my bedroom. I began to think he had radar for witnesses, the way he suddenly calmed—and then, within seconds, Andy knocked. I told him to come in. Nate walked to the top of the stairs, and prevented Andy from coming all the way up.

"Could I have a few minutes alone with her?" Nate asked. I tried to have Andy stay without saying so but was unable to get the message through. Andy left.

Nate began to cry.

"Here I go again," he said.

I just listened again. I examined the bloody scratch on my face, put a cold rag on my throat, and listened.

He finally got up to leave and I followed him down the stairs. The last thing he said as I let him out the door was, "Please don't say anything bad about me." The similarity between Nate and his father filled me with a sudden, numbing dread.

About twenty minutes later, Andy walked upstairs with Joe, and, in a few minutes, so did Nate. He was smiling now, and calm.

"You're going up the Arrow, right? Why don't you stop at my place for coffee before you go?" Nate said.

I thought Nate was nuts.

Chapter 55

We didn't stop at Nate's, drove right past the driveway. I looked up the driveway quickly as we passed by. The cable was down. I didn't tell Andy and Joe what had happened at the apartment. Being with people this way made me feel safe, and I tried to relax into it.

We hiked in to the lake on snowshoes. The snow was deep and my pack large so that I fell backward coming around a bend. We gathered wood, sat by the fire, drank pine-needle flavored snow melted with hot-chocolate mix, ate gorp, and walked around on the frozen lake on our snowshoes. Andy took a photo of me for an article he was writing on singles in Alma, for Valentine's Day.

In the morning, we were nestled like filaments are inside three light bulbs, with the sun glowing through the golden nylon tent. Frost forms on the sleeping bags from the moisture in your breath. The sheet of frost over us cracked with our first movement.

"This is the crack of dawn," Joe said. We laughed.

Upon return from camping on Monday, I told Jim Weeks what had happened with Nate. He suggested I call the police.

"Why don't you have a phone?" he said.

"I couldn't afford one at first, and then I just thought I would save the money. I'm never more than a block or two away from a phone."

"It's something people have," he said. "You're trying to live a civilized life now, out of the woods. How about getting a phone? Besides, you need to be able to call the police."

I signed a statement at the Alma Police Department with Jim as witness. I talked to Norman Koivisto, whom Nate had described as an asshole, from the city attorney's office. I cried, expressed my fear, showed the scars on my face.

"I want a restraining order," I said. Norman Koivisto led me to believe there wouldn't be any problem getting one. I had lunch at Angelica's. I saw Hal and my old neighbor from Tupa, Dale Adams, the artist, there. I asked Dale if he could help me get locks installed on my door.

"You know Nate," I said. "You know how he thinks. I need someone who can secure my place to prevent him from getting in. Can you help me?"

"No. I don't think so. Nate's a friend of mine," Dale said.

Something became clear. Dale and Hal both knew that Nate had chased more than one young woman out of town. Hal didn't say anything, neither of them did. Cowards, like meteors, leave a glowing tail.

"He's been trying to kill me. I need help. Is there anyone you can recommend?"

"You might try Ricky True."

"Do you know him? Do you know his number?"

"No."

I looked up the Ricky True Lock Shop in the tiny Alma phone book, smaller than a school notebook, hooked to the phone booth placed outside the Alma Police Department building. I called him.

Ricky was young and new in town or he wouldn't have helped me either. No one wanted to do anything to make Nate mad at them. I told Ricky I needed to make my apartment impossibly secure.

On Tuesday, I met him over my lunch hour. I had bars put on the door and window at the bottom of the stairs, a new, heavy-duty deadbolt lock which had to be locked with a key from the inside installed in the front door. Ricky bolted two brackets on each side of the door frame just above the door knob on the door in the bedroom, which led to an impossibly small porch. Then he rested a two-by-four in the brackets, so that if you crawled on the roof and tried to enter the house through that porch, the door couldn't be opened. (If Nate ever got in while I was home I planned to beat him with the two by four.) He charged me fifty-five dollars. I paid by check.

The same day I got the bars put in, the phone was installed. I was watching my back, as they say.

I could walk to a skating rink from my apartment. I invited Andy over that night to skate with me. We found the light switch on the pole, and laced up our skates on the bench. We skated to the sibilant sound of our blades on the ice until our feet got cold. The rink was two blocks from my house and one block from the Alma Hospital. At night, the hospital was as quiet as one of the wilderness lakes.

Norman Koivisto had promised to have Nate in court by Friday. I called him Thursday and Norman said Nate wouldn't be in court for another week.

Nate disappeared during this time. I'm sure someone told him what I was up to. He stayed at home, didn't drink, and didn't so much as call me. But I didn't know that this was his new intent. I was still frightened every day. Several Fridays passed and no court date had been set.

Finally, I got a call from Mr. Koivisto that Nate had been served a summons. Now, I was worried that Nate would be angry. I wanted a restraining order to protect me from further violence. I didn't want to put Nate in jail; I only wanted to be able to feel safe in my home.

Norman said the court date was set two weeks out to give them time to deliver the summons. I called Norman Koivisto on Thursday before court. With three jobs, especially one as a waitress, it was difficult to take time off work. I learned that I would not have to appear in court and that Nate had been charged with assault. I worried that night.

Friday morning, I called to ask about the assault charge. Norman explained that the charge was coming from the City of Alma and was necessary for the restraining order. Then he explained that Nate would make his plea that morning and then there would be a trial.

I asked him to call me after court and tell me what Nate said.

Norman Koivisto called about 1:30 and said Nate had never appeared in court because he had never been served a summons.

"Why not?"

"Because he doesn't have an address."

"This is a town of five thousand people. Everyone knows where he lives!" I was flabbergasted. I knew his address.

"We only have a post office box. We can't serve a summons to a post office box."

I had been harassed and beaten, my life had been threatened, and I had done nothing to provoke it. I couldn't do anything to protect myself. This inefficiency just put me in greater danger.

"As long as this has happened, would you like to forget it?" Norman asked.

I said, "No. I don't want to forget it."

He said it would be another two weeks before a summons could be served, and meanwhile, Nate was leaving me alone, which is what you had hoped to gain by the charges anyway, he said. So if I didn't do anything, the charges could lie dormant.

"They could?" I said.

"Yes."

"The case will just sit here as it is, ready, in case anything else happens. The statute of limitations is two years," he said.

Chapter 56

On Friday, I found letters from Andy in my post office box.

Dear Anna,

Wednesday night.

The stove is finally hot so I can close the damper part way. Steam pours up out of the kettle. Pink Floyd's "Us and Them" is playing over the radio and I can see the full moon light through the window. I am still thinking about skating with you the other day, me with my hockey stick and you doing gentle pirouettes.

I missed you today, even checked for you at work, but you weren't there. I agreed to give Katie Baxter a ride to her cabin at 5:30, so I left town early only to get stuck on a steep hill leading up to her place. Boy was I stuck. The sun was setting a beautiful orange and I could see it was a race against available light. I shoveled like Hell, got out, and then couldn't control skidding backward, then sideways, down the hill. When my rear end went in the ditch, I was stuck broadside on the single lane road vulnerable to traffic coming either way. The downhill cars would be unable to stop, and cars going uphill would be building speed to get up. I was frightened. I shoveled like mad, scraped some gravel, laid out my chains, then inched around until finally I was heading in the right direction. That's what I get for messing around with another woman, huh? I can't get over the shock of seeing the bars being put on the door and windows of your apartment. And you tell me there's no need for concern. I am wondering if that could be true. Incidentally I'm writing this letter after reading your two to show you who is the writer around here.

What can I say about our Alma relationship? God must have willed this. Who else or what else would have been so clever? Who could arrange such subtle pain and emotional confusion. I wish I could see a great good in all this mire the way I could have done ten years ago. I have no answers, just a gut level feeling that all will work out, if we will it to hard enough.

You are young, energetic, intelligent, and you have formed no lean handful of appealing values. When you speak, for some reason I feel I know precisely where your heart is, where you're coming from. But then I realize we're strangers. I hope the rest of you lets as much light shine through as what I've only seen on the surface.

I wish I could say something that would make it all easier.

Andy

Anna,

Thursday night

"Only Women Bleed" is playing on WAKX as I befriend my stove again. Men bleed too. I saw Chuck today. He visited with Nate, and listened to his side of the story. Nate told Chuck about your bond with him. What Chuck implied was so different from what I have heard from you, it shook my confidence. I decided not to hunt you down, for I knew my confusion would only promote a night of analyzing. This situation is getting so bizarre I don't know what to think anymore. All I want is peace of mind. I am not sure how I will get it, but I will be cooling our friendship. Sometimes I feel that all this has killed my Alma experience, at least its innocence. I can't see how we'll ever live in peace together in Alma country as long as Nate loves you. I need to feel your freedom in order to give myself fully to you. There is too much fear and suspicion, too much tension, too many half-truths for me to be anything but confused and cold. My chimney caught fire tonight and burned with a roar. No apparent damage except I aged a year. I cleaned myself of the past. "Tomorrow," Thoreau said, "is the first day of the rest of our life."

Andy

I had started to like Andy with the first letter, but the second irritated me. People were always fair and neutral when it came to Nate.

Andy wanted to cool our relationship? Fine with me, I thought.

❦

April twenty-first the Miss Alma Pageant committee met at the Alma High School. Women ages eighteen to twenty-six were welcome to attend. Ben's wife, Wendy, was involved in the Miss Alma Pageant.

"Won't you join us?" Wendy asked.

"What would be my talent?" I said. "Could I stand on stage and embroider?"

She laughed.

Wendy was kind to ask me, but her invitation made me feel lonely. I was sure she had never invited an Arrow Trail hippie into a local contest. Her pity hurt.

⚬

I found the Battered Women's Advocate office by accident. It was located right next to the Suds-Yer-Duds Laundromat. I happened to see the sign. I met with Liz Hane, informally at first, and then I scheduled an appointment.

"I've been washing my clothes here since 1978. Have I missed your office all this time?" I asked.

"No. We just opened this office in April," Liz said.

Liz had short curly hair. She wore gold hoop earrings and pastel colored pantsuits and skirts. She was soft-spoken and soft-skinned. She listened to me with a serious look on her face. I found out later that she was Wes Hane's sister. Wes had helped Nate's third girlfriend leave town. Wes also owned the car full of garbage I had slept in one night. I didn't know if Liz knew that this was the same Nate. If she did, she never let on, and I didn't tell her, either.

I talked for an hour non-stop. My story came out with force to her sympathetic ears. She advised me to contact Norman Koivisto again.

⚬

From Norman, I learned that what he told me previously was a lie. Suddenly, there was no such thing as putting charges on hold. Norman told me that when I didn't follow through it had become "an incomplete process of law." The charges I had filed could no longer be used against Nate. It was the equivalent of starting over. I couldn't figure out why he had lied to me. I didn't understand this system. I was disillusioned by what I had always vaguely believed about society, about authority, about systems of protection.

It pushed me over the edge. Any human compassion for Nate that I was holding onto left me. I went to the police department, and got a handful of statements, three-part forms used to describe one's involvement in or witness to a crime. I typed up my memory of every incident I had with Nate in our whole history for the police, all in one day.

&

I smoked pot after work and withdrew into myself. Ellie approached me at the Tippy Canoe while I was in one of these inner reveries. I tried to tell her that I thought I could almost see the purpose of life, as if it were actually right in front of my face, separated by a skin-thin membrane. If I could only find a way to get through to the other side, everything would be clear. I could feel it.

"You're crazy," she said, and walked away.

Chapter 57

Ben gave me some old paint he had, and I painted the kitchen in bright orange and green. He said he had it left over from painting a child's room. Ben's kindness pleased me. I had just enough for one orange and three green walls. I hung a Finnish fabric painting, fabric stretched over a square wooden frame, that I bought at a local gift shop on the largest green wall. The stretching had orange in it along with the same green in the paint, so it tied everything together. It was bright, friendly, and felt promising. I did my best to be the way I thought other people were.

I set my bottle collection up in the living room. I even looked at local antique stores some afternoons to see if I could find any additions to my bottle collection. I left the shades open so the rips in them didn't show.

On my way to the post office one summer day, I saw my boss, Dave, from the *Messenger*, go into the VFW. On my return, he came out of the bar and was weaving around, unsteady on his feet. I hurried to get up behind him as he crossed the street to tease him about weaving around. He fell over before I had a chance. He didn't even brace himself, so he landed on his thumb. He broke it, we found out later. He also hit his forehead. I helped him up off Sheridan Street and Central Avenue, and brought him back to the office. I looked for a hint of embarrassment for his drunkenness, his clumsiness, and he didn't have it. He seemed lost, as if he'd been pulled into a black hole.

His family sent him to the hospital and he dried out in there.

"He plans to drink again," Emma said.

❧

On Dave's first day back at work, I noticed the smell of booze on his breath. I took myself to lunch at Angelica's. I ordered homemade toast and jelly, and read the paper slowly. Something urged me to look up and out the large picture window overlooking Central Avenue, and I happened to notice Jim and Katie talking to each other on the sidewalk. I noticed them laughing together, and I got a bad feeling in my throat. Katie put on a helmet and rode off on the back of Jim's motorcycle. The next time I saw him, he had a hickey on his neck. I assumed that Katie and him were having an affair. Poor Chuck, I thought.

❧

I saw Andy again. I had just finished work at the New Moon, and stopped at the Tippy Canoe on my way home. I was just sitting at the bar, counting my tips, and drinking a glass of beer.

"Where did you live before you lived here," he asked.

"Spring Lake."

"Did you live on Spring Lake?"

"No. Lake Elizabeth."

"You're kidding. I used to spend time on Lake Elizabeth. When I was a child. My dad took retreats there, and I went with him."

I learned that Andy's mother had died in childbirth. His father and he had often visited the Society of Jesus Retreat House on the shores of the second bay of Lake Elizabeth. That was his start at the contemplative life and led to him becoming a priest.

I told him that our house was on the shore of the first bay of the same lake and though he was older than I, we were both floating around on that same lake fifteen years before we met.

"I dreamed of a white bear last night. I knew something special was going to happen to me today," he said.

With this link of history, we became closer. It was as if he could see me now from a different side, and he wasn't so scared of Nate's point of view. I was comforted by the change in him.

We talked until the bar closed. He walked home to my apartment. He read me an essay titled, "Where We Are," by Gary Snyder, from the magazine *Parabola: Myth and the Quest for Meaning*, from an issue called "The Old Ones." Gary Snyder said he perceived more in a place than its location on a map. I was entranced by these ideas and by Andy's voice reading to me. I was as if in a dream—soft inside, and filled with color and possibilities.

⌘

Chuck, Katie, Lee, DeeDee all told me that Nate had stopped drinking again. They all said that he had changed. They urged me to see him and I agreed. We talked. He listened. I told him I was proud for him, but I didn't want to have a relationship. He took the news as if he were a changed man.

Chapter 58

Nate called me Friday, June 27, 1980, and said, "Hear that?" he said, and I heard him opening a bottle. "That's a beer," he said.

He showed up at my apartment and started drinking a bottle of brandy I had there. I seized it out of his hands and dumped it down the sink. He told me he was going to spend the next day at the Tippy Canoe and he left.

I was afraid to do anything all day.

I went over to DeeDee's and did not go home. Nate crawled up on the roof of my apartment, and came in through the window in the living room. Of course, Ricky True and I never thought he would get on the roof to enter a window, so those windows had not been secured. Dale probably would have known that Nate would think that way, if he had been willing to help me.

DeeDee's house was right next to work, about three blocks from Harvey Street. I hid there, mostly in her unrented apartment in the back of her store. I was afraid to be seen. I was afraid for Lee and DeeDee that Nate would figure out I was there.

DeeDee got her laundry off the line in her backyard and told me Nate's truck was parked on the road alongside of my house; there was a ladder leaning against the wall. No one had rented the basement apartment. The owner lived in Minneapolis. Nate could have moved in and no one would have done anything about it.

He was at my apartment—DeeDee kept checking—on into the

afternoon on Sunday, June twenty-ninth. When his car was finally gone, I went home just for a visit and got my laundry. I saw the sign outside of the Lutheran church:

A Switch in Time Saves Crime.

What an aggravating sign! Maybe you can beat a horseshoe into shape, but human beings need some other treatment.

I saw Nate on Chapman Street, on my way back from Suds-Yer-Duds. He was on foot, as though he were looking for me.

"I'm not drinking," he said. "I'm not going to be."

"Nate," I said, "Remember when you used to put the cable up in front of the driveway to let people know you wanted to be alone? The cable is up; stay away. I don't want to see you any more."

Chapter 59

It was nearly four years since I had moved to Alma. My parents had never visited me. My parents had never seen the cabin where I had lived with Nate or Tupa. Of course, my parents had not seen my apartment. I had it in my mind that they hadn't been free to visit me before because I was living in sin, but they never said that was the reason. They never gave a reason. I forgot my training from Holy Mary, and gave up being honest about my feelings. I never asked if the feeling I had that they were ashamed of me was correct.

My parents were going to be in Duluth for some reason, and they planned to visit me in Alma on Friday for the parade on July Fourth. I told them that Don Blix, who wrote for the *Alma Voice*, would be there.

"Whitepine" Don Blix, as he was known, who founded the Independent Firsherman's Party, announced his presidential campaign on June eighteenth. Joe Weir, who worked both at Ben's shop, and the *Alma Voice*, told us all about it at work. "Whitepine" Don was going to have a float in the Fourth of July parade. Joe was going to ride in it. My parents wanted to see the parade. They said they would arrive in the morning around eight or nine.

Thursday night, the smell at the bottom of the stairs when I first opened the door reminded me that Max's cat box needed cleaning.

At nine o'clock, I noticed my apartment was filthy. I started in the bathroom. I turned on the light and I could see all of the dirt. Every piece of dust amplified my revulsion that I half recognized as self-hatred. Mom would be sure to notice. She would instinctively know that I was miserable if she saw those fuzz balls around the toilet; the hair curled around the feet of the old-style bathtub and stuck to the painted white bathroom floor would give me away.

Mom did everything for us when we were children. I thought of how many times she made us supper. She cleaned and scrubbed. As I cleaned the bathroom, I could hear again the water running in the bathtub at my parents' house; I could hear the bus coming down the hill, see the May flowers blooming along the fence as I carried the mail up the driveway—I could smell the sweet, damp mail: bills, book clubs, Publisher's Clearing House. The past seemed so smooth now and rhythmical, with all the jags missing.

I could recall the way I ran away at age twelve, but not why I ran away. I thought my mother must have enjoyed some parts of being my mother: watching me run up or down the driveway to the school bus, calling my friends, having the friends call me, eating supper: our tater tots and hot dogs, hamburgers on the grill. What was so bad? What was wrong—when now I remembered it as so beautiful? It was beautiful. I thought my parents weren't happy then and I had wanted them to be. I wanted them to be happy now, too. I wanted people to be happier than they were.

When I was twelve-years-old, I was grounded, but my mom said I could still work. I cleaned Susan Stone's house for her mom. I called in sick. I had some money. I waited on the corner just down from my house. Larry picked me up and drove me to Stillwater. I bought a tiny ashtray in a shop there and then walked to the armory dance. Susan knew where I was going. She told my dad where I was.

The sound of running away was better than the reality. The music was playing and I wasn't having fun. I was too shy to dance, so I just stood near the door. My dad didn't have trouble finding me when he showed up—I suppose he told the police that I was in there, so they let him enter without paying. I didn't notice a stamp on his hand. All of this must have been planned, but I didn't remember planning it; I certainly hadn't made any long-term plans. My dad took me out of there but not before I twisted my gum around my finger so many times he finally wrapped his hand around mine and took the gum away.

Another time I ran away from home, I got sent to an emergency foster home. Several single beds filled a large bedroom downstairs of this house where all of the foster children slept. I was on speed. I had a candy bar for supper. My legs were so thin I had a space between my thighs when I stood with my knees together. I stood there in the hall light looking in the mirror. I didn't live anywhere. I didn't go to school, and all was good because of the space between my legs. I sat out in the hall in the unfinished basement on the cement floor. I wrote lists of things to do—lots of lists of things—mainly projects. I had lots of projects; lists of projects were even better. To do was to be; to be was to do (as long as I was thin). If I wasn't thin then: to be thin was to be. I was thin and had long lists of good intentions. I shut off the hall light, groped in darkness back to the room, and saw a witch standing right by my bed. I froze. I knew it could have been the speed messing up my mind, but I wasn't sure. I stared at her, trying to read the witch's mind, to determine what she would do. I finally risked my life and decided to touch her. She was a lamp.

As I frantically cleaned my apartment in Alma, I wondered if my life was any better now than it had been. Having my parents come to visit felt like a test for which I was not prepared.

Less than twelve hours before their arrival; the place was under a microscope and everything looked dirty and clumped, instead of beautiful and complex. I scrubbed, first with a scrub brush; then I brought a lamp from my bedroom, one with a movable head so I could focus. Why did someone put white paint on the floor in the bathroom? Why didn't they leave the wood alone like the rest of the apartment? I took a toothbrush, and a rag and attacked the dirt. I opened the closet in the bathroom, pulled on the yellow screwdriver that was wedged in the hole where there should have been a door knob, and was just going to put the scrub bucket away, and God—what a mess! Why hadn't I ever got a doorknob? And why did I keep so much junk? I took everything out of the closet. I wiped the dust from the white plastic first-aid kit. I threw out the six-year-old jar of Vaseline. I refolded my towels and my washcloths and restacked them neatly.

The place needed to be clean beneath the surface. I planned to shake the rugs out in the morning and vacuum. Dirty dishes next. On my way through the foyer I heard the door creak. Why hadn't I locked the door? Tonight of all nights.

Nate came up the stairs, and walked into the living room as if he lived there, as if I didn't matter, and I felt my rage, that rage, can't control it, if I let go he will kill me and if I don't—

"Hi," he said, with the arrogance of kings.

"What do you want? What are you doing here?"

"What's up?"

"My parents are coming tomorrow." I could already hear the pathetic appeal in my voice. Why did I always have to beg? "My parents will be here in the morning, Nate, they—I have things to do, and I have to get some sleep."

"Can I see them, too?"

He had to be kidding. He had to be.

I said, "No. You aren't even supposed to be seeing me!"

What happened next happened fast. He threw a coffee cup. Then it looked as though the 1890 Mason jar full of my favorite antique buttons, the white sailor and the five-pointed star, just flew through the air and exploded. Tommy had given me that jar on my twelfth birthday; they were MY buttons.

"Damn you—damn you!" I said.

He reached for me, and scratched my face, while he choked me.

"How dare you!" he said.

"Nate, Nate I'm chok—"

"How dare you tell me what to do! If I want to see your parents, I will. I will!"

"Nate—Nate, please, I can't breathe, " I squeaked.

He let loose, and I cried and started to pick up the glass and the buttons, no time to feel, no time for madness, have to pick up the buttons, the glass.

"Oh, Tommy, I'm sorry, sorry Nate broke your jar," I said as I started to sort through the buttons, taking out the glass.

My neck and jaw were bruised. My face had a scratch on it. He was sober. I knew he was sober. This detail entered my mind as if I were witness to a fact in a mystery that changed everything. It occurred to me that he usually drank only so he could be violent and have a socially acceptable excuse. He was smart enough to see that unacceptable behavior became tolerable if you said you were drunk, especially in a town where so many people drank. He was sober now to let me know he had more control over himself than he pretended to have. This was the truth: he acted out of control, but he wasn't. He was acting.

Finally he left. My shame prevented me from calling the police. I was so focused on impressing my parents. I was shattered that my life was the way it was. All the pretending I could muster wouldn't cover up the mark on my face and throat. Nate came in with his impeccably cruel sixth sense and made sure my day would be spoiled; then he left. He had the accuracy of radar and the instability of a tornado. How would I explain the scratch, I wondered? I decided to put make-up over it. Even if they noticed I didn't think they would ask. I'd tell them that things were all right with Nate because I was ashamed of the truth.

I vacuumed to get the rest of the glass off the floor. Another mess. How I resented cleaning up another mess caused by Nate. I still had to shake out the rug in the morning, and empty Max's box, and breakfast—they will want breakfast, I thought. I finally lay down on the double mattress with no frame or box spring. The early morning light came through my cracked yellow shade. Why hadn't I ever made curtains? If I slept it was only sleeping halfway, as if my dreams occurred six inches outside of my head.

In kindergarten, we had practiced pretending. We had a big box painted orange with windows cut in it, and a door that split in two the way a real bus door opens. Wooden chairs were lined up inside for seats. We pretended we knew how to act properly on the bus. I watched Miss Nancy on Romper Room. I remembered the Do-Bee song about always doing everything right.

The day with my parents was a refresher course in pretending. Miss Nancy, from Romper Room, would have been so proud of me.

My parents knocked on the door just after 9:00 a.m. Everything that was wrong in my life seemed magnified, the way the dirt had seemed the night before. But I pretended I didn't notice. I pretended the coffee I made campfire-style—because the core had broken from my clear glass pot—was not too black. I pretended I was not ashamed that I had a screwdriver for a doorknob in my bathroom closet door. I pretended the eggs I made for Dad were not too hard, the way I knew he hated them. I pretended I was frantically, frantically happy, frantically, frantically clean. I pretended the scratch on my face wasn't there. I pretended I had never had a Mason jar full of buttons.

We visited at my apartment. Then drove around town, and up the Arrow Trail. We drove down to Grahek's and I showed them where my car had been held.

I introduced my parents to Chuck and Katie, and Lee and DeeDee, at the Tippy Canoe. Dave even stopped in, so they met him. I drank more than I usually did because that, too, was a sign of happiness. We watched the parade. We saw Don Blix's presidential float. I told my parents that in Don's most recent article, he had named Hal Maki as his Secretary of the Treasury, as no one was closer with a buck than Hal. The newly crowned Miss Alma floated behind Don Blix.

I gave my parents a tour of the *Messenger* office, and of Ben's print shop. I showed them the New Moon, where I worked, but we had dinner at the Habit Asylum, in the basement steakhouse part, because they served food they liked better.

They showed some interest in my show-and-tell, where I worked, where I drank, where I lived. I didn't want to tell them about what had happened with Nate. I didn't want to tell anyone, as though by not telling I could keep pretending. I just wanted it to go away.

Then I must have had enough to drink, because I just fell into my despair. "Mom and Dad, Nate is terrible to me. He won't leave me alone. Just last night he came in my apartment and choked me. Do you see the scratch?"

If they had seen it before, they didn't say.

"What are you going to do?" my dad said.

"I'm trying to get him to leave me alone. I've called the police, and filed charges, but nothing happens. I don't know what to do," I said, foggy from the drink, uncertain what I was looking for, or hoping for. They looked sad of course which made it worse for me, but I also couldn't tell if they were judging me. It's sort of my comeuppance for having a bad reputation. History was never solid with my parents because we never talked about anything, and we never agreed on what happened. Without language, there is no solidity. So, though I sought sympathy and love, maybe even some help, in my weak moments I felt even more alone and ashamed.

Chapter 60

I heard from Nate five minutes after my parents drove away on Saturday, July fifth. The phone lines now reached up the Arrow Trail, and Nate had a telephone. He hassled me all afternoon and into the evening over the phone. I kept answering so that he wouldn't come into town.

He said, "Who are you expecting to call you that you answer the phone so sweetly?"

I got mad so the next time he called, I left the phone off the hook. As I predicted, he came to town saying he thought he would catch me on the phone to "him."

My phone continued to ring and ring and ring, day after day, all week long. Saturday morning without thinking, I picked up the phone when it rang. The phone sat in the foyer of my apartment on the neat piece of particle board atop the radiator just at the top of the stairs. The bulletin board above the phone still had the same notices on it plus Andy's poem.

"Hello," I said.

"Hello. This is Nate. I was on my way to Alaska because I can't live without you. I was all ready to start a new life, and I realized that I can't stand it. I'm going to end it."

I heard a gun shot, and the sound of the phone dropping.

"Hello. Nate, Nate? Nate?" I dropped my phone, too, and ran to DeeDee and Lee's house. They called Katie to ask her to check on Nate.

It would be faster than sending an ambulance. Back at home, I heard the phone ring again. I picked it up thinking it would be Lee, and it was Nate.

"Nate?"

"I know that was a dirty trick, but I am going to do it now."

I heard another gun shot, the same dropping phone. This time I had already called, already sent a neighbor. I couldn't think of anything else to do, so I walked down the stairs and sat on the angled steps of my porch. I just sat there. The leaves were slowly dropping off the elm tree onto my crooked porch on the corner of Harvey Street. I didn't cry. I was beyond tears. I looked outward and inward at the same time, focused on my future. I wondered what it would be like to live the rest of my life if Nate actually killed himself. It would be a mark for sure, but if he wasn't dead, I likely would be. If he killed himself, would that be a victory?

DeeDee found me sitting there, staring out.

"Katie just called. She drove to Nate's and found him sitting at the sawmill."

"Alive?"

"Alive."

"Wounded?"

"No."

"He won't stop, will he?" I said.

Chapter 61

On Sunday I decided to go to Ben's shop to work on the American Legion book. About twenty minutes after I arrived the phone began to ring.

Ring, ring.

"I just want you to know that you are still a fucking cunt." Click.

Ring, ring.

Ring, ring.

"Remember I'm going to make your life so miserable that you'll have to leave town." Click.

I locked up at Ben's, walked home, locked up my house, and sought shelter with company in public.

I walked into the New Moon, where Ellie was just getting off work. I told her I needed to get away from Nate. She said she would join me for dinner. We ate downstairs at the Habit Asylum, as we thought Nate wouldn't expect that.

The formal dining room was in the basement, where I had just eaten with my parents. The bar took up the front half of the upstairs, and the game room took up the back half. There is a front and back stairway to the dining room. The back stairway led to the game room, the front stairway led to the bar. We were paying for our meal, when I saw Nate on the back stairs. Our eyes met, and he turned around. We went up the back stairs, trying to avoid him. I saw him sitting at the bar. I turned to leave.

Ellie said, "Would you like to go back to the Moon?" We headed for the rear door of the game room. Nate rushed at me and put a cigarette out on my back. He started to push me toward the door. He knocked me down. He yanked on my legs and tried to pull me out the door.

I jumped down and got my hands around a booth to get back inside and prevent him from taking me with him.

"Could someone please help me?" I yelled.

One of the men playing pool yelled, "Hey!"

Nate left the room for a moment, and then he turned and squeezed my arm to the bone. "When the cops catch me, I'll kill them, and if I get away I'll kill you, too," he said.

Ellie pulled a toothpick out of my cheek, and gave me a napkin to stop the bleeding. When Nate first approached me, he had had a toothpick in his mouth.

"I guess he must have stuck this in my face," I said, dabbing the blood.

He returned, and there were people around me.

"You poor baby," he said.

Ellie and I signed statements at the Police Department.

We tried to press charges, again. I got my wounds documented at the hospital: X-ray elbow, multiple abrasions, contusions, superficial scratches, and puncture wound, face.

There were witnesses.

I talked to Liz Hane again from the Battered Women's Advocates. She encouraged me.

"You're not alone in this. This is America," she said. "You don't have to live in fear for your life."

Nevertheless, I stayed that night in Lee and DeeDee's empty apartment, in the back of their store. I was too afraid to stay alone.

It got more difficult for me to go out. I didn't feel right. It was as if I had woken up to find my nose growing out the side of my head. I tried to get my nose on right before I could leave, but I didn't know how, so I went out all screwed up. Nothing was right.

The phone rang no less than fifty times in a row, non-stop, whenever I was home. Once I was at work late, and the phone rang there too. It just kept ringing. I found out later that Nate used to drive by a phone booth, dial my number and drive away.

I stopped at home after work on Friday; I walked up the stairs into my apartment, cautiously. For some reason I was hypervigilant. I looked in my bedroom. The two-by-four rested where I had placed it, over the wooden brackets in front of the porch door in my bedroom. A claw hammer was hanging over it, a cruel statement from Nate. I noticed my pillowcase was missing from my pillow, and my legs began to shake. My nickels, the ones I had counted endlessly while Nate had cried his apologies to me, were gone. The display case was unharmed, but every single bottle, marble, and box in my collection was missing, even the ceramic ashtray, and the bottle from Andy.

I called the police.

Chapter 62

On Sunday, Nate broke into my house again, through the window, making off with my jewelry. I notified the police on Monday morning. They said they couldn't arrest Nate because they didn't have any proof.

On Monday, during my lunch shift, I found a letter from Nate left on a table at the New Moon. Nate flattered me for being wiser than he was, but selfish. He said that I didn't want to share with him what I knew, and so his life was miserable. Right! Just withholding the secrets of the universe from *you*, Nate. He went on with another apology of sorts. He surrendered, and said his habits weren't going to change much. Yes. He is in the habit of chasing women out of town. Hard habit to break. Then he started talking about the monster, his monster, as he called it. "At one point, I thought you'd be strong enough to help me with it," he said.

That's exactly what I had thought: I had thought I could help him. He no longer believed I could, and neither did I.

Another Tuesday. I was back for the long day at the *Messenger*. I still had not slept at my apartment since just after the fifth of July, eighteen days ago. Katie called me twice at work to make a deal: she said that Nate would promise to leave me alone, if I would agree to drop the charges against him. She said that I could get my personal property back if I would make this deal with Nate. I didn't understand why Katie was involved. Sometimes she thought that she understood Nate so that made her safe from his antics. It was true that he never bothered some people; that's what people said. What he was doing to me was known as *bothering me*, something he didn't do to everyone. It was a mystery.

I had lunch with Chuck at Angelica's.

"Have you heard from Nate?" I couldn't resist asking.

"He told me that he was going to kill you. He didn't know when but that eventually he knew he would," Chuck said. I was only hearing what I already believed, so I just sat there looking blank. Chuck was nice enough not to blame me for my situation. He never told me what to do.

❧

I visited again with Liz Hane, the Battered Woman's Advocate. She gave me some pamphlets and flyers with statistics and general information about Battered Women. I felt so different from her. Her clothes were neat. She wore matching jewelry: post pearls with a matching necklace or pin. I knew I could never be like Liz Hane.

I took the pamphlets to my apartment, sat on the brown rocker, and read them carefully, again and again. The words on these flyers fascinated me as if they contained a candle flame. Staring at them, I lost track of time.

One flyer listed statistics with bullets:

- Women are victimized by an indifferent society as well as by men.
- Only ten percent of battered women ever call the police.
- When women do sign complaints, only ten percent of the batterers are ever prosecuted.
- If a woman decides to prosecute, the only witness is

usually the victim, and she is usually called a "bad" witness.

- In Kansas City in 1976, eighty percent of the women murdered by their husbands and boyfriends had called the police one to five times before being killed.
- It is unrealistic to expect the victim to sign the complaint and press the charges when she is given no protection from further assaults. The legal system interprets this reluctance as a desire to remain battered rather than fear of punishment by the batterer. It is inferred that the woman likes to be battered, or that she lacks courage.
- Sometimes the psychological bond between the couple is the equivalent of a physical restraint.
- If the couple is not married and does not own joint property, an order for protection should be issued simply with evidence of violence.
- The Woman:
  > has the ability to withstand intense pain. She
  > readily assumes the blame for things.
  - The Man:
  > perceives himself as inadequate.

I was amazed to see this written down. The words spared me from total blame.

Another sheet discussed the "Provocative Nature Myth."

Many women are made to feel that they want to be abused and that they are somehow bringing the abuse on themselves, for some pleasure. In reality, many women have emotional problems caused by their victimization. They do not choose to be battered because of some personality defect. They develop behavioral disturbances because they live in violence. Some women suffer from learned helplessness as they become out of control of their environment, so they may not leave even if the opportunity arises."

The "Phases of Abuse" were described in a neatly done, tri-fold brochure on lime-green paper. I admired the typestyle and layout.

- Phase One: Tension building.
- Phase Two: Acute battering.
- Phase Three: Kindness. The woman chooses to believe this stage represents what the batterer is *really* like. The woman may trade psychological and physical safety for this temporary dream state.

On the next panel were the "characteristics of the batterer."

- Low self-esteem
- Believes the myths about females who submit to violence.
- Believes in male supremacy.
- Blames others for his actions.
- Is pathologically jealous.
- Presents a dual personality.
- Suffers severe stress reactions: uses drinking, and wife-beating to cope.
- Uses sex to enhance his self-esteem.
- Does not believe violent behavior should have negative consequences.
- Is unpredictable.
- Engages in unusual sexuality.
- Has a history of economic deprivation.

I thought about this as I walked to work. What I read said that women were aware of the potential for death. The women knew that the man was capable of killing her and himself. At the same time, women believed that the man was fragile and could fall apart at any minute; they also believed that their lover was omnipotent and could do things that others couldn't do.

I wondered whether my behavior was ineffective self-defense or provocative in nature. I had believed that Carol must not have loved Nate well enough. That's why they didn't get along, I thought. I wanted to believe that loving him would be enough.

I didn't fit the mold of the battered woman entirely. I was glad to be one who broke away, or at least tried to break away. If I was going to die, I was going to die trying to get away.

Chapter 63

On Friday, July twenty-fifth, Nate appeared in court and was instructed to leave me alone. I moved back into my apartment. The next day he called me. I called the police. The following Tuesday he was arrested. On Friday, August eighth, he was released from jail.

The next day, Jim said he saw Nate two houses away from my apartment. He saw him at the Tippy Canoe a few hours later.

On Sunday, Nate knocked on my door at ten-twenty p.m. I called the police and he disappeared.

Nate called me at work at nine-fifteen p.m. on Monday. I called the police.

Nate was supposed to appear before his probation officer on August twelfth. I called and learned that he hadn't shown up.

No local official was making a serious effort to keep him away from me. I called the newspaper in Duluth on Wednesday, August thirteenth, to tell them what was happening to me.

Chapter 64

DeeDee called early on Sunday. She woke me up. She got papers delivered to the store, so she had seen it right away.

"Hello," I said.

"You made the front page."

"My God! I'll be right over."

It was a cool, bright morning. The sun was just coming through the trees at the horizon. It was quiet in town. The church goers hadn't even begun to stir. I knocked on DeeDee's door.

"Can you believe it? You're on the front page!"

The paper was on the table by a full cup of coffee. I could see the headline before I sat down:

Fear of retribution leaves battered woman scared, angry

"The reporter didn't tell me it would be on the front page. I bet they ran it because of that woman in Duluth who was just killed by her boyfriend. He had been stalking her, too, same as Nate," I tried to sound logical, but my knees were shaking.

I read aloud. "No matter where twenty-two year old Kristin (not her real name) goes in Alma, she can't quite shake the feeling that someone is stalking her.

"In her apartment, at her three jobs, out on the town with friends, she never feels safe.

"It's not that Kristin is paranoid. She has been followed and assaulted before. And despite the cooperation of Alma police, her fear grows every day."

"I feel relieved about that," I said. "I asked her to make the Alma police sound cooperative."

"Why'd you do that? What have they done for you?" DeeDee said.

"It just seemed smart. I can't have them mad at me. I need them."

I read the rest of the article quickly, and then slowly, while I drank my coffee. I didn't like seeing the quotes, and misquotes, things I had sort of said but not actually said.

"This is the reporter quoting me: 'I hear that most battered women drop charges they initiate. I didn't drop them. It's not easy to charge someone with battering you. People keep saying to me, "You're not badly hurt, you're not dead, why do you have to charge him?" Do I have to be dead for it to mean anything?' That isn't what I said, exactly. It's not a direct quote."

Chapter 65

On Monday morning, a stranger walked up to me and said, "Are you Kristin?"

I said, "Yes."

"I don't think it's right of you to ruin the reputation of a bar and restaurant. You made it sound as if women are beaten there all the time."

What? I couldn't believe it. I was shocked. I just stood there looking at her, and then she walked off. I worried about that comment all day. The reputation of the restaurant was more important than my safety? It must comfort them somehow to blame me. But how bold they were to tell me they were blaming me! They didn't have to worry that I would slash their tires after hearing their opinion, the way they would if they told Nate what they thought of him. I bet no one in town had approached Nate after the article.

This was a war of sorts. Some people's lives don't unfold like a boxed blue shirt; mine sure didn't. Messy lives and the people living them were seen as a threat to the even seams.

Chapter 66

For most women there were two reasons to avoid sex: one was because you might get pregnant and the other one was that it would ruin your reputation. When I left Nate I couldn't get pregnant and I'd already ruined my reputation by living with him, and by living on the Arrow Trail. I discovered that I needed to develop my own inner sense of morals, to stop making decisions based on what others wanted of me. In order to make my own decisions, I needed my own opinion.

I began to think.

Chuck heard that Nate was dating a young girl; this one was sixteen, and lived in Babbitt,

"Nate is sure lucky to get all those women," Chuck said.

"You needn't feel so envious of young women who get involved with Nate," I said. "They'll be miserable before long."

"It's just that I love women, and I've had so few of them."

"Nate is screwed up and so am I and probably so is that young girl," I said.

Chuck looked stunned, as if a stereotype had just broken inside of his head.

Chapter 67

Katie came over and cried. Chuck didn't like that she was having an affair with Jim Weeks. He was making her choose. She didn't know what to do. She didn't think it was fair that she had to choose.

"I don't understand," I said. "Why is he making you choose this time?"

"He found a note that Jim wrote to me. He said he loved me. That bothered Chuck. He always thought that I had a bigger sex drive than he had. I guess this is different to him, but not to me," Katie said.

She loved Jim, but she preferred her life as it was; she didn't want to change. She wasn't sure what she would decide.

It was nice for me that she came over. I had spent so many hours on so many of my friends' couches it was a relief to be able to listen to someone else's troubles.

Max jumped up on the couch with me while we were talking. I felt better that I had been able to care for Max without Katie's help.

"Katie. I'm not sure how to help you decide," I said. "I think I'd pick Chuck because you're settled with him, because you have Jeff together. But look at my taste in men. What do I know?" I said.

We laughed.

Chapter 68

I was free of Nate for about a month. I assumed mostly because of the new girlfriend. But whatever the reason, it was a relief. I signed up for a class at the Community Center and took square dancing lessons from the local "Wilderness Whirlers." I admired the members' flared skirts. It was acceptable to wear a jean skirt as long as I wasn't a member. If I joined the full group, I'd have to get the clothes.

On September seventeenth, Victor Zorman called from the County Attorney's Office in Duluth.

"I am sending a letter to you in response to the charges against Nathan Rohr. You have some inconsistencies in your statements, especially around the December incident. I am wondering if you can help clear this up for me."

"Clear up for me what you mean by the 'December incident,'" I said.

"It's the time you stated that you were threatened with a knife."

"When I gave that statement, I was afraid. The police forced me to sign it. They said they wouldn't help me again if I didn't. Nate was there. I was afraid to tell everything that happened. Later on when the pattern continued, and I was trying to make charges that would stick, I rewrote the statement as the incident actually happened. I put in the part about the knife. I wrote this second group of statements all at one sitting. I got the date wrong for that incident by one week."

"It looks as if you are trying to make two incidents out of one," Victor said.

"I realize it may look as if I was trying to make two incidents out of one, but I wasn't, and I'm not. It was just a mistake. I only meant to add to the description of the complaint that had been filed already at the police department, but I made a mistake on the date. The police were actually there the night this happened. They took Nate to the station, though they didn't keep him. It can be verified."

"Mmm," was all I heard on the other line.

"Don't you believe me? I was confused about a date. There have been so many assaults; it is difficult to keep them all straight."

"It's hard to charge someone when you have these inconsistencies in your statements," he said. "It appears that Mr. Rohr has been rude to you on several occasions. But we don't have laws that say you have to be nice to people. I can't take away a person's freedom simply because they are rude."

"Now I know that I am being victimized, not just by Nate, but by society," I said, quoting from the brochure.

"What?"

"At the time I didn't feel I had any protection from the police. It is unrealistic for me to sign complaints and press charges, which ends up being provocative behavior, increasing the chances of more assaults, and when those assaults happen I am given no protection by the law," I said.

"We have statistics that women drop the charges nine out of ten times. We don't want to proceed with this when there is such a high likelihood that you will drop the charges."

"Drop the charges? I haven't been given the chance to drop them. It's as if you are all against bringing them. Perhaps women drop the charges out of frustration with working with the law. I am being terrorized. I am clear that what is being done to me is wrong, and I think there are laws to protect me. But I can't enforce what laws there are without your help. Maybe ninety percent of the women figure out they have no chance, so they give up. I can't get Nate to leave me alone. I've been trying on my own for one year."

"I am willing to take this matter to trial if you feel this is necessary to prevent Nate from doing further harm to you. I am concerned about going to the trouble if you are simply going to drop the charges. When you get my letter, I want you to think about this for a few days, and then write me back."

❧

Nate got a job roofing the building where Ben leased his print shop, right next door to Angelica's Cafe. From the roof, Nate spat on me as I left the building.

In a few days, true to his word, I received the exceedingly white letter—it was so perfectly white—from Victor Zorman at the County Attorney's Office, dated September 17, 1980, typed in clean black print. Nate was charged with the following things. I read and reread them.

Count I. Assault in the Second Degree

This is a five-year and/or a $5,000 felony, contrary to Minnesota Statue 609.222. Specifically, this count revolved around the allegations that the defendant placed a pocketknife to your throat, but without inflicting great bodily harm.

Count II: Terroristic Threats

This is a five-year felony, contrary to Minnesota Statute 609.713 Subd. 1. Specifically, this count alleges that the above-named defendant did threaten to tear your eyeballs out of your sockets.

Count III: Assault in the Fourth Degree

This is a misdemeanor punishable by 90 days in jail and/or a $500 fine, contrary to Minnesota Statute 609.224. Specifically, this count alleges the above-named defendant slapped you.

⚜

Mr. Zorman let me know that a conviction would put Nate in Stillwater State Prison for two and a half years. However, he reminded me again that this case would not be a good case to try because of my inconsistent statements. He said that I was a "bad" witness, a shame that stuck.

He also added that Nate might be planning to leave me alone as he had a new, young girlfriend. So he suggested, given all this, that I go along with a plea agreement with nine special conditions; none of them would do anything to protect me or change the situation I was in.

Mr. Zorman asked me to think about the letter for a week, and talk about it with my advisors. I assumed he meant Liz Hane, the battered woman's advocate. Then I was to write him back to let him know what I thought.

In the meantime, I did my best to create a new life for myself. I was independent, took care of my things, made my own money. I square danced with friends at the Community Center on Monday nights. I enjoyed the rhythm of life in town, beauty everywhere, belonging. I waitressed and my new-old coin collection grew and grew with the coin tips I collected.

Though some people would never like me because of the Nathan Rohr saga, I had friends and the beginning of a creative life. I walked to work. I didn't ride in cars much, so when I did take a trip to visit my family I was initially struck by how fast I was moving.

Lee, DeeDee, Chuck, Joe, Andy started liking me for myself instead of as Nate's girlfriend. They began to introduce me to another life, and slowly things improved for me. Strangers wanted to know my last name and I told them, "Books."

"Oh, from Babbit?"

I would offer them half a nod, not a direct lie, but I let them think I was almost a "local," from the nearest town to Alma.

I had my own friends, and I knew that made Nate mad. He wasn't used to having people like his girlfriends. It was a glimmer, but it was a glimmer of a life that was genuinely my own.

I bought a journal. I read *Yoga, Youth, and Reincarnation* by Jess Stern, a book I had previously owned but never read. Jess Stern could concentrate so thoroughly that the clouds would move, he said. I bought another book about Yoga and practiced it at night when I got home from work. I signed up for a Yoga class at the Community Center. I wanted to be able to concentrate thoroughly enough to make a cloud move. It was a new goal of mine.

The yoga gave me dreams of health, of getting off cigarettes. I spent time in my bedroom at my desk practicing calligraphy and writing letters. I bought another desk, a wooden library table, from the second-hand store up the street because I needed more table space to work. This all fit in my bedroom.

I heard that Carol moved to Alaska. I thought that maybe that was where I was going to end up, exiled the way all of Nathan Rohr's exes were.

I re-read the charges and the letter. I read them to Katie, and to Andy. I read the letter to Chuck. I sought help from Liz Hane. First, she read the letter.

"They are saying there is no crime against being rude. This is just rude domestic behavior—can that be right?" I asked.

"He is more than rude, Anna," Liz said.

"Is it a crime to be immature, to have made a poor choice of boyfriends, to have emotional problems?" I said.

"Anna, it isn't a crime to have emotional problems."

"Why did they want to let him off, I wonder?"

"It doesn't make sense," Liz said.

"Why would they not want to punish him? And mostly get him off the streets?"

"It's a problem I can't answer," she said.

"The Duluth News article said that if all of the men in domestic violence situations were arrested, the jails would be full. Is that the reason they don't do anything? Is that why I feel as if I've committed the crime? I thought the police and laws were in place for citizens' protection."

❧

I wrote to Mr. Zorman. I told him I wasn't impressed with his choice of charges or his arguments. I told him I didn't desire to remain battered, as he insinuated. I wasn't afraid to go to trial even as a "bad" witness. I told him that his calling my injuries simple assault minimized the impact these crimes had on my life. I told him it sounded as if he were giving men permission to beat women because to hold them responsible for their choices would be inconvenient for them. I accused him of trying to manipulate me by getting me to pity Nate.

Finally I told him I was concerned about his logic that simply because Nate was "leaving me alone" now that he had a girlfriend, that this condition will stick. I asked him why he thought I knew what motivated Nate. And finally, I said, I wasn't interested in dropping the charges.

Chapter 69

People loved Dave and the *Northern Messenger*, but we all knew that Dave wasn't going to live much longer. He was sick with the late stages of cirrhosis of the liver. Dave's legs got sores on them. I wanted to go to the VFW and ask them how they could take Dave's money day in and day out. Didn't they realize they were killing him? Jim talked me out of it, at first, but I finally went to talk to the bartender.

"Why do you serve him alcohol? Don't you know he's dying?" I asked.

"He'll just drink somewhere else," he said.

Dave collapsed again on September fifteenth and died the next day.

I went to the funeral at the Catholic church on West James Street. The sky held just a few high clouds. It was afternoon and the bell rang in the tower. The priest came through with his heavy incense and said Dave was one with the wine of Jesus. No one at the church could keep a straight face after that. Hadn't anyone told the priest about Dave's drinking? I was humiliated for his children.

Chapter 70

Andy visited on Halloween with a few friends. He brought me Martin Buber's *I and Thou*. He had read to me from the book previously, and I learned from it that, according to Buber, love was a cosmic force. I told him I'd seen Nate's truck parked across the street from the *Messenger*. I hadn't seen him in a while, and I didn't know what he would do. He said I should come along with them. It was Friday night, and I didn't work Saturday so I agreed to go. We went to his cabin for the evening, and stayed there overnight. We built a fire near the shore, and sat around it talking. Andy taught me a prayer:

Holy Spirit within me
Go before me and open the way.
Infinite wisdom shows me just what to do.

∽

It was raining in the morning, so we stayed in the cabin and waited for the rain to stop. I was surprised when he began kissing me tenderly in the morning amidst the sounds of the lake. He was a kind lover. This time I was passive and afraid of lovemaking. For some reason he stopped. He just stopped and I was relieved, but I didn't talk about it.

Chapter 71

Two weeks past Halloween, it was Nate's birthday. I was uneasy. Chuck Baxter was staying with me, because Katie had left him. I was making up his bed in the living room. I moved the trunk close to the couch to make a wide enough space for his sleeping bag on the floor.

He had confronted Katie about her affair with Jim. He thought it was right to make her choose. She was going to move in with Jim. He hadn't counted on this. Chuck was lost and sad.

He had just got in his sleeping bag, when Nate began banging on my locked apartment door. I called the police immediately.

"Nathan Rohr is at my house. This is a violation of his probation. I want you to arrest him," I said to the phone without even saying hello or identifying myself. I had Vic Zorman on my mind.

Chuck tried to let himself out to save Nate.

You get an idea of how people truly are in a crisis. He was my friend, but he was *afraid* of Nate. His fear was primary. He didn't want Nate to think he was on my side, even though I think he was.

Chuck hadn't figured Nate out yet, but I had. I realized that just as I could be emotionally disturbed *and* physically ill, Nate could be wounded *and* criminal.

"DON'T LET HIM IN CHUCK," I yelled.

I repeated the plea that he not be let in several times. I had locked the door from the inside, but had unfortunately left the key in the deadbolt. Chuck could not seem to manage getting the door unlocked.

Nate was still outside trying to get in. Finally the door was opened. I remained upstairs. Nate was not interested in being saved from the police, as I knew, or being grateful to Chuck for saving him from the police, as I knew. He wanted to get me.

Chuck must have finally figured that out because he tried to block Nate from coming up the stairs. Chuck and Nate tangled for a few minutes at the doorway and then tumbled out onto the porch. At one point the window on the outside door got smashed. They were hollering at each other and kept working their way closer and closer up the stairs to where I was standing.

Nate and Chuck were struggling this way when Officers Crayon and Hitch arrived. The two officers, Chuck, and Nate all began to struggle on the steps, making their way closer and closer to me. The only way out of the apartment was down those stairs, so I was stuck watching.

Nate swung at Officer Hitch. Several times I saw how easily Nate could have reached one of the officer's guns. In fact I thought I saw him think it, too. Chuck continued to try to calm Nate in order to bring him home. He kept calling him "Buddy," which pissed me off.

The struggle finally stopped. They got Nate down the stairs. I assumed they were going to arrest him. Then they all four left the house. I called my mom. I was just telling her that I thought it would be all right, when I heard voices outside.

"Hang on, Mom," I said. I walked downstairs and onto the porch and discovered my key lying on the porch floor.

The key to the front door was broken off in the lock. I saw the Alma Police car drive away with no one in the back seat. Neither Nate nor Chuck were anywhere in sight. I ran up the stairs.

"I'll call you back," I yelled into the phone. I dialed the Alma police immediately.

"Alma Police Department."

"This is Anna Books. My lock is broken and he's back. He's back. YOU LET HIM GO! I thought you arrested him. Nate isn't supposed to be at my house and I want him arrested. Do you understand? I want him arrested, at least until my door can be locked again." My voice rose in hysterical dismay, "Certainly by now this is not *domestic* violence. It has been a full year since we've lived together."

At this moment, Nate came through the door and started up the stairs. He was alone.

"He's coming up the stairs. He's going to hurt me right now—!"

Nate pulled the phone from my hand and began punching me full force in the face. He knocked me down.

When you take a beating one has consciousness in blocks instead of in a fluid path. One is there, and now here, with no awareness of the in-between. He knocked me into the bedroom and punched me several times in the eyes.

He said, "You haven't ever been beaten before and this time I'm going to kill you."

He took my hair and slammed me against the floor.

He was on top of me, striking repeated blows to my head. I heard their radios first, before their feet. Nate stopped beating me and got up. I peeked my head out the bedroom door and Chuck, Hitch, and Crayon were attempting to restrain Nate. Someone shut the bedroom door and that is where I stayed.

The two-by-four I had near my bed lay there still as a road; at the crucial time I hadn't even remembered it was there.

A moment later, I came out to see the officers on top of Nate on the floor.

As if someone else were speaking, I heard myself say, "And now you have to kick him," but I couldn't get my legs to move. I didn't want to kick him.

I moved back into the bedroom and watched as they got him handcuffed. I watched them walk down the stairs.

I was bleeding from my nose and eyes. Nate had reopened a recent wound on the middle finger of my right hand; it was bleeding, too. The officers came back upstairs and they wanted me to ride with them to the hospital.

"With Nate in the car?" I said.

"I guess," they said.

"Why don't you take him to the Police Department and come back."

"Oh. Okay," they said.

Chuck stayed with me until the two officers returned. I got my coat and the four of us drove to Alma Hospital, where my injuries were documented in the Emergency Room.

I stayed overnight in the hospital. The emergency room nurses asked their questions. They couldn't give me anything for the pain without a doctor's orders. The doctor wouldn't be in until morning. They led me to a room.

The hospital seemed deserted. I don't remember seeing anyone except the nurses. I didn't have anything with me because I didn't know I'd be going, didn't know I'd be staying. The nurse gave me hospital pajamas and a robe, and I put them on.

My nose wasn't bleeding anymore, but my head hurt. Everything hurt. I didn't look in the mirror. My eyes hurt. I wondered why the doctor couldn't come in now so I could get something. I got into bed because I couldn't stand the pain. The blanket was thin as a snowflake and too light. The pillowcases were crisp, not soft. My teeth were chattering.

I didn't feel safe.

I lay there in the room along the quiet hallway all alone. I didn't think about Nate. I moved my right foot back and forth along the inside of my left foot. The skin was soft there. What happened next I don't completely understand. My body didn't leave the bed, yet it felt as though a volcanic force, a force from somewhere else, entered through my feet and split open the top of my head. My body was released through my skull as though all along I hadn't been alive, but trapped. Now I was free. I flew with the vigor of a launched bullet, traveling faster than memory. I wasn't in pain. I heard a watery sound as though I were hearing the future as wind.

I will never understand why, but it felt as if my dislodged self snagged on the skull of the body I was leaving behind. This awareness made a sound like a bone cracking and I snapped back into my head. I had the sense that if I fell asleep I would die. I didn't know why, but I wanted to live.

I lay awake. I thought about what Nate had just done. He had pounded my head with his fist, pounded me against the wall, pounded me, smeared my old pink-flowered wallpaper with blood.

I spent the night quietly walking the shiny gray-tiled halls of the Alma Hospital. I couldn't lean into any mysterious aspects of myself or whatever thread held me to life would have severed as easily as a burnt match head falls off its stick.

In the morning, Dr. Beane ordered skull X-rays and an X-ray of my right elbow. I was released following examination and the X-ray results. Whatever had happened to me didn't appear on an X-ray.

Chapter 72

Nate was charged for assaulting a police officer, and held briefly in the Alma jail before being transported to Duluth. It was instantaneous. I had spent a year trying and failing to get charges against him to stick, but strike a cop and you go to jail right away. No further charges were filed.

I heard from Chuck that Nate hadn't learned whether or not he had killed me until he was transported to the Duluth County Jail. When in Duluth, he was able to talk to Chuck. Chuck said, "It took me a while to convince him that he hadn't killed you. I explained to him that you weren't dead."

I didn't believe that for a minute. It was so odd: all of a sudden, I could see clearly. I never knew for sure whether people still talked to Nate because they were afraid not to, or because they liked him, or because they just didn't know what I knew about him.

From jail, Nate told Chuck where he could find my coin and bottle collection. He'd buried them in my blue pillowcase in a sawdust pile by the sawmill. The bottles weren't broken, but the papier maché boxes were destroyed. I got my coin collection, though, even the nickels.

Chapter 73

I examined my wounded face in my bathroom mirror as I got ready for work at Ben's. It was Wednesday, the fourth day after the beating. My eyes had started to open, enough so I could see out of them. The bruises always looked worse when they were healing. I asked Ben to photograph my face. The picture didn't turn out.

A customer came into the office to order some printing.

"You have a bruised face and a tattoo. What sort of person are you?" he said.

"Strange." I smiled at him. "We should have a proof for you by Friday," I said.

❧

I told Ben that I had some bad news.

"What?" he said.

"I've decided I'm going to quit," I said.

"It's the money, isn't it?" he said. He thought he wasn't paying me enough.

"No. It's just that Nate's going to be out of jail in March and it's time to go."

I gave Ben thirty days notice, because it was hard for him to find people. It overestimated my importance to him, but I wanted to be fair. I planned to leave in March, before Nate was released. Now I knew he would never leave me alone if I stayed in Alma. It was too much for other people.

It took me the whole month to pack. I was dragging out packing because I didn't want to do it. Moving would be the end of the tiny life I had started to grow.

It's sad to see something die that has just started to grow. But here I was murdering it, for no reason. Or for a bad reason: simply because there was no forest big enough to support the undergrowth of a fragile young woman. I would never again grow in that tender direction, or love a place the way I loved Alma. I was sad. I couldn't stay, though, and put myself, or worse, my friends, through the next round of Nate drama. He would never give up. I knew that.

☙

On the day of my going away party at Ben's printing, I was at the New Moon getting drunk. At about 7:30 I decided to go home, and on my way I saw Ben on the road. I accepted his offer of a ride home. He asked me if he could come in to use my bathroom and I said yes. He followed me in the living room and pulled me toward him as if to kiss me.

He said, "All you need is someone who will love you."

I said, "Ben you don't want to be doing this."

He agreed, I guess, because he left.

He called the next morning, early, to apologize.

He said, "I know how much you are bothered by things like that and I am sorry. It was wrong of me. I drank too much. Don't be afraid to come around. I'm sorry."

"It's okay, Ben. Thanks for calling," I said.

Chapter 74

I met DeeDee for the last of a six-part lecture series—part of a community promotion for healthy living. The lecture took place at the Community Center, one block past the Post Office, where I square danced on Monday nights, and where I used to shower on Thursdays.

The last session, was a videotaped talk by Leo Buscaglia. He talked about the class he held on "Love" despite criticism from his colleagues. He said, "Think of what you are and all the fantastic potential of you."

His message was about loving life: autumn leaves, fresh bread, each other. He began to weep at the beauty in a single loaf of home-baked bread. I thought of my books and my bottle collection, of the marvel of the bear at my window. I smiled. I cried. I felt hopeful, content, and determined. DeeDee walked me home.

I washed the dishes before going to bed. My apartment was clean even though I wasn't having company. I took the time to put on pajamas before bed. The humming of the refrigerator calmed me, as did the streetlight showing through the crack in my window shade. I still didn't have curtains, but I had food in the refrigerator.

I dreamed I was in a colorful field with a crowd of people. We were at an art class, drawing flowers. I began to draw my flowers. It felt as if I were drawing with my mind because what I thought seemed to have an effect on what was on the page. My flowers kept multiplying effortlessly. Eventually I held a bouquet of marigolds. Everyone in the class held their own bouquet. I awaited further instruction. While waiting, I painted the centers of the marigolds red. Everyone was told to say what their flowers represented. I wanted my flowers to represent reconciliation. In the dream I said, "Reconciliation is the most important thing for me."

When I woke up, I stayed in bed, considering this dream.

I thought you could love someone enough to get them to come around. I thought love would move a person the way a strong magnet can lift a car from a junk pile. I thought I could love Nate so much the cloud in him would move. It was sad that it didn't work that way.

I didn't have to give up on love; I could get better at it. Maybe I needed more practice. I could still love the world. I realized you'd have to coax a cloud in order to get it to move. I bet even Jess Stearn didn't do it the first time he tried. Something good might happen if I kept trying.

I'm not giving up, I thought. I might move a cloud or heal the wounded or love the unlovable, or I might still save the world.

Acknowledgements

Gratitude for faith in Mercy
and for all who have shown me some.

Special thanks to:

Carol Bly for telling;
To Connie Devich for seeing;
Steve Chandler for reaching;
Chris Nelson for doing;
Richard Severance for loving.

About the Author

Melissa B. Severance is a writer, artist and psychologist. She founded Be Somebody, Inc. in 2001 and works there as a private-practice licensed psychologist and coach. Her credentials include degrees in psychology and writing; certification as a life, executive, and creativity coach; certification in Dream Tending from Pacifica University; certification in EMDR from the EMDR Institute; and a lifetime membership in the Minnesota Jungian Association. She lives in Stillwater with her husband, Richard, and two cats: Butter Oak and Yibble Emmanuel.

You can reach Melissa at:

www.besomebodyinc.com

Made in the USA
Monee, IL
16 February 2024